JUDGE DREDD
SWINE FEVER

Trotters. Curly tail. Large, pointed, hypersensitive ears. Refusing to believe what her mind was telling her, Psi-Judge Zandonella opened her eyes again and looked around at the big room full of red light. She was seeing the room from about a metre above floor level. That was the height of her head, as she stood here on her four trotters, her little tail testing the air behind her.

Gradually, like sipping a viciously bitter medicine, Zandonella let the truth trickle into her mind: the appalling, unavoidable, awful truth.

She had jumped into a new body all right. A body that should by now have been covered in the oily sweat of fear.

But pigs don't sweat.

Judge Dredd from Black Flame

More 2000 AD action

Judge Dredd created by
John Wagner & Carlos Ezquerra.

Chief Judge Hershey created by
John Wagner & Brian Bolland.

JUDGE DREDD

SWINE FEVER

ANDREW CARTMEL

BLACK FLAME

For Rosie Alvarez, who laughs in all the right places.

A Black Flame Publication
www.blackflame.com

First published in 2005 by BL Publishing, Games Workshop
Ltd., Willow Road, Nottingham NG7 2WS, UK.

Distributed in the US by Simon & Schuster, 1230 Avenue of the
Americas, New York, NY 10020, USA.

10 9 8 7 6 5 4 3 2 1

Cover illustration by Patrick Goddard and Dylan Teague.

ISBN 13: 978-1-84416-174-4
ISBN 10: 1-84416-174-9

A CIP record for this book is available from the British Library.

Printed in the UK by Bookmarque, Surrey, UK.

MEGA-CITY ONE, 2128

ONE

The moon shone down on Mega-City One. It was a full moon, high and white, its ravaged face pouring steady cold light on the expanse of the city that stretched endlessly away across the dark half of the world. The moonlight probed the shadowed valleys between the high towers, stirring excitement in the mental hospitals dotted plentifully throughout the urban sprawl and shone, too, in the worshipful upturned eyes of the occasional lunatic roving free in the streets below. The moon was also reflected in a cold perfect circle on the steel and glass spire of the building called Justice Central.

"Full moon tonight," observed Judge Carver as he struggled with a food-vending unit in the mess.

"Is that significant?" asked Psi-Judge Zandonella, peering over his shoulder. Belinda Zandonella was a tall young woman with long, straight, lustrous black hair and the golden skin you might expect from the interplay of Filipina and Irish genes.

In contrast, Carver was a tall young man with a pasty white complexion spattered with reddish freckles. He had big hands and a boyish face, and large blue eyes that promised loyalty and dogged devotion to duty, but not vast vistas of intellect. Now those moist blue eyes flickered nervously in their surveillance of Zandonella.

He was not at ease with her, and with good reason. Carver was a street Judge and had never met a Psi-Judge before this assignment. He found Zandonella strange and a little unnerving, although so far she'd behaved much like any other Judge, never giving any hint of her special powers, which were rumoured to be highly unpleasant.

"Crime goes up seventeen point five per cent during a full moon," said a low, harsh voice. Zandonella and Carver turned to see a tall figure looming over them. Zandonella hadn't heard his approach and she was a little spooked at this sudden appearance of her field commander for tonight, Judge Dredd.

"Didn't you know that, Judge?" said Dredd.

"No, sir," said Zandonella. "That's high."

"The rate's even higher for certain offences. Like sexual assault." Dredd's face was expressionless. "Or murder. So it won't be making our assignment tonight any easier. Now let's get going."

He moved off. The young Judges hurried after him. Zandonella and Carver had both fought to get places on tonight's task force and they were eager to show what they were made of. Carver hastily swallowed the last oily fragments of the munce morsels he'd purchased and tossed the empty packet into a recycling bin, which whirred and flashed purple as it malfunctioned.

The full moon summoned something up in the minds of the vulnerable citizens of the Mega-City, firing unknown circuits in their addled brains, burning like a bright drug in their bloodstreams.

Staring up at the beautiful purity of the streaming silver moonlight, a man in Kylie Minogue Block decided he could fly like a bat. He didn't have the necessary membranes under his arm but he hypothesised that these would naturally grow out under evolutionary pressure as he fell. After all, nature provides. So he put on his best clothes, stepped out of his sitting room window and promptly tumbled into the void. His fall was arrested on an illegal balcony extension seventeen floors below where he survived thanks to landing on an extremely overweight and therefore well-padded cyborg dog. The dog was destroyed in a messy fashion but the jumper lived to be charged with failure to hire a psychiatrist and was locked away in a suitable institution.

Elsewhere, other full-moon fiends were busily obeying the siren call of their own chosen satellite. They were mixing explosives, sharpening knives and polishing telescopic sights.

"For some, the full moon is like a dangerous intoxicant," announced Judge Darrid. He was an older street Judge, an experienced officer with more years on the job than Dredd, although not remotely the same level of reputation. He was a florid, portly man with a cherubic face that was lent a slightly eccentric air by the large walrus moustache that he sported. The moustache was as grey as the hair on Darrid's head.

Darrid was sitting in the back of the H-Wagon, buckled in between Zandonella and Carver, while Dredd sat on his own in the cockpit and steered them through the night. The vehicle was a new design of H-Wagon that was being brought on stream by the Tek-Judges. Rumour was that the prototype had been a tricky vehicle to operate and several had indeed come to grief in the vast canyons of the Mega-City. Zandonella had heard a story about an inexperienced Judge steering too close to a building, over-correcting and sending the H-Wagon sailing too close to the building opposite. Panic had then set in, the pilot over-correcting again, and on the next terminal swing the vehicle had crashed into a building, ripping a deep groove in the densely populated structure and killing citizens as well as the crew, who had been charged with post-mortem negligence and had their ashes sealed in secure units at the penal crematorium.

Until the technology was perfected it was volunteers only on the new H-Wagon, and Zandonella had volunteered. Her tour of duty with the street Judges had been intended as a disciplinary assignment – a form of punishment. Or penance. But that was no reason it couldn't also be fun.

And Zandonella was delighted Dredd was flying the craft tonight. The H-Wagon was only dangerous if the pilot panicked, and Dredd didn't seem the type to panic.

The H-Wagon had been as steady as a rock since take-off, and if Zandonella hadn't looked out the windows she would

have believed that the craft was still floating in the docking
bay in the vehicle pool instead of streaking across the city
skyline. Despite the smoothness of their flight, Carver had
already begun to look a little air sick. Zandonella devoutly
prayed that he wouldn't throw up, not here in this tiny
space. As far as she could tell, Carver had the makings of a
good Judge, but his personal habits left a lot to be desired.
He ate junk like those munce morsels and then went on
assignments in a small personnel carrier like this and then
of course the inevitable happened.

Judge Darrid's nostrils suddenly twitched. "What is that
grud-awful smell?" he said.

"Malfunctioning exhaust," said Zandonella, which in a
way it was.

Carver suddenly seemed eager to change the subject.
"What was that you were saying? Just now? About the dangerous intoxicant, Judge Darrid?"

Darrid took the bait and began expounding his pet theo-
ries about law and order. As far as Zandonella was
concerned, he was an old bore with a superfluity of nostril
hair. She looked away from Darrid and Carver, out through
the side window of the H-Wagon at the glittering towers of
the Mega-City as they streamed past.

"The narcotic of lunacy," said Darrid, "has tonight joined
the multitude of other illegal substances coursing through
the collective bloodstream of Mega-City One." He pointed at
the endless landscape of gaudy urban deprivation flowing
past beneath them. "Down there are literally millions of per-
petrators squirming out from under their slimy stones to
obtain illegal substances because they want a thrill that ordinary life can't provide. Squirming like vermin! Like
squirming vermin! Millions of them. And we have to try and
find and arrest every single one of these rotten, wriggling,
squirming vermin."

Zandonella felt a sudden clench of excitement. "Is that
what tonight's assignment is about?" The task force's mission was strictly confidential. Only Dredd had been officially
briefed and he wasn't saying a word. But perhaps Darrid had

heard something. "Are we going after some kind of narcotics ring?" Perhaps it was sugar smugglers.

"Well—"

"Is that right?" broke in Carver, eagerly leaning forward. "Are we going on a drugs bust?"

"Well," said Darrid, "have you heard of a gang called the Mob Better Blues?"

"Darrid," said Dredd from the driver's seat. "Shut up. And the rest of you too. And buckle up. We're stopping to pick up one more member of the task force." The H-Wagon slowed as Dredd dropped it out of the traffic flow, falling one hundred and fifty metres in a smooth dive and drifting neatly into alignment with a Justice Department docking station. The umbilical port hissed and opened, extruding a clear plastic tube the same diameter as the hatch in the side of the H-Wagon's cockpit. A woman stepped into the tube and Zandonella's heart sank as she recognised Psi-Judge O'Mannion.

"Who's that?" said Carver.

"My immediate superior," said Zandonella.

"What's she doing here?"

"Evaluating my progress." She watched O'Mannion climb into the empty seat in the cockpit as the tube retracted, the door hummed shut and Dredd lifted them smoothly back into the traffic stream.

Two and a half city blocks, or fifty-five kilometres away, a hydrogen-filled airship floated silently against the moon, leaving two long, cigar-shaped shadows on the roof of William Holden Memorial Trauma Unit below. The top "cigar" was the buoyancy module, filled with hydrogen, which kept the airship afloat. The lower shape was a large cargo container and a smaller control gondola. In the gondola there were crowded four young men and a young woman. All of them had been so densely and comprehensively tattooed that their skin appeared to be a uniform shade of blue.

One of the men was extremely thin and he was called Blue Streak. "Why an airship?" said Streak. "There are plenty of more sophisticated vehicles we could have used for this job. Why are we stuck on this zeppelin?"

"What's a zeppelin?" said one of the two extremely short young men who were standing rather than sitting on their seats in the gondola.

"Ignorant dwarf," said the other extremely short young man. "Ignorant tattooed dwarf," he added.

"The tattoos were your idea!" said the other blue dwarf.

While they bickered, Blue Streak turned to the tattooed young woman. Even her eyes were blue. They gleamed at him in the moonlight, burning like blue coals in her beautiful depraved face. Her tattoos stopped at the neck and the shock of their interruption and the sudden appearance of unsullied white skin above made her face look positively naked. "Why are we using this archaic mode of travel?" he asked her.

The girl was called Blue Belle, though the men in the gang secretly referred to her as Blue Balls. She ran her fingers through her close-cropped, bleached hair, shrugged and said, "Ask Big Blue."

The fourth young man, Big Blue, was a giant product of an overactive pituitary combined with illegal steroids and many years of weight lifting. He crouched over the airship controls, occupying both the pilot and copilot's seats. Blue Streak leaned over one of his huge muscle-bound tattooed shoulders and addressed the man's strangely small, tattooed face. "Why?" But Big just ignored him, as if his task of piloting the airship was too important to allow him to indulge in pointless conversation. Deeply offended, Streak turned away and began to check the weapons.

"Hey there," called Big Blue suddenly from the front of the gondola. He turned to look at Streak with a big white smile in his tattooed face. "Are you sulking back there, old Blue Streak old buddy?" The dwarfs and the girl laughed and Streak felt his face heat up. If he hadn't been covered in blue tattoos, he would have been turning red. "Are you sulking because I didn't answer your question?"

"No," said Streak tightly.

"Aw, yes you are. You are sulking. Here buddy, come on up here, old buddy, and give us a hug." Blue Streak put down the magazine of incendiary ammunition he'd been about to load into his PW7 Peaceful World fully automatic assault rifle. He set the weapon aside as he made his way past the escape pod, towards the front of the craft. Here the gang's leader Big Blue was turning from the controls, rising from his seats, his white teeth gleaming as his tiny blue face smiled and he welcomed Blue Streak into his enormous muscular embrace. Blue Streak winced at the pressure of the big arm as it wrapped around his shoulder. "We're the Mob Better Blues," crooned Big Blue into Streak's face. "That's because we're better than other mobs."

"And we're blue," added the first dwarf helpfully.

Big Blue hooked his thumb towards the cargo container hanging behind the gondola. "Better at mob jobs like smuggling contraband."

"Contraband!" repeated the dwarf.

"We're a better mob because we plan better. When we smuggle contraband we do it right, in a hydrogen-filled airship made of plastic. Which makes us harder to detect," said Big Blue. "It allows us to smuggle in our contraband in a silent, stealthy manner. Wouldn't you agree, old buddy?"

"I suppose so." Streak nodded reluctantly, wrestling with a half-formed memory. "But wasn't there a problem with zeppelins bursting into flame?"

"Bursting into flame!" roared Big Blue, pounding at the controls as he bellowed with laughter.

"Bursting into flame," echoed the dwarfs, chuckling.

"The only reason airships kept bursting into flame," said Big Blue, "was because those old idiots back in the old days filled them with an inflammable gas called helium. That's why Big Blue got you a nice safe airship filled with hydrogen."

"Hydrogen?" said Streak, struggling again with that half-formed memory.

"That's right. It's helium you've got to worry about. Good old hydrogen is as safe as houses." Big Blue smiled and steered their airship towards its destination.

. . .

"Normally a vehicle like that, virtually silent and with a polymer airframe, would be almost impossible to detect," said Judge Darrid, passing his night vision glasses to Zandonella. The twin cigars of the airship floated into visibility in the glasses, a ghostly lilac image.

"How did we know to look for it?" asked Zandonella.

"What?"

"If it was undetectable, how did we know to look for it here?"

"We were tipped off," said Judge O'Mannion from the cockpit. She was a petite woman in her early thirties with witchy silver hair. Even her ironic eyebrows were silver. Her foxy features and coffee-brown eyes, dark and bitter, reflected her wicked and often malicious sense of humour. Those bitter-coffee eyes were watching Zandonella now. She could feel them, weighing and appraising her; summing Zandonella up for the fitness report she'd soon be writing. The report would determine Zandonella's future as a Judge, and Zandonella wasn't sure what worried her the most, the arrest of the multiple felons that she was about to participate in, or the thought of this woman watching and evaluating her.

"Most drugs arrests are tip-offs," added Darrid knowledgeably. "The rats weasel on each other. I mean the weasels rat on each other. In any case, the vermin betray each other as they buy and sell the filthy merchandise they're addicted to."

"So it *is* a drug bust?" said Carver. He checked his sidearm for the hundredth time.

"Something like that," said Judge O'Mannion.

"Get ready," said Dredd. "We're going to go down and take a closer look."

Big Blue steered the airship onto the roof of what had once been the Neverland Fun Fair and Orphan's Home. Almost the entire roof had been given over to a swimming pool, now dry and drained. Giant, cartoonish castle towers rose out of the pool and jostled against mushrooms and trees and flowers that had been designed by someone who had never seen a mushroom, or a tree, or a flower. These tall, abandoned structures housed various water slides and pipe rides, all now disused and as dry as a bone while they awaited redevelopment. A sign at the far end of the roof promised the imminent construction of the "Aquatomic Fun Pool and Fission Reactor Complex – a Nuclear Excursion for the Nuclear Family!"

Big Blue brought the airship down in a feather landing on the fringe of tarmac beside the swimming pool, then opened the hatch in the wall of the gondola, lowering the ramp to the roof top.

"If we're selling contraband, where's the buyers?" said Streak.

Big smiled. "Well, I guess that's them over there." He nodded towards the shadowy superstructure of a castle tower water slide. Emerging from the plastic mouth of the slide, a tunnel encrusted with dry algae, were two men. They were both tall and heavily built, though neither as massive as Big. One had short-cropped blond hair and a black moustache. The other had short-cropped black hair and a blond moustache. Their features were similar, though not so similar that they could be identical twins or clones. Streak judged them to be brothers.

"Evening," said Big. "The Barkin brothers, I presume? Good to see you fellas. Are we on time or are we on time?"

"You're on time," said the blond with the black moustache.

"Now which of you fellows is Theo, and which is Leo?"

"I'm Leo Barkin," said the one with blond hair. He seemed to be the spokesman.

"I'm Theo Barkin," added the brother with the black hair.

The blond frowned at him. "You didn't have to tell them that."

"Why not?"

"Because it was obvious. By a simple process of elimination it was obvious."

Big Blue chuckled and lifted his large hands. "Hey now fellows, let's not have any sibling bickering. We've got ourselves some business to conduct."

The Judges' FWP was floating in concealment behind the largest giant mushroom sprouting from the dry swimming pool. From the cockpit of the platform Dredd and O'Mannion could peer over the mushroom cap and watch the transaction taking place below. O'Mannion was staring through night glasses. Dredd was listening to an aural feed. "Any moment now and we'll have all parties incriminated." He switched off the headphones and turned to look at Darrid, Zandonella and Carver. "Judge Darrid," he said. "I want you to follow me in."

"Follow you in? Just say the word. Let me at those substance-selling scum."

Dredd turned away from Darrid's avid, florid face and looked at Zandonella. "Judge Zandonella, I want you and Carver to follow us and cover our backs. Do not fire on the perps unless I specifically instruct you to. Do not needlessly expose yourselves to their fire. Stay back and do as you're told."

"Yes, Judge," said Zandonella and Carver.

Dredd eased back into the cockpit. "Judge O'Mannion, stay with the platform. Keep it out of the line of fire and bring it down when we're ready to make arrests. You know how to operate the controls?"

"Don't worry, Dredd, you're not the only one who's qualified to fly these things."

"Good. Then perhaps you'll demonstrate your skill for us. Let me see you program a steady hover pattern and once you've done that I'll hand the controls over to you." Zandonella smiled at Dredd's words, imagining Judge O'Mannion's impotent fury at being treated like a novice. O'Mannion remained silent, though, and began to punch commands on the flight computer. Dredd watched her for a moment then glanced back at Zandonella. "And then we go in."

. . .

"That's right," said Leo, "we've got some business to conduct." His beady little eyes gleamed in the moonlight. Streak decided he didn't like him. He felt his hand tightening on the butt of his Peaceful World. It occurred to him that the incendiary ammunition he had loaded into the assault rifle would make a terrible mess of a human body. He moved behind Big Blue, who seemed unaware of any tension.

"We're here to sell and you boys are here to buy, correct?" said Big Blue.

"If what you've got is worth buying," said Theo, who seemed eager to participate in the negotiations as an equal with his brother. Leo frowned and said nothing.

Big Blue just smiled an even wider smile and swept his big hands towards the airship's cargo container, as if he was offering it to Theo as a gift. "Nothing but primo merchandise. You have my word, and if you don't want to take my word, take a sample. Hop into the container and choose a sample at random and try it."

"What?" said Theo. "Right here? Right now?"

"Sure, why not?" smiled Big. "Satisfied customers are what we want. Test the merchandise, my friend."

"But we'd have to cook it up..."

"Well then, cook it up. We got a gas burner you can use," said Big. "Go on and cook up a big old sample and try it."

"We don't need a sample," said Leo in a decisive voice that seemed to cut through all the negotiations and conclude things once and for all. He looked at Big. "You come highly recommended to us."

"Well, that's nice to hear."

"We know that you only provide quality merchandise and you'd never try to rip anyone off."

"Well, that's really nice..." Big fell silent. He was looking at the gun that was now in Leo's hand, and the identical one in Theo's.

"Shame everyone isn't so reliable," said Leo, and he shot one of the dwarfs. Theo shot the other dwarf and then they both turned and shot Big Blue in the chest.

. . .

In the cockpit of the FWP, Judge O'Mannion was making final adjustments to the flight computer when Dredd suddenly sat up and tore the headphones from his head. "Gunfire. It's a double-cross. We're going in now." The cockpit door on Dredd's side of the platform snapped open and Dredd was out, jumping across to the cap of the giant mushroom and running towards the opening in its centre that led to the long, spiral tube of a dry water slide. He had already vanished into the water slide before Zandonella could begin to react. She followed Dredd out the door, landing on the mushroom with an impact that knocked the breath out of her. As she staggered to her feet she heard O'Mannion cursing in the cramped cockpit and Carver struggling past her, followed by Darrid. The men jumped out onto the cap of the mushroom but by that time Zandonella had already caught her breath and was following Dredd into the evil-smelling slide.

Despite all his weapon preparedness and his distrust of the Barkin brothers, Streak froze up as soon as the gunfire started. He saw the dwarfs going down, and then Big, and then the dwarfs struggling to their feet painfully and the brothers exchanging a puzzled look. And then Leo and Theo simultaneously said, "Vests."

Both dwarfs were on their feet now, their carbon fibre vests having protected them from the gunfire. The first dwarf pointed his large weapon at the brothers and opened fire. Unfortunately, just as he did so, the second dwarf bobbed to his feet and got in the way. The blast from the first dwarf's gun blew his head off. Meanwhile, the recoil from the weapon sent the first dwarf scooting across the tarmac on his buttocks. The Barkin brothers turned to each other and roared with laughter.

By now Big Blue was also struggling to his feet, the two bullets having given him a double pounding on his own vest. Looking at him, Blue Belle screamed and lifted her assault rifle. "How dare you shoot our leader, you bastards!" She opened fire on the brothers but the powerful weapon bucked and twisted in her hands and Blue Belle missed, her stream of bullets flashing towards Big instead, splatting into his vest and knocking him off his feet again. Blue Belle screamed and dropped the gun, which continued spraying bullets indiscriminately in every direction for a vicious instant before falling silent.

Only now did Streak remember that he too had a weapon. He lifted his assault rifle and blazed away at the brothers, or at least in their general direction. Leo and Theo ducked away unharmed, disappearing neatly over the rim of the swimming pool into the echoing depths below. Streak ran eagerly to the edge of the pool, looked over, and snatched his head back from a hail of bullets that came so close that he could feel a slipstream of displaced air on the tip of his nose.

A powerful hand clenched on his shoulder. He turned to see Big frowning at him. "Come on, let's go," he gasped between clenched teeth. "Before they come back." There was the sound of gunfire from down in the swimming pool. Streak and Blue Belle helped Big limp back towards the airship and climb the ramp into the gondola. The surviving dwarf stood for a moment looking at the decapitated body of his fallen comrade. Then he too hurried to the airship. The sound of gunfire from the swimming pool continued in a steady roar.

Judge Zandonella slipped and slithered down a long, dry plastic tunnel that stank of chlorine and mould until she finally burst out into the moonlight and found herself in the middle of a crossfire.

"Get down," roared Dredd. Zandonella ducked behind the stalk of the giant mushroom and watched as Dredd exchanged fire with two suspects, one blond, the other black-haired. They blazed away at the Judges, then turned and fled behind a tall water slide shaped like a dandelion. Dredd rose to follow and Zandonella moved to follow him when she felt a rush of air from above. She looked up to see the weapons platform, O'Mannion at the controls, descending on them fast. O'Mannion landed at the foot of the mushroom and clicked open her hatch.

"I told you to stay in position!" shouted Dredd.

"The airship is taking off," said O'Mannion. "I thought you ought to know."

There was an ironic note in her voice, but Dredd ignored it. "We can't let the airship get away," he said. "We need the contraband as evidence."

"Precisely," said O'Mannion dryly.

Zandonella heard a scuffling sound and turned to see Carver and Darrid finally emerging from the mushroom water slide. They were both badly out of breath. "Where are the perps?" said Darrid in a strangled voice.

Dredd looked at him and then at Zandonella. "Zandonella, you come with me and O'Mannion on the platform. We'll pursue the airship. Darrid, you and Carver apprehend the two here in the swimming pool. Proceed with caution, they're heavily armed."

"Don't worry," said Darrid. "We'll get the vile substance-abusing parasites."

But Dredd was already in the FWP, and Zandonella was scrambling to follow him.

Big Blue had recovered from the impact of the bullets on his vest and he was once again piloting the airship with skill and enthusiasm. "Can you believe those bastards? Trying to hijack us like that?"

Blue Belle massaged his bulging shoulder muscles as he bent over the control console. "We should have stayed and taught them a lesson," she said.

"One thing's for certain," said Big. "We're not doing business with those two again."

"Mob," said the dwarf. "Better. Blues."

"That's right, little fellow." Big chuckled as he steered the airship between the tower blocks. "We're the Mob Better Blues and we're still alive and kicking."

"What's that?" said Streak, peering out the rear observation port of the gondola.

"What's what?" said Big, craning his head around quizzically.

"Don't distract the driver," said Blue Belle.

"That vessel pursuing us," said Streak.

Big squinted into the display screen for the rear airship cameras. "Looks like one of those new Judges' hover-wagons," he said thoughtfully.

Aboard the FWP, Zandonella strapped herself in at the weapons station. "Ready?" asked Dredd.

"Ready," said Zandonella.

"She's not qualified for this," muttered O'Mannion.

"I'm ready," repeated Zandonella.

"She has to learn some time," said Dredd as he pushed a button on the control panel. The roof in the rear section of the FWP cracked open like the back of a beetle, admitting a cool spill of racing night air. Zandonella held tight to the weapons station as the roof slid quickly back overhead, folding in on itself and descending into a well at the rear of the platform. Now the entire rear section of the FWP was open to the fleeting night sky. Only the cockpit remained sealed, with O'Mannion staring unhappily back at Zandonella while Dredd concentrated on flying. The air whipped past Zandonella as she performed a final weapons check.

The airship was directly ahead of them, floating in the deep canyon formed by two tower blocks. "Fire a warning shot," said Dredd over the intercom. "And be careful. Tyson Stadium is approaching and there's a game tonight. We don't want any stray rounds going into the crowd."

Zandonella locked onto her target, said a silent prayer, and pressed the twin fire controls. At that instant the airship suddenly veered upwards and to the left, causing Zandonella's pattern of fire, which was intended to pass harmlessly in front of the gondola, to rip into the cargo container of the airship, piercing it with hundreds of holes.

"She missed," said O'Mannion.

"They took evasive action. She couldn't anticipate that." Dredd glanced back at Zandonella. "Hold your fire. The stadium's coming up."

Zandonella was cursing her lousy aim and her lousy luck as the vast ear-shaped open bowl of Mike Tyson Stadium floated into view below them. Light poured out of the stadium, catching the airship in a web of searchlights. Zandonella blinked. There was something pouring out of the container on the airship, a liquid running out of the numerous bullet holes. A red liquid that gleamed in the stadium light and spilled in long, twisting streams towards the street below.

"What's that?" asked O'Mannion.

"Looks like blood," said Dredd.

"They've hit the cargo," said Streak.

Big Blue shook his head sadly. "I wish they hadn't done that. Now we have to get the side windows open and return fire." Blue Belle was already tugging open one of the windows. She had an assault rifle slung around her shoulder. Streak watched her doubtfully. He looked at Big.

"That thing's loaded with incendiaries," he said.

"So what?" snarled Blue Belle. She had the window open now and a raw breeze tore through the gondola. Blue Belle clicked the safety off on the assault rifle. She looked ready to shoot Streak.

He turned to Big. "She might hit the balloon."

"Doesn't matter if she does," said Big breezily. "That plastic's self-sealing. Put as many holes in it as you like and it still keeps the gas in."

"But the bullets will go through the gas, the flaming bullets–"

"You forget, son. That's hydrogen gas. Nice and inert and safe, won't catch fire, not like helium. Good old, safe old hydrogen." Big beamed at him as Blue Belle began to take aim through the open window. "It's the most common element in the universe."

"And in the hydrogen bomb," said the surviving dwarf suddenly.

For the first time a shadow of uncertainty crossed Big Blue's face. "The hydrogen bomb?"

"Are you sure it's not helium that's inert?" said Streak, his eyes flicking nervously towards the escape pod. "Are you sure it's not hydrogen that's highly flammable?"

Before Big had a chance to reply, Blue Belle opened fire.

Luckily, the anti-dazzle device on Zandonella's helmet visor instantly darkened and protected her eyes from the huge sphere of flame that erupted in front of her, filling the night sky where the airship had been but a moment earlier.

The harness that held her to the weapons station saved her from the worst of the shockwaves of flaming gas that rippled out from the exploding airship. The titanic sound of the explosion, magnified by the endless walls of concrete, deafened Zandonella, and even attracted the attention of the crowd down below in Tyson. They stared up at the fireball in the night sky and then returned to watching the half-time holographic advertisements, which were slightly more spectacular.

Dredd lowered the roof of the vehicle again, like a beetle's shell closing to conceal its wings, and came back to help Zandonella unstrap herself from the weapons station. The huge flare of burning hydrogen faded in the night sky.

"So much for the evidence," said Dredd.

When they returned the FWP to Tek-Division they found Darrid and Carver waiting for them. O'Mannion sized up the situation at a glance and stalked off without bothering to hear their report. Dredd said nothing as Darrid haltingly explained how the two men from the rooftop swimming pool had managed to escape. Dredd simply waited for Darrid to stop talking, then turned and walked away. Carver gave Zandonella a shame-faced look. She took pity on him.

"We didn't do much better," she whispered as they walked away from the docking bay. "The airship we were pursuing managed to blow itself up."

"I heard, but not before pouring blood everywhere." Zandonella's stomach turned over at the memory. Carver lowered his voice. "I heard that they were cannibals."

"What?"

"Selling human meat. That's what they were smuggling. It wasn't drugs at all."

"Cannibals?" said Zandonella. "Human meat?"

Carver shrugged. "That was the tip-off your boss O'Mannion received."

Zandonella stopped and looked at him. It was possible, she decided. Stranger things had happened in the Big Meg. "Well the blood will tell us if it's human. Has it been analysed yet?"

"They haven't been able to find a sample."

"What? All that stuff that spilled out of the container? Some of it must have fallen somewhere."

"It did, but it was licked up."

"Licked up? By cyborg pets?" The latest craze in cyborg pets had led to synthetic dogs and cats that ate and defecated with such alarming authenticity that several new public hygiene laws had to be introduced and rigorously enforced.

"Well," said Carver, "by cyborg pets and also, er, their owners." He glanced over her shoulder and Zandonella turned to see Dredd standing there, holding a pale blue sheet of plastic. She recognised it as a report facsimile from the pathology lab.

"No blood," said Dredd, "but a number of pieces of scorched meat fell onto the crowd in Tyson Stadium where they were promptly devoured."

"Devoured?" said Zandonella, feeling faint.

"Judges on the scene managed to retrieve a few pieces intact and they've now been analysed."

"Human?" asked Carver. There was almost a hopeful note in his voice.

"No," said Dredd. "Pig. Mutant pig."

TWO

The small hairy Judge from Tek-Division kept looking at Zandonella's legs, which annoyed her. Not least because it was practically impossible for anyone to determine the shape of Zandonella's legs under the regulation fat padding and armour that were standard issue for a Judge's uniform. Nevertheless, the hairy young man from Tek-Division, Judge Turan by name, kept trying, peering gamely at her legs as he offered his report. "Preliminary analysis confirms what Judge Dredd's FAU told you at the CS."

Zandonella shook her head in silent exasperation. Turan was the sort of technician who loved to make everything more technical. And it all had to be official-sounding. Acronyms were his lifeblood. CS meant crime scene, FAU a Forensic Analysis Unit – a needle-nose pliers and glowing ping-pong ball arrangement that Dredd had applied to a bleeding hunk of meat found in the refrigerator at a crime scene that morning. Zandonella had been there, looking over his shoulder when he found the pork, an unexpected bonus at the scene of a routine domestic double-homicide. An obscenely fat man called Denzil Whitelaw and his equally obese wife had killed each other fighting over who got the last pork chop.

"Genetic comparison established to a certainty of one in fifteen billion," chattered Turan, "that this sample of tissue, as found in the DOA's kitchen, came from an animal closely related in lineage to the animal that provided the sample you apprehended as the result of your recent HSAP."

"HSAP?"

"High-Speed Air Pursuit."

Zandonella remembered a ball of pink flame in the purple night sky, twisted blackened wreckage falling from that sky, fragments of scorched meat raining down on Tyson Stadium. "And what exactly does closely related in lineage mean?"

"The animals came from the same family group. The same litter, as it's called."

Strange word, thought Zandonella. Litter. As though the groups of baby animals were merely garbage, to be discarded.

"They were in fact, siblings," said Turan with satisfaction.

"So what you're saying is that the pork from the fatties' homicide came from the same source as the stuff in the exploding airship."

"To a very small statistical possibility of error, as I said, approximately one in fifteen billion, it did in fact, indeed match the Whitelaws' sample, yes. That is indeed what I said, yes." Turan smiled at her, swallowed nervously and cleared his throat.

He was evidently finally finishing his report, a report that he could have sent just as easily – more easily in fact – over the computer. But Turan had insisted on coming down in person to the mess hall in Justice Central where an off-duty Zandonella had been trying to enjoy her quiet meal between tours of duty.

Turan smiled and cleared his throat again. It's coming any moment now, she thought with glum resignation. The smile was beginning to stiffen on Turan's face as he nerved himself to take the plunge. If he clears his throat again, thought Zandonella, I'm going to scream.

"You know, I happen to have observed you several times on the firing range in recent times when I was getting in my MQ of HTS..."

By which he meant his monthly quota of hologram target shooting.

"And I was firing my Lawgiver," babbled Turan, "and I must say..."

"Yes?" said Zandonella, in the most chilly voice she could muster. He was looking at her legs again.

"What a fine shot you are and what a great addition to the Psi-Judges you are and, and, and..."

"And?"

"And I was wondering if perhaps sometime you and I, we, that is, perhaps the two of us together, could have together, well, have a meal."

"A meal?"

"Yes. We could for example purchase something from the vending machines right now." Turan glanced wildly around at the munce dispensers that lined the walls of the canteen. The food substitutes provided by these mechanisms were as disgusting as they were cheap, and accounted for the chronic gastric offensiveness of all the Judges who used them as a mainstay of their diet. The notoriously flatulent Carver was a good example.

The coloured lights on the dispensers gleamed with the same flickering uncertainty as Turan's desperate eyes. "I'll pay. My treat."

"NIYL," said Zandonella.

"NIYL?"

"Not in your lifetime." Zandonella turned away from Turan. She had noticed Judge Dredd entering the room. He was now approaching down the blue-tiled length of the canteen, his tall figure striding between the rows of silver tables. At these tables off-duty Judges tried to look at him without staring. They were watching a walking legend and they knew it.

"Isn't lifetime two words?" said Turan. "Shouldn't it be NIYLT?" Then he saw Dredd approaching, and beat a hasty retreat, hurrying out the rear entrance of the canteen, no doubt heading back to the Genetic Analysis unit.

"Fraternising with Genetic Analysis?" Dredd said.

"Not fraternising, sir, although that buffoon–"

"That buffoon is a fellow Judge," snapped Dredd. But Zandonella could have sworn that there was a fleeting undertone of something that had sounded suspiciously like amusement in his voice. "What did he report?"

"Judge Turan confirmed your hunch, sir. The meat came from the same source. The same group of animals."

Dredd nodded grimly. "In that case you had better get down to the Armoury."

"The Armoury sir?"

"I suspect we're going to need some heavy weaponry for the next phase of this investigation."

"Another one of your hunches, sir?"

"And take Carver with you. I don't trust him to find the Armoury on his own."

"Yes sir. Sir, can I ask why we're still on this assignment?"

"Still on it?"

"Well, judging by the resources that the department is throwing at us, they're taking this investigation pretty seriously. For a bunch of black market meat, it's commanding some senior personnel." Like you, she thought. "And why would an experienced street Judge like you be stuck with a rookie like me?"

Dredd looked at her. She couldn't read that grim face. "Justice likes to use rookies on really dangerous assignments," said Dredd. Was there still a hint of amusement in his voice? "No point risking the lives of more valuable seasoned officers." He turned and walked away, past the bilious lights of a bank of malfunctioning munce machines. Zandonella couldn't decide whether he was joking or not. She followed him.

Outside the canteen they went their separate ways, Zandonella sighing as she set off in search of Carver, reminding herself once she found him to take separate elevators down to the Armoury. She didn't want to be sealed in a small metal cubicle for any length of time with Carver and his malfunctioning exhaust pipe.

In the corridor to the Armoury, Judge Dredd caught up with Zandonella and Carver. He had two more rookie street Judges with him, both young women, though of dramatically differing height and build. "These are the Karst sisters," said Dredd. "Judge Karst, E and Karst, T."

"Esma and Tykrist," said the smaller, plumper Judge confidingly to Zandonella as they fell into step on the long corridor that led to the Armoury. "I'm Esma and that tall drink of waste fluid there is my sister, Tykrist." The lanky girl nodded lugubriously at Zandonella and Carver. "She's the shy one," continued Esma. "I'm the outgoing, vivacious one."

"Why have they sent you on this assignment?" interrupted Carver in a hissing voice which clearly he intended to be a whisper. "This is our assignment. We broke the case open." Zandonella found herself strangely pleased to hear Carver use the word "we". She realised that in the bloodshed and violence of the past few days a bond had been forged between herself and the other rookie. She had become a comrade in arms with this ill-smelling young street Judge. And now he was jealously defending what he saw as their territory against the newcomers. Personally, Zandonella felt the sisters looked promising, and she would welcome having more women on the team, as long as they weren't anything like Psi-Judge O'Mannion.

Esma Karst was looking at Carver with contempt. "Well, they obviously felt you needed the assistance."

"More cannon fodder," said Zandonella. "And very welcome too." She smiled at the Karst sisters. If they were going to all serve together on a dangerous mission like this, they would have to form a rapport and all pull together. Carver would do well to realise that.

"What do you mean, cannon fodder?" asked Carver in genuine puzzlement.

"What's that terrible smell?" said Tykrist.

"Quiet, all of you," said Dredd. "I believe Psi-Judge O'Mannion has a briefing for us."

Zandonella looked up to see her commanding officer standing in front of the huge vault door of the Armoury. It rose twenty metres into the air, a seamless, monstrous gate that formed a gleaming silver cliff of reinforced steel. The Armoury was one of the best-guarded divisions in Justice Central. Heaven help the Mega-City if any of its more psychopathic denizens managed to get their hands on the experimental weaponry that lay beyond these

doors, sleeping in dreadful readiness in the Judges' special
arsenal.

O'Mannion's silver hair was reflected in a bright burnished zigzag on the monstrous doors behind. Her sardonic
smile was a slash of red on her pale, vulpine face. She stood
with hands on her hips, legs braced wide in an attitude of
defiance. "You're late, Judge," she greeted Dredd. "We were
supposed to rendezvous here for weapons familiarisation
two and a half minutes ago."

"Sorry to waste your precious time, O'Mannion," snarled
Dredd. "Next time I'll let you round up the rookies and I'll
take the briefing with the Council of Five. Now what have
you got to tell us?"

"Well, the Council is taking very seriously indeed the matter of this contraband meat."

"Why?" said Esma.

"Why?" O'Mannion turned to Dredd. "Who is this?"

Dredd grimaced. "Judge Karst, E."

"And why does she feel she has the right to question the
Council's ruling?"

"All I meant," said Esma, "is that it's just meat, for grud's
sake. Just like the stuff they grow out in the Cursed Earth on
Sausage Tree Farm."

"Well that shows how much you understand, Judge Karst,
E." O'Mannion turned her withering bitter-coffee eyes on the
unfortunate Esma. "It is absolutely not like the farmed meat.
It couldn't be more different."

"How so?" said Esma.

"It doesn't grow on bushes programmed with animal
DNA."

"What do you mean?" asked Carver; as always, he was
struggling to keep up.

Psi-Judge O'Mannion rolled her eyes and then went on to
explain in the simplest possible terms. "It contains no plant
DNA. Sausage Tree Farm could not possibly be the source."

"Then where did it come from?" persisted Carver. "If meat
doesn't come from genetically modified plants then where
do you get it?"

O'Mannion smiled indulgently. She seemed to forget her impatience, as if she was suddenly glad to share her specialist knowledge. "It grows on an animal."

"Really?" said Tykrist and Esma in a simultaneous chirp.

"In the past all meat was grown on animals," said Zandonella, who was an avid viewer of the History Channel.

"Really?" said Esma. "That's sick."

"It's awful," said her sister.

"It's disgusting," agreed Esma.

"Not to mention unsanitary, unhygienic and possibly lethal." O'Mannion looked at Dredd. "If this meat didn't come from Sausage Tree Farm, then where did it come from? Possibly some tainted source in the Cursed Earth. We don't know."

"And we can't take chances," said Dredd.

"Precisely. That's why the Council wants all trade in this potentially dangerous meat of unknown origin stamped out." O'Mannion went on, but Zandonella was by now hardly listening. It was a standard, motivate-the-troops pep talk.

O'Mannion finally said something interesting and Zandonella started listening again. "We don't know where this meat comes from and we don't know its long-term effects on human beings. If we're not careful we might be facing a public health crisis like the great American BSE epidemic of 2017."

Carver and the Karst sisters stared blankly at O'Mannion, but Zandonella knew what she was talking about, thanks again to the History Channel.

"Only about fifty million people were wiped out in that," added O'Mannion cheerfully. She could afford to be cheerful. On the scale of Mega-City size populations, fifty million souls was just a drop in the bucket. "It was nonetheless considered one of the first great public health disasters of the twenty-first century. And we don't want any repetition of it."

"So we shut these meat dealers down," said Dredd, putting an end to the lectures and turning to the vast vault door that sealed off the Armoury. Zandonella felt her pulse quicken at

his words, and at the rock steady tone of determination in
Dredd's voice. It was the voice of a man who knew his job
and intended to do it, and she felt sorry for any perps who
got in his way.

"Now let's look at the weapons we're going to use for the
job." Dredd stepped closer to the door. With O'Mannion at
his side, he moved to an oval screen recessed in the steel
door at waist level and began to punch in code words on a
keypad. After a moment he stepped aside and let O'Mannion
type in her own entry code. Access to the Armoury always
required at least two Judges with top security clearance to be
in attendance.

O'Mannion smiled with satisfaction as she typed. "Right.
That's almost it. We should be cleared for entry any moment
now..."

But just then the lights in the corridor went out, to be
replaced a split second later by an eerie amber glow. The
milky light from the entry screen also suddenly went out
and the oval portal that covered it snapped shut. O'Mannion
cursed as she snatched her fingers back from the keypad,
the descending steel cover almost slicing them off.

"What's happening?" said Carver. The red glow etched an
expression of surprise and confusion on his boyish face.
Then he said something else, but his words were lost in the
sudden high-pitched whooping sound that Zandonella
remembered from drills during her cadet days.

"Intruder alert," she said, turning to look at Dredd, who
simply nodded in confirmation and drew his Lawgiver from
its holster.

"You mean someone has broken into Justice Central?"
shouted Esma, her voice echoing violently in the sudden
silence as the alarm cut off and the strange amber glow
faded. The white lights returned in the corridor, coming
smoothly back up to the usual level of illumination.

"Does that mean they've been caught?" said Carver.

"No," said Dredd. "It means that every Judge in the vicinity is assumed to be aware of the danger and to devote all
their attention to finding the intruder until the all-clear is

sounded." He moved off down the corridor, his gun held ready.

"Where are you going?" said O'Mannion.

"To find the dirtbag who has entered Justice Central without due authorisation." Dredd was heading rapidly back in the direction they had come from.

"But how do you know they aren't heading here?" called O'Mannion. "Maybe they're trying to break into the Armoury."

"Now it's locked down, they won't be able to get in," said Dredd, his voice fading down the corridor. "Even we can't get in."

A few hundred metres down the corridor the group caught up with Dredd again. He had paused in his swift striding to talk to Judge Darrid. The moustached veteran seemed agitated. "I could have stopped him."

"Him," murmured Dredd. "Are you sure there's only one intruder?"

"Sure," said Darrid. "I was in the Waste Processing section when the dirtbag arrived."

"Waste Processing?" Zandonella said. Darrid looked at her. There was something furtive in his eyes and she wondered why.

"You know," he explained haltingly. "Where they have the floating platforms taking the garbage cans away from Justice Central and bringing the empty cans back?"

"What were you doing there?" said O'Mannion, echoing Zandonella's own puzzled, unspoken question.

Darrid's corrupt face flushed pink. "Official departmental business," he said.

"Like heck," said Carver in Zandonella's ear. "He goes there to check out the kitchen waste. That's where the old boy gets his meals. And doesn't have to pay anything for the privilege."

"You're kidding," murmured Zandonella. No wonder he'd looked furtive. He'd been eating garbage.

"No," said Darrid. He'd overheard them. "He's not kidding." He kept his eyes down as he spoke and wouldn't meet her gaze, but his face was flushed with anger. "A lot of the old veterans eat for free that way. What's wrong with it?"

Eating food thrown away from the departmental canteen, rejected meals, scraps from trays? Zandonella's stomach heaved. As hard to believe as it seemed, there were Judges with worse eating habits than Carver.

"Anyway," said Darrid, "I was there when one of the hover skiffs arrived. They're robot piloted, you know. No humans on board. They just plug into the docking port outside Waste Disposal and they load the empty waste cans in like bullets into a magazine. The cans are transported back into the building in position, ready to receive the next load of garbage, and–"

"What happened?" said Dredd tersely.

"Well it seems someone stowed away on board the garbage skiff."

"Stowed away?"

"They must have been hiding in one of the empty cans. They got into it somehow when the kitchen waste was shipped to the Trinny and Susannah Municipal Dump. Then the stowaway was shipped back to Justice Central, inside one of the cans, his cunning plan being–"

"To be automatically shunted back into Waste Processing," said Dredd impatiently.

"That's right, and once he was inside the building he had access to all the rest of Justice Central. They snuck in right under our noses, or at least right under my nose. I was there when it happened." Darrid's long, grey moustache twitched with regret. "I could have caught him."

"Has the perp been spotted on any of the video surveillance cameras?" said O'Mannion.

Darrid shook his head. "No."

"Isn't that strange?" said Zandonella.

"He must have managed to duck under the line of sight."

"How do they know there's an intruder at all, if they haven't seen him?" demanded O'Mannion.

"The weight sensors for the waste cans recorded the movement of a body mass which approximates one adult male human being."

"Which way is the perp headed?" said Dredd.

Darrid flushed again, this time on behalf of the entire department it seemed. "No one seems to know."

O'Mannion's silver eyebrows scissored with cynical surprise. "No one knows?"

"Like I said, he's pretty good at avoiding the video surveillance and no one's actually laid eyes on him in the flesh. This dirtbag is smart and he's moving fast."

"What about internal security?" said Dredd. "Everything is on lockdown automatically after an intruder alert."

"That's right," agreed Darrid with a knowledgeable nod. "They seal themselves off. There are whole areas of the building where he can't possibly go."

"So that means there are still some areas where he can go?" said O'Mannion tartly.

"Well yes, I guess so." Darrid shrugged. "That's why I'm here. There are two areas in this section of the building that aren't locked down and remain vulnerable to intrusion by, er, an intruder..." He glanced anxiously upward as the lights in the corridor flickered off. After a fleeting moment of darkness, the peculiar amber lighting returned.

Zandonella stared at the other Judges. They looked unearthly in this strange glow. Carver tried to ask a question but he was drowned out by the eerie wailing of the alarm. After a while the alarm faded and the lights returned to normal.

"A little reminder," said O'Mannion.

"You mean that wasn't the all-clear?" asked Carver.

O'Mannion looked at him with cruel amusement. "No, Judge. The all-clear isn't likely to consist of flashing coloured lights and disturbing warning sounds, is it?"

"So we should go and reinforce these vulnerable areas immediately," said Dredd to Darrid.

Darrid nodded. "That's right. I was just on my way there when I bumped into you."

"On your way where?" demanded O'Mannion. "What are these two unprotected areas?"

"Well, one's the map room," said Darrid. "And the other is the Bio-Chem Weapons Lab."

"The Weapons Lab?" said Esma, her voice rising an octave. "The place where they store the nerve gas and killer viruses and stuff?" Darrid looked at her and nodded in silent response.

O'Mannion shook her head ruefully. "I think what the Judge is implicitly asking, Darrid, is why this area isn't under automatic lockdown."

"I suppose no one ever thought an intruder would target the map room..."

"Not the map room," snapped Dredd. "We're not talking about the map room. Why isn't the Bio-Chem Weapons Lab sealed off?"

Darrid shrugged. "Technical problems with the security auto-response system apparently."

O'Mannion stepped in front of Darrid, putting her face in front of his, their noses virtually touching. "You're saying this intruder could be heading to the Weapons Lab?"

"Yes."

"And it's unguarded?"

Darrid looked helplessly away from her hot brown gaze and turned to Zandonella. He clearly felt he was being unjustly blamed for events beyond his control and that he might get a fairer hearing with her. "I was just on my way there..."

"Come on," said Dredd. He was already moving down the corridor, his Lawgiver held ready for action. "O'Mannion, you and the Karst sisters follow me to the Lab. Zandonella, you, Carver and Darrid take the map room in case the perp heads there." Dredd never moved slowly, but now he was heading down the corridor with the casual speed of a large jungle cat. O'Mannion and the Karsts had to run to keep up.

Zandonella watched them go and then turned to Carver, who still seemed puzzled about the whole situation, and Darrid, who despite his seniority seemed to be waiting for Zandonella to take charge.

The two men stared at her expectantly. Zandonella had the sinking feeling that she'd been stuck with dud colleagues on

a dud assignment. "All right," she said. "Let's head for the
map room."

Although the map room itself wasn't deemed sufficiently
high risk to merit a lockdown system of its own, several of
the departments adjacent to it were, and these had been
duly sealed off. Zandonella soon discovered that there was
only one viable route that any intruder might follow. This
led through the labyrinth of the Vehicle Confiscation unit.

"This place is really something," said Carver eagerly as
they entered the echoing warehouse space. "I always wanted
to look around here."

The confiscation unit was just one room, but it was a room
big enough to have its own weather. It had to be, to accommodate some of the more grandiose vehicles that had been
confiscated from the tirelessly industrious and ambitious
miscreants in the Mega-City. "You see that over there?" said
Carver, his voice rising with boyish excitement. He seemed
to have forgotten that they were in the process of hunting
down a potentially deadly intruder; an intruder sufficiently
intelligent and cunning to have penetrated deep into the
heart of Justice Central.

Zandonella looked in the direction that Carver was pointing and yawned. It was merely the replica Apollo 13 space
rocket and launch vehicle that a wealthy businessman had
used in an attempt to get rid of his wife permanently, by
sending her into a long, gentle orbit that took her out past
the moon on its leisurely eternal elliptical sweep through the
solar system. Unluckily for the rich murderer-to-be, Dredd
had got wind of his plans and rescued the heavily doped
spouse from the capsule on the launch pad, just as the
countdown was dropping to zero.

Now the spaceship sat here in Justice Central with other
seized vehicles, its nose cone pointing towards a milky
sphere that hung in the ceiling high above them, like a coun-
terfeit moon left there to taunt the stranded spacecraft.

Zandonella was all too familiar with the Apollo. All the
news broadcasts had featured pictures of it for days

afterwards, usually with headlines like "Mega-City One, We Have a Problem!"

The rocket ship was one of the larger crafts in the room, but it was far from being one of the most interesting. Had this been a sightseeing expedition, Zandonella would have made a point of checking out the full-sized wooden pirate ships *HMS Depp* and *HMS Flynn*, which were floating in a purpose-built tank. But it wasn't a sightseeing expedition. "Pay attention to the job at hand, Carver," she said.

Carver looked at her, a hurt expression in his liquid bovine eyes. "I am paying attention." He turned to Judge Darrid. "I just think this place is awesome."

Darrid snorted dismissively, his grey moustache twitching. "I guess a rookie would be impressed, but I got bored looking around this dump years ago."

"Yeah, I guess you'd rather be sniffing around the kitchen garbage cans, looking for scraps." Carver stared pugnaciously at the older Judge.

Darrid's face reddened. "At least I don't stink like–"

"It's strange, isn't it?" said Zandonella quickly, interrupting Darrid and forestalling the time-wasting argument that threatened to distract the men even further from the job at hand. "It's strange that this room isn't under automatic lockdown."

"What? What's that?" Darrid turned his red face from Carver to Zandonella.

Zandonella smiled. The old walrus had taken the bait. "I was just saying it's strange that the Vehicle Confiscation unit isn't locked down. You'd think it would be a primary target for any intruder with all of these..." She gestured at the exotic array of vehicles that surrounded them, ranging from bicycles to hovercraft, jet-packs to hot air balloons. Immediately in front of them was a sand-coloured tank designed for desert warfare, its long deadly cannon projecting from a pilot turret spattered with graffiti. The tank had been the property of a gang who had stolen it from a war museum, planning to use its uranium-enriched shells to blow open a bank vault. Judge Dredd, however, had once again interfered with the scheme and the gang had been forced to settle for lengthy prison sentences instead. Zandonella patted the armoured treads of the massive tank.

"You'd think a vehicle like this would be a prime target for any perp who broke in here," she said.

Darrid snorted derisively. "Any perp who did that would have to be pretty stupid. Certainly a hell of a lot more stupid than our intruder has proved to be so far."

"Why?" said Zandonella in her most innocent voice. She knew the answer, of course, but by letting Darrid explain she knew she could defuse the tension between the older Judge and Carver. "Please explain," said Zandonella.

"Because all these vehicles are on inertial lockdown." The old Judge pointed at the milky globe that hung above them in the dim recesses of the distant ceiling. "There's the inertia projector up there. It has a computerised map of all the confiscated vehicles stored here and it's got them on permanent scan." Zandonella nodded as if all this was news to her. "It will automatically project a heavy inertia beam at any vehicle that so much as budges a centimetre. Anybody trying to steal one of these babies will find that it's like driving through swamp mud or quick-drying cement."

"Didn't you know that?" said Carver.

"No," said Zandonella sweetly. "It's all so fascinating." But as she spoke, a thought suddenly occurred to her. "But you can still get into the vehicles?"

"Get into them?" Darrid frowned. "I suppose so. But what's the point of getting into them if you can't drive them away?"

Zandonella had already pulled herself up onto the gun platform of the desert tank and scrambled up to the turret, the hatch of which was indeed unlocked, and descended into the bowels of the tank itself. She emerged a moment later to see the two men staring up at her as if she'd gone mad.

"What are you doing up there?" said Darrid.

Zandonella smiled and held up the three small handheld screens she had retrieved from the supply niche of the tank.

"Motion detectors," she said. "Just exactly what we need for tracking down an intruder. I remembered that these combat vehicles were outfitted with all kinds of supplies, including motion detectors. They're a bit old-fashioned, but they'll work."

Carver eyed the motion detectors with distaste. "Why don't we get some proper, up-to-date ones from the Armoury?"

"Because the Armoury is under lockdown, remember Stinky?" Darrid accepted one of the motion detectors from Zandonella. She offered the other one to Carver, who was reluctant to accept it. "Go on, take it," Zandonella urged.

"What's the point?" Carver shrugged. "No one's coming in here anyway. The intruder won't come for a confiscated vehicle he can't drive."

"He might be on his way to the map room," said Zandonella.

"Oh sure," snorted Darrid. "The map room. That would be the first port of call for any perp invading Justice Central. No, I have to admit Stinky's right." He nodded at Judge Carver. "Any action is going to be taking place outside the Bio-Chem Lab."

Carver nodded gloomily. "That's why Dredd sent us here. To keep us out of trouble."

"To keep us out of the action," agreed Darrid. The two men seemed to have forgotten all about their earlier altercation. They were now united in dismal contemplation of the boring mission they'd been assigned.

Zandonella felt her own spirits sinking. "Oh well, we might as well take up defensive positions since we're here." She turned and walked in the direction of the map room, past a towering yellow bulldozer fitted with machine guns, and a jet-assisted cherry-red fire engine whose water tanks had been converted into gasoline tanks, changing the emergency vehicle into a deadly platform for a flame-thrower. Darrid and Carver followed slowly behind her, their lack of enthusiasm palpable.

When she idly flipped the switch of the motion detector to its ON position, four glowing white dots appeared on the orange handheld screen, all moving slowly in the direction of the map room. Three of the dots were clustered close together. The fourth dot...

"He's here," hissed Zandonella. "The intruder." Darrid and Carver stopped and stared at her. "He's here in this room with us," she whispered.

THREE

The three Judges moved swiftly between the ranks of parked vehicles. Zandonella signalled to Carver to keep up with her. Darrid was already ahead of both of them. Despite his age and his burgeoning paunch, the old Judge was moving more quickly than they had specified in the plan. Watching him go, she had a sudden strong longing for Dredd's presence. But Dredd was protecting the Weapons Lab. She would have to handle this herself.

They had agreed in a minute of swift whispered deliberation that they would head for the door of the map room, fanning out so that they would overtake the intruder and surprise him, coming at him from three different directions in a coordinated swoop.

The plan was in danger of falling apart if the idiot Darrid continued to hurry ahead. Was Darrid going to attempt a single-handed arrest? Zandonella wouldn't put it past the old walrus. She tried to signal to him but he wasn't looking in her direction, and he was already too far away to speak to without shouting and tipping off the intruder.

Darrid was moving faster with each passing second, his Lawgiver extended out in his right hand, finger ready on the trigger. Zandonella turned and signalled urgently for Carver to catch up. If they could intercept Darrid's bid for glory maybe they could still salvage the operation. She broke into a run herself, just as Darrid disappeared around the side of a red double-decker bus that was parked across from a curious antique bicycle with an enormous wheel at the front and a tiny wheel at the back.

Almost as soon as he was out of sight, they heard Darrid begin to shout. "Halt, or I'll fire!"

Zandonella cursed under her breath as she forced herself forward at top speed, boots slapping on the concrete floor, trying to catch up with the old maniac. Behind her she could hear Carver panting as he followed. Then there was the sound of gunfire, like a miniature thunderstorm ripping at the air, and erratic flashes of blue light flared under the bus. Zandonella reached for her Lawgiver and flung herself around the front of the bus. There she found Darrid, legs braced and one eye squinted shut as he took aim with his weapon.

The Lawgiver fired and twenty metres away a pink and yellow hovercraft, turbocharged for use by sugar smugglers, exploded into a million fragments. Jagged pieces of flaming shrapnel caromed all around the hall, ricocheting off vehicles and bouncing across the floor. A superheated fragment of metal went hissing past Zandonella's cheek, close enough that she felt the warm breeze of its passage. Another larger piece smashed the windscreen of the bus above her. Fragments of glass showered down on Darrid and Zandonella and the tardy Carver as he came stumbling around the bus to join them.

Darrid took his hands away from his face and grinned sheepishly at Zandonella. "I must have hit the gas tank." Zandonella ignored him and hurried over to the smouldering remains of the hovercraft. There was no sign of any intruder, living or dead, anywhere in the vicinity. She checked her motion detector. It only registered three moving shapes. Darrid joined her as she studied the small screen and he shook his head.

"I guess I missed him."

"Did you even see him?" demanded Zandonella.

"What do you mean? What are you implying by a remark like that?"

"If you saw him, describe him," said Zandonella tersely.

"Well, I only got a glimpse."

"A glimpse?"

"A glimpse of a shadow."

Zandonella curled her lip. "A glimpse of a shadow. I see." There was a startled cry behind them. She turned to see Carver drop his motion detector and raise his Lawgiver.

"There he is," he yelled as his gun went off.

The murderous cough of an explosive shell detonating was heard, and in the next row of vehicles a tractor burst into flames. A moment later a limousine and a motorcycle parked adjacent to it also caught fire and then exploded. These in turn set off an ice-cream van and a jet ski. Finally, the chain of exploding vehicles came to a stop when it reached an old-fashioned stagecoach, the kind that used to be pulled by a team of horses.

The stagecoach was made of wood and began to burn enthusiastically, but at least it didn't explode. "Stop using explosive ammunition!" yelled Zandonella. "You'll blow us all up." Carver had the good grace to look a little ashamed as he altered the setting on his Lawgiver.

Zandonella jogged over to the burning wreckage of the tractor. The air was full of fumes and the stink of smoke and burning fuel. The hot air wavered in front of her and the dancing, towering flames from the tractor cast strange, writhing shadows on the floor. Something landed on Zandonella's head, as light as a feather, and she looked up to see fat white flakes descending in a cloud from the ceiling.

For a surreal instant she thought it had begun to snow. Then she realised that the fire control system had finally kicked in and was dropping dry extinguisher flakes onto the flaming wrecks. In no time at all, white flakes were blizzarding down in a churning cloud and within seconds, the fires were all out and the wrecked vehicles were buried in neat, white piles. Zandonella lifted her face to the strange snowfall. She caught one on her tongue and almost gagged at the acrid, chemical taste. She turned to see Carver and Darrid approaching. They were both staring at their motion detectors, but she could tell by the expression on their faces that they had found nothing.

Then the sound of wood scraping on concrete was heard. Zandonella turned to see that what remained of the stagecoach, now concealed under a white mound, was moving. Or rather, something was moving under it. As she ran towards the white pile, something began to dig its way frantically out from underneath. A pink face appeared, staring at her, two dark eyes fixed on hers. Zandonella stopped dead in shock. The face was followed by two horribly deformed pink hands, digging madly at the white powder. A long, pink body followed, with two more of those dreadfully deformed hands; or were they feet?

And then a tail.

A corkscrew of pink tail. It wiggled madly at her as the intruder finished digging his way out and turned and fled across the concrete floor, feet clicking in a determined staccato.

"Why didn't you shoot?" demanded Darrid as he ran up to join her, and only with his words did Zandonella's shock recede. She looked at the Lawgiver in her hand. It had never occurred to her to fire once she'd got a good look at their intruder.

Carver joined them. "Did you see him?" he asked breathlessly. "He was some kind of hideously deformed mutie."

"No," said Zandonella. "He was a pig."

"A pig?"

"Correct," said a voice. They all turned to see Judge Dredd standing there. Zandonella felt a warm wave of relief wash over her. With Dredd to watch her back, maybe she could finally get down to business here. Although it was probably she who would end up watching Dredd's back, as he took over. Either way, it compensated for being saddled with Darrid.

"What are you doing here, Dredd?" said Darrid. "I thought you were guarding the lab."

"I heard your weapons being fired. And some other explosions." Dredd looked grimly around at the smouldering wreckage surrounding them courtesy of Darrid's quick thinking. "So I came to see what in grud's name you were up to. I told the others to remain guarding the lab in case it was some kind of diversion."

"It's no diversion, sir," said Zandonella. "It's a pig."

The pig led them a merry chase. From the Vehicle Confiscation unit it had gone scampering into the cavernous depths of the map room. Only slightly smaller than the gargantuan vehicle unit, the room was designed to accommodate a highly accurate multi-scale map of the Mega-City. The scale of the map was variable according to the Judges' needs. It could zoom in from an overview of the city equivalent to that glimpsed by a satellite from low orbit all the way down to a close-up representation of blocks and buildings so accurate and detailed you could read the graffiti on the walls.

The map appeared as a hologram projected in three dimensions on the glowing semi-transparent mist that filled the room to about Zandonella's chest height. She looked at Dredd wading through the hologram and saw that the map image hardly rose above his belt buckle.

"What's with those holes in the floor?" asked Carver. He was peering around in fascination, never having seen the map room before. He had been absent on the day that Zandonella and the others had received their orientation training. As usual with Carver's absences, it had been the result of some gastric disorder, a consequence of his grisly diet. He knew nothing about the place and it would be up to her to fill in the gaps of his knowledge.

"It's not a hole," she said. "It's a control pit."

They were approaching one of the pits now, a hemispherical indentation in the floor big enough for one or two people to crouch in. The pit was painted a bright red that made it visible through the shining fog of the map, part of a huge number of similar pits arrayed on the floor of the vast room in a neat polka dot geometry, receding in all directions in a repeating grid pattern.

As they neared the pit Zandonella saw a pink shape squirm and launch itself upwards. It was the pig. The animal scampered up out of the pit, moving quickly on its startlingly delicate little feet. Or trotters, as Zandonella remembered that they were called. She was raising her weapon and taking aim at the pig, but Darrid had beaten her to it. He was sighting his Lawgiver and he began to fire at the scuttling pink fugitive.

Or at least, he would have begun to fire at it if Dredd hadn't seized Darrid's arm and twisted it so the old Judge's Lawgiver pointed upwards and blasted harmlessly towards the ceiling. Darrid stopped firing and turned to stare at Dredd, his face red and his moustache flapping with outrage.

"What are you doing? I could have hit him."

"Hit him with what, Darrid?" demanded Dredd in an icy voice. "What kind of round are you using?"

"Not explosive, if that's what you're thinking. This snotty young Psi-Judge here has already given us an earful about that." Darrid glowered at Zandonella. "So I'm just using good old-fashioned armour piercing. They'll go right through that little pink bugger and tear him to shreds in the process."

"Exactly," snarled Dredd. He took Darrid's Lawgiver from him and began to adjust the ammunition selector. "You would have killed the perp."

"Damned right."

Dredd looked at Darrid. "Aren't you aware of the directive requiring us to keep all intruders in Justice Central alive for questioning?"

"Ah, well," blustered the old walrus. "I might have heard something along those lines..."

Dredd finished adjusting Darrid's Lawgiver and handed it back to him. Darrid took it and turned to Carver. "Come on then, what are you waiting for?" he demanded, as though all this was in some way Carver's fault, and he shooed the rookie off in pursuit of their pink quarry.

"Adjust Carver's sidearm as well," yelled Dredd after him as the two Judges hurried off into the holographic mist of the map room.

"Yes, *sir*," replied Darrid tartly as he vanished into the glowing fog of the map.

Zandonella moved to follow them but Dredd stopped her. "Let's see your weapon, Judge. I noticed that you were about to fire on the perp if Darrid hadn't beaten you to it." She showed him her gun and Dredd nodded. "Anaesthetic darts. Not bad."

"Better than armour piercing anyway," she said.

Dredd shook his head. "Better, but not good enough."

"What do you mean?"

Dredd began to alter the setting on her selector. "What makes you think that the same drug that will anaesthetise a human perp will also work on a pig?"

"Uh, I guess I never thought about it, sir. I just kind of assumed."

"Don't make assumptions, Zandonella. You might get us both killed." Dredd finished adjusting her gun and handed it back.

Zandonella peered at the ammo selector. "What kind of round have you chosen, sir?"

"Net burster," said Dredd.

A net burster was an exploding round that erupted into a sticky spray of resin when it hit its target, wrapping the perp in an immobilising web of restraints that adhered like a cocoon. Zandonella kicked herself for not thinking of it. "Good choice, sir."

Dredd shrugged impatiently. "Darrid and Carver's Law-givers are set on net bursters now too. Now let's go and see if we can't catch that pig before our two colleagues manage to burst nets all over each other."

"Wait a moment..." said Zandonella, staring around at the portion of map that now surrounded them. "Something's changed, sir." She was standing up to her collarbone in a holographic mist that represented the section of the Mega-City adjacent to Trinny and Susannah Municipal Dump. As she walked forward she was moving like a giant striding through the ghostly yielding effigies of entire city blocks, crossing a street, a small park, and then into another city block, heading towards the great circular arena of the dump.

"We're moving through a different location on the map," said Dredd. "It's been adjusted."

"Adjusted by who, sir?"

"By whoever just climbed out of the control pit."

"Do you mean the pig?" said Zandonella.

Dredd said nothing as he disappeared into the holographic mist, Lawgiver held high. She hurried after him. Dredd managed to stay ahead of her for perhaps two minutes before they saw Darrid and Carver.

The old Judge and the rookie had stopped fifty metres from the next control pit and were both taking aim with their weapons. Dredd hurried to intercept them, with Zandonella close at his heels. But they weren't quick enough to get there before the action started. A familiar pink shape came lunging out of the control pit and both Darrid and Carver instantly fired. Their Lawgivers spat flame and Zandonella saw a blur of motion as the net burster shells began to blossom into twin clouds of expanding translucent tentacles. They opened wide as they splattered into each other, locking and encircling as they fell to the floor in a heaving, sticky mess.

Darrid and Carver had managed to shoot down each other's web bursters. Dredd and Zandonella caught up with them as they stood staring down at the floor, where a double-sized cocoon was blossoming and hardening around nothing at all. She looked at the cocoon, then at the distant figure of the pig, its little pink corkscrew tail wagging cheerfully as it evaded them yet again.

Zandonella's attention then shifted away from the vanishing pig, to the holographic mist she was wading through. Once again she was striding like a behemoth along a cavernous Mega-City avenue leading straight towards the T&S Municipal Dump.

"Judge Dredd," she called.

"I know," he said. "Our friend was in the control pit and he adjusted the coordinates again."

"We're back at the same place on the map."

Dredd didn't answer. He moved off after the pig.

"What friend?" said Carver.

"Who adjusted the coordinates?" demanded Darrid querulously. "What the hell are you driving at?"

But Dredd didn't answer them either. Zandonella hurried after Dredd, and as soon as she caught up with him, she said aloud the things she'd been thinking.

"If that pig really did change the settings in the control pit..."

"I don't think there's any doubt about that," said Dredd.

"He could have done it accidentally. The settings are touch-sensitive. He could have hit them as he scrambled through the pit. I mean, that could happen. It could even happen twice..."

"Exactly the same settings twice?" said Dredd.

"That's what I'm worried about," said Zandonella. "That's exactly what I'm worried about."

"Well, save your worries until we apprehend the perp."

Three more times they caught up with the pig waiting for them in a control pit. Each time he fled before they could get in effective range to use their net bursters. And each time as he fled, he somehow managed to reset the controls so that they were surrounded by a certain section of the map. And each time, it seemed to Zandonella, the map moved a little closer to the municipal dump.

But the fourth time they encountered the pig, Dredd got off a shot. Zandonella thought he was wasting his time. They were well beyond the net burster's range of effective use. But the blossoming tentacles of the shell arced through the air and landed at exactly the spot where the scampering pig arrived a moment later. There was an audible plop as the synthetic web locked onto the scurrying animal, enveloping him.

"Lucky shot, Dredd," said Darrid. "We've got the little bastard." A moment later they were all standing over the cocoon. The pig didn't seem unduly upset about being immobilised in the adhesive strands. His trotters jerked for a moment, then stopped moving and he just lay there, gasping a little but looking otherwise relaxed and cheerful, fine golden bristles twitching sleekly on his pink neck and shoulders. Nestled at the base of his long, pink snout, the pig's eye seemed to be smiling up at her.

Zandonella could have sworn he winked at her.

"And each time the pig led us through a control pit in the map room, the map was reset to a certain district," said Zandonella. She looked at O'Mannion and wondered if the senior Psi-Judge was even listening.

But O'Mannion was listening, all right. "What are you saying? That a pig was adjusting the map?" Her silver eyebrows twitched upwards in twin sardonic chevrons. "A pig?" Her wicked eyes glowed with amusement. "Don't be ridiculous, Zandonella. He was just accidentally hitting the controls as he scuttled through."

"That's what we thought at first, but–"

"No buts. It was accidental."

"Every time taking us back to exactly the same section of the map?"

"Coincidence," said O'Mannion.

"Four times? That's not coincidence. It would have been five times if Dredd hadn't managed to hit him with a net."

"What are you trying to say here, Zandonella? You asked especially to speak to me and I agreed but as far as I can tell you're not saying anything. Not anything that makes sense, anyway."

Zandonella fought to keep her temper. "What I'm saying is that the pig was trying to tell us something."

"Tell us?" O'Mannion's eyebrows quirked up again in amusement.

"Show us, then. He was trying to show us that there is something special about that area. Specifically, the municipal dump."

"Oh, come on, Zandonella. You're reading a lot into this little escapade. You're reading a whole damned library into it."

"The pig was exhibiting intelligent, directed behaviour," persisted Zandonella. "Ask Carver or Darrid."

O'Mannion leaned back behind her desk and lazily smiled her malicious fox's smile. "I have. They say there was nothing out of the ordinary in the pig's behaviour."

Zandonella could feel herself finally losing her temper. "Then ask Dredd."

"Judge Dredd is seeing the Council of Five, receiving instructions on the security arrangements for the Cetacean Ambassador's visit. He's far too busy for me to bother him with such nonsense." O'Mannion lifted her thin, pointed chin and shook back her long mane of silver hair. "You're dismissed, Zandonella."

A Judge, even a rookie like Zandonella, commanded certain privileges, and a decent-sized con-apt was one of them. When she came home to her con-apt in Rosemary Moore Block at the end of the day, she could get undressed in her bedroom without having one foot in the living room and the other in the kitchen. The con-apt had its walls painted creamy white and the floor was covered with plush, red carpet deep enough for you to sink your feet into. Zandonella's bare feet sank into it now as she took off her uniform and changed into a kimono. She could her feel her skin breathe again after being buried all day in armour.

She was crossing to the kitchen to get something to eat, maybe some vegetable soup with real vegetables in it, when the doorbell chimed. Zandonella tightened the belt of her kimono as she hurried to the door. Just before she opened it, she checked her hair. She had a funny feeling that it was going to be Judge Dredd and for some reason, Zandonella didn't want him to see her with her hair looking a mess.

But it wasn't Dredd; it was O'Mannion. Her own silver hair billowed out as she took off her helmet and stepped into Zandonella's con-apt without waiting to be invited. "Good news, Zandonella," she said.

"So good that you had to deliver it to me when I was at home, off duty?"

"Absolutely had to." O'Mannion smiled, looking around at the furnishings of Zandonella's con-apt. Her smile seemed almost sincere. "What a bijou residence. I like the colour scheme. Sort of strawberries and cream."

"Thank you. Now what was so important that you had to tell me?" Zandonella felt ridiculous, standing here talking to her superior officer, wearing nothing but a silk kimono. At least, the label said it was silk.

"The good news is that Dredd confirmed your story."

"My story?"

"About the pig in the map room. Dredd says the pig was definitely trying to tell us something. To show us a place."

"That's what I was trying to tell you," said Zandonella.

"Don't bother offering me a hot beverage or anything," said O'Mannion lightly. "This won't take long. As I was saying, Dredd thinks the pig was trying to get us to look at a certain location."

"The municipal dump," said Zandonella.

"Correct. And so Dredd and I authorised surveillance and it transpires that the dump is being used by black market meat dealers."

"Used for what?"

"To grow meat and slaughter it."

"Grow meat? You mean they have animals there?"

"Finally up to speed?" O'Mannion smiled. A strand of her silver hair had drifted into her mouth and was caught between her full, red lips. Zandonella wanted to gently pull that annoying strand of hair free and then punch O'Mannion full in the face.

"It's called a farm," said Zandonella.

"A factory farm to be more precise. Full of pigs like the one you and Dredd apprehended."

"With the help of Carver and Darrid."

O'Mannion held up her hand. "Do you have to be so tediously loyal? I know those two mediocrities only slowed you down. But in any case, you caught the pig and we believe it is one of the animals from the factory farm."

"You mean he escaped from the farm?" said Zandonella. "Good for him."

"Him? Actually the animal *is* a male, yes, as it happens. And he did escape. And now he's leading us back there."

"But why?"

"So we can smash the factory farm and free his companions. Perhaps that's exactly what he wanted us to do. If you believe that a farmyard animal can have that much intelligence." O'Mannion smiled wickedly. "And it seems you *are* willing to believe that, Zandonella."

"Yes, I am."

"In fact, you seem to be almost fond of the animal. And that's good."

Zandonella had a sudden sinking feeling. "Why is it good?"

O'Mannion's eyes gleamed with amusement. "Because the pig has now gone from being an animal in the pound to being a potential witness."

"Witness?"

"And there's a small matter of witness protection." O'Mannion stepped back to the door of Zandonella's con-apt and swung it open again, revealing the pig standing there, patiently waiting. He looked up his narrow pink snout at Zandonella, dark little eyes glowing at her.

"I don't understand," said Zandonella. "Witness protection?"

"You've got yourself a new roommate." O'Mannion ushered the pig into the living room where it stood, staring alertly up at Zandonella, poised on its little hooves as though ready for mischief. "He's staying here with you tonight."

"For grud's sake, why me?"

"You had a very high opinion of his intelligence. I'm sure you won't mind his company. We'll pick you both up tomorrow at 06.00 sharp, for the raid on the factory farm."

O'Mannion left, smiling back through the diminishing slit of the closing door as she went. In the suddenly silent con-apt, Zandonella and the pig looked at each other.

The first thing that Zandonella did was take down the shower curtain and spread it across her beloved carpet in the living room, so that when the inevitable happened she would merely have to clean pig excrement off the plastic curtain and not out of the deep, rich ruby fibres of her carpet. Then she sat nervously, legs curled under her on her pale blue, synthetic leather sofa, watching the pig.

The pig lay disconsolately on the plastic shower curtain, strangely subdued. The mischief seemed to have gone from its dark eyes as it watched her. The sunlight gradually faded from the window of the living room and the room eventually fell into darkness.

Her guest seemed disinclined to move from its spot on the living room floor so Zandonella went to bed and left it there. What else could she do? She turned off the lights and climbed onto the sloshing softness of her waterbed. Normally, she found sleep as soon as she put her face to the cool liquid slope of the double membrane. But tonight she was keenly aware of another breathing presence, another living thing, out there in the darkness of the next room.

When Zandonella finally managed to go to sleep she was almost immediately jolted awake by a noise. It was a familiar roaring sound, but so unexpected that she snapped awake in response to it, all her faculties honed sharp by a burst of adrenaline. The toilet was being flushed.

Who was flushing her toilet? Zandonella lay there for a moment, disoriented, and then she heard the clatter of hooves in the hallway. Little pig hooves crossing the tiled floor of the bathroom, and then falling into silence again as they passed out into the carpeted softness of the living room.

Zandonella sprang to her feet, walked to the living room, and put the lights on. The pig was sitting there on the plastic shower curtain in the middle of the floor looking up at her, patiently, attentively. The only noise was the hissing and the gurgle of the pipes as the toilet patiently finished its automatic refill.

At exactly 06.00 hours, Dredd came and collected Zandonella and the pig from the rooftop of her building with the

Floating Weapons Platform. The FWP also contained Darrid, the perennially ill-smelling Carver and the Karst sisters. No sign of O'Mannion though. Zandonella relaxed and buckled herself into a seat. The pig came and sat at her feet, his warm back pressing into her shins. As the weapons platform rose into the Mega-City sky, Zandonella found herself absent-mindedly scratching Porkditz behind the ear. He responded by rolling his head with pleasure.

Zandonella had dubbed the pig Porkditz because the History Channel had recently featured an obscure programme about the daring escape of a number of prisoners from the World War Two castle prison called Colditz, and somehow she associated the pig with daring escapes.

As Dredd sat in the cockpit piloting them towards the city dump, a holographic briefing appeared in the rear of the FWP, showing the Judges, and the oddly attentive Porkditz, the details of their mission.

"This is the target," said Dredd over the intercom. The glowing hologram showed a pale green donut shape floating in mid-air. "It's the factory farm which is being concealed in the municipal dump. A big operation, large enough to house thousands of animals and the facilities for slaughtering them. The unit was salvaged from a high orbit space station, and it has been adapted for use in the atmosphere. It is a steel structure in the shape of a toroid."

"What's that?" whispered Carver.

"Like what you see there," said Zandonella. "Like a donut."

"I wish I had a donut," said Carver.

"Shut up," said Darrid. "I'm trying to listen."

"The factory is not, repeat, not, in the municipal dump itself," said Dredd. "It is floating above it."

"Floating?" whispered Carver.

"It is suspended from a large helium balloon which is hanging in the air above the dump," said Dredd. Above the donut hologram appeared a pale green ball, its diameter somewhat larger than that of the donut itself. "High tension alloy cables attach the circular farm unit to the balloon." A series of glowing white lines appeared, attaching the balloon to the donut and then the view swung around so that the donut could be seen floating edge on, suspended flat in mid-air with the ball floating above it.

A small glowing dot appeared a metre away from the ball and donut. "That dot is our vehicle," said Dredd. "As you can see we will be making contact with our target shortly. Prepare for assault, using hover-chutes."

The hover-chutes were triangular shapes that hung above the wearer like a conventional parachute, but jet propulsion units on the convergent sides of the triangle allowed the user to hover and to steer. They were the ideal means of deployment for a raid on the factory farm and Zandonella was glad to be using one. Porkditz the pig, however, didn't seem so pleased.

The armourers at Justice Central had adapted a harness on one of the chutes so that it could be used for the pig. It was Zandonella's job to strap Porkditz into the harness and then push him out of the weapons platform into mid-air. The first part of the procedure went easily enough, the pig submitting trustfully as she adjusted the padded black nylon harness around his tubular pink body. Porkditz seemed to think it was all some kind of game, his tail wagging cheerfully. But then Zandonella fastened the Velcro fasteners on the harness and began to urge Porkditz towards the door of the FWP. The door was open and cool air was blowing in. Below was a straight drop of over one hundred metres to the streets of the Mega-City. Porkditz sensibly refused to go out, digging his trotters into the metal floor of the weapons platform. Zandonella had to grab him and push him out.

The controls for Porkditz's chute had been linked to Zandonella's, with thin, silver umbilical cables into an improvised tandem unit. All of which meant that when Porkditz went out the door, Zandonella had no choice but to follow.

She tumbled out into thin air, heading for their target.

FOUR

The Trinny and Susannah Municipal Dump was a landfill site, a huge circular crater into which, as the name suggested, countless tonnes of city garbage were dumped every day. The angry smoke of millions of burning tyres perpetually hung over this giant crater as a mountain of discarded rubber was consumed in a slow, endless inferno, giving the place the appearance of a sullenly smouldering volcano here in the very heart of the Mega-City.

It was inside this permanent cloud of choking, acrid brown smoke that the factory farm was concealed, hanging on its balloon, although Zandonella couldn't see any sign of it yet, and she and Porkditz were already deep inside the sour, billowing dark cloud. The floating bulk of the weapons platform had vanished in the distance behind them, set on autopilot by Judge Dredd to hover unmanned at a constant altitude, obediently awaiting their return.

Dredd's voice crackled on Zandonella's headset. "Switch to infrared." She adjusted her goggles and immediately through the smoke she could make out the ghostly sweeping shape of the farm in the distance, like a giant metal pipe curved in a circle, hanging suspended from the bloated sphere of the helium balloon which rose like an eerie full moon above it. Porkditz gave a little yelp and Zandonella realised that even if he couldn't see the farm he must somehow sense its closeness. Perhaps his sensitive nose could detect the smell of it, even through the sulphurous stink of the smoke from the dump. Or perhaps his eyes were more sensitive than a human's.

In any case, the pig seemed aware of where they were going and didn't seem entirely pleased by the prospect. After all, reflected Zandonella, this was the giant killing machine from which he'd only recently managed to escape.

Zandonella switched off her goggles. She could make out the shape of the farm now without the help of the infrared, and it emerged as a vast dark shadow within the depths of the smoke.

Dredd's voice came over her headset again. "Zandonella, you're drifting off to the left. See to it."

She realised that Dredd was right and promptly corrected the controls of the tandem hover-chutes, aiming them once again, straight and true, at the middle of the farm. As they grew closer she could see the dark oval shape on the sloping steel hull that was their point of entry. The oval hole was an exhaust duct intended to vent gases from the toroid when it was used as a space station. It was the best way into the farm for a clandestine penetration by the Judges.

Zandonella steered herself towards the oval opening, Porkditz hanging glumly from his hover-chute beside her. The dark oval grew and grew as they floated silently forward, the tiny jets of the propulsion units on the hover-chutes above them snorting quietly and shedding a fine spray of water vapour as they powered Zandonella and the pig gracefully through the air. The brown curtain of smoke began to part and the true dimensions of the exhaust opening – and therefore the entire structure – became clear to her for the first time. The oval duct was big enough to accommodate perhaps three of the jumbo-sized Floating Weapons Platforms. So why had they left the FWP back there and taken the hover-chutes?

The ring-shaped space station itself was big enough to house a population of several thousand personnel, especially if they were packed together Mega-City intensive-housing style. Several thousand... Zandonella began checking her weapons. Intelligence reports suggested that the farm was automated and virtually unmanned, so they should only meet with the minimum of resistance.

Zandonella hoped the reports were right.

As she entered the oval aperture she realised why they'd used hover-chutes for their approach rather than simply flying the weapons platform into it. Directly inside the opening there was a lip several metres deep. But beyond that the opening was sealed with metal strips three metres high and forty metres across, like the slats of a giant venetian blind. The slats were angled, evidently, to allow a certain flow of air into the farm, and consequently they were open just wide enough to allow access for a human being, or a pig.

On the lip below, the other Judges stood waiting, dismantling their chutes and checking their guns. Zandonella's arrival had been slowed down by the need to steer for her companion and she was the last to get there. She set down on the lip and unbuckled quickly, making up for lost time. As soon as she was free of the chute's harness she unbuckled the pig. Porkditz instantly squirmed free and dashed towards the edge of the lip. Zandonella's heart leapt in her chest and she ran after him.

"Don't lose the pig!" shouted Dredd, but Porkditz had already come to a halt, staring down over the lip of the duct at the hellish smoke billowing up from the dump far below. There was clearly no escape in that direction. He raised his head and looked at Zandonella as if to say, "It was worth a try," then he turned back to the wide metal slats where Dredd and the others stood waiting. Zandonella breathed with relief and followed him.

Dredd was waiting impatiently. "I want everyone clear on this," he said. "We want to bust the gang that runs this place. But to get to them we have to penetrate through the slaughterhouse itself. Surveillance has managed to provide a schematic of the interior and intelligence has acquired access to the plans originally used to convert the place, so we have some idea of what to expect, and it's not good. This whole structure is a vast killing machine, designed to eviscerate, decapitate, slice and dice thousands of pigs every day."

Zandonella couldn't help stealing a glance at Porkditz while Dredd was speaking. The pig gave every appearance of listening attentively to the Judge, his broad and surprisingly delicate-looking pink ears spread wide as if to receive every word. She felt like covering those big floppy ears to prevent him hearing about the bloody fate of his brethren.

"This is what makes the place so well fortified and so dangerous to penetrate," said Dredd. "We can use this exhaust port as our point of entry, but as soon as we're inside we're going to have to make our way through the abattoir tunnels and the killing chutes."

"Why?" said Darrid. "Surely there's another way?"

"Negative," said Dredd. "The farm is designed like two circular pipes, one inside the other. The big pipe on the outside is the farm itself. The smaller pipe running through the centre contains the control rooms and the living quarters of the perps."

"I don't get it," said Carver helplessly.

"We have to go through the big pipe to get at the little pipe inside," said Zandonella.

"Correct," said Dredd. "We have to go through the slaughterhouse to get to the perps. Now this slaughterhouse is equipped with mechanical swing blades and chainsaws and razor-sharp killing knives. They are designed to be triggered by the approach of a pig, but any animal will do." Dredd looked at Carver and Zandonella. "Including rookie Judges. Do I make myself clear?"

"All except for one small point," said Darrid. "How the hell do we get through this fun house in one piece?"

Dredd looked down at Porkditz, sitting patiently and alertly at Zandonella's heels. "Our little pink friend, here. He obviously found a safe route through the place on his way out. Now he will be our guide on the way back in."

"You've got to be kidding," said Darrid.

"No," said Dredd.

"We're going to follow that pig?"

"Yes," said Dredd.

"And what the hell are we supposed to do once we get inside?" demanded Darrid. "There's only six of us." Seven, thought Zandonella, who was already beginning to think of Porkditz as one of the team.

"Reinforcements are already arriving," said Dredd.

"I don't see any. Where are they?"

Dredd nodded towards the enveloping cloud of foul-smelling brown smoke that rose from the crater below. "Dump ships are arriving out there all the time. The perps in this factory farm are accustomed to the comings and goings of these dump ships. They know they're just independent waste contractors bringing garbage in from all over the Mega-City. But we've borrowed some dump ships and modified them and now we're using them to bring in reinforcements who will be deployed as soon as we have secured a staging post." Dredd looked at them. "Securing that staging post is our responsibility."

He turned away without another word and clambered through the gap beneath the vast metal slats. Darrid stared after him for a moment, then followed. Carver shot a nervous look at Zandonella, then went after him. The Karst sisters went next and Zandonella brought up the rear, urging the squirming mass of Porkditz through the opening with her. The air inside was warm and smelled of engine oil, manure and something else, something heavier and sweeter and choking. The hairs on the back of Zandonella's neck stirred. If death had a smell, this was it.

"Wait up," she called to the others. "I've got our guide here."

"So this place is held up by a balloon?" said Blue Belle.

"That's right," replied Mac the Meat Man, smiling and nodding at her. Mac was a small, cheerful man with a tight, round little paunch that made it look like a basketball was tucked into his pink and turquoise horror of a Hawaiian shirt. He also wore khaki shorts over his knobbly and pathetically spindly white legs, and flip-flops that exposed egregiously hairy toes. His toes disgusted Blue Streak. As did his fat white eyebrows and his attitude. Mac was annoyingly eager to please and never happier than when he was agreeing with someone. "When I decided to build the Mega-City's number one meat farm and slaughter–"

"Who says you're number one?" interrupted Blue Streak. He couldn't take any more of the little man's posturing.

"Let him finish," said Blue Belle. Streak fell silent, glumly reflecting that he'd only been with this woman a few days and already she had him firmly under her thumb. Sneckin' Blue Balls. That nickname was perfect, because she was a real pain in a very personal place. Not that he'd ever dare hint as much to her. Streak was infatuated with the girl and he knew it.

Blue Belle turned back to Mac the Meat Man. She was wearing combat boots, ski pants, a bra and a bandolier full of ammunition; all matching in black leather, and that was all. The astonishing detail of the blue tattoos on her naked torso made it hard not to stare at the splendid contours of Belle's body. He could see Mac, that red-faced old fraud, trying hard not to stare. The old, sick bastard was turned on by her sexy outfit even now, with death staring him in the face.

Belle, at that moment, was pointing her pistol, a wicked-looking silver automatic with twin ammunition clips, right in Mac's face. But still Mac was trying not to stare at her breasts. And of course Belle's tattoos stopped abruptly at her neck, and this along with her short hair, cropped close to her skull, made her pale unblemished face look obscenely naked. Obscenely, or arousingly, thought Streak. But definitely naked.

"Go on," Belle demanded. "What were you saying?" She held the gun steady, pointing right between Mac's eyes. The laser-assisted gun sight projected a hot pink dot on his forehead between the bristling white eyebrows that looked disgustingly to Streak like two fat white caterpillars. The white caterpillars danced and jiggled on either side of that hot pink spot that indicated where the first bullet would go in.

"Ah yes, where was I? My farm, my slaughterhouse, the finest in the Mega-City, yes. The finest anywhere. I had other farms before, certainly, little back street operations, but nothing like this. The big one. The big one I knew I had in me. And when my operations began to turn a profit, a pretty profit..."

"There's money in meat, all right," said Streak, suddenly feeling left out of the conversation.

"Stop interrupting," said Belle, a now familiar note of irritation creeping into her voice. Streak suppressed his own annoyance. It was hard to believe that this ill-tempered shrew was the same, feverishly passionate, almost violently responsive creature he'd made frantic love to in the sweaty confines of the escape pod as it drifted safely down through the burning sky of the Mega-City night.

"So I invested all my profits," said Mac, "in this fine operation you see here. A Tatou-class Russian space station bought for a snip from a military surplus supplier, converted and armoured and reinforced–"

"Fat lot of good that did you," said Streak.

Belle turned to look at him. "Stop interrupting," she hissed.

"But you two *infiltrated*," said Mac, obviously stung by the remark. "We never expected an infiltration. We were braced for a frontal assault. We thought the Judges might try and raid us, smash down the front door and so on." He twitched his sweaty gaze towards Streak. Streak tried not to look at those fat white eyebrows. They made his stomach turn. "But you two..."

"Just ignore him," said Belle, "and answer my question."

Mac's gaze returned to her, the beautiful half-naked tattooed woman who was pointing the gun at him. "What question?" he said politely.

"This thing is held up by a balloon," repeated Belle impatiently, the gun twitching in her hand.

"Yes," said Mac, his rheumy old eyes dancing nervously as they followed the gun barrel. "That's right. The station is a toroid design, a fat ring in effect, hanging suspended from a balloon."

"Well, my question is," said Belle, "what's in the balloon?"

"Oh, here we go again," said Streak. He sighed and rolled his eyes with exasperation, pointedly turning away to look at their other prisoners, all of whom seemed to be still unconscious. Even the robot.

"Put a sock in it," said Belle. She looked at Mac. "Ignore him. What I want to know is, what's in the balloon?"

"In it? You mean the gas? The gas that makes it float?"

"That's right," said Belle. "Is it hydrogen or helium?"

"Why, helium," said Mac. "Why do you ask?"

"She just can't stand to lose an argument," said Streak over his shoulder as he wandered down the length of the cramped control room to check on their other prisoners. The control room was long and narrow, circular in cross section, like a length of pipe just big enough to stand up in. Like a sewer pipe, thought Streak. And it didn't smell much better, because the air conditioning system was interconnected with the slaughterhouse that encased them and the pervading odour of pig, pig excrement and pig blood drifted in, opposed only by the feeble synthetic pine odour of the little green, tree-shaped air fresheners some optimistic soul had used to festoon the control room.

The control room was a galley-style design, with banks of controls and computer screens running down both sides of the pipe. The labels on the control panels were all in Russian. On the monochrome Tri-D screens above the controls were pigs, pigs and more pigs. Some of them were feeding greedily on a flow of slurry, splashing pale gobbets of unknown origin. Others were in the process of evisceration, silently screaming in terror as whirling blades hacked them to pieces and their blood was sluiced away to serve as, among other things, a component of the slurry for their companions. Others still raced furiously down corridors, being urged along by small electric shocks in the metal floor beneath them, stampeding towards feeding or to slaughter. Some were simply standing still, trying to sleep or play or find some meaning in their little piggy lives in this steel circle of hell in which they had found themselves.

But all of them, whatever they were doing, were jammed together, jowl to jowl, snout to tail, in as dense a mass as could be physically packed into the metal passages of the slaughterhouse. The more pigs, the more profit. So you were always cramming in the maximum amount of livestock.

Streak understood that. He looked away from the screens and scanned the prisoners. The Barkin brothers and the robot were secured along the length of one side of the control panel. Streak kept his gun, a fat-barrelled machine pistol, carefully aimed at them, but they appeared to still be out cold.

"Yes sir, it's helium, all right," repeated Mac, still eager to please, sweating with fear, trying to smile into the gun that Belle was pointing at his fat face. "And it works like a dream. We float just dandy."

"All right, all right, so it's helium. But it could be hydrogen, couldn't it?"

"Oh yes, certainly," said Mac. "Hydrogen certainly does cause a balloon to float, too."

"He's just humouring you," said Streak.

"No, no," said Mac, staring into the gun. "The young lady's absolutely right. Hydrogen works perfectly well as a gas in a balloon. It's all to do with valencies, or something, I believe."

"And hydrogen," said Belle. "It isn't flammable, is it? I mean it's not likely to explode."

Mac fell silent, momentarily stalled in his campaign to enthusiastically agree with everything anyone said. "Ah well…"

"Go on, tell her the truth," said Streak. "Tell her you didn't use hydrogen in the balloon because only a fool would." He looked closely at Belle. "Only a fool like Big Blue."

"Big Blue was not a fool," snarled Belle, hot indigo eyes flashing at Streak with rage. It wasn't the reaction he'd hoped for. Her old boyfriend was dead, thoroughly dead, had been a cinder for days as a result of the airship explosion, but it seemed she wasn't over him yet. Streak couldn't help glancing at his own spindly arms and remembering Big Blue's biceps. They had been like boulders. Maybe he should start doing some push-ups.

Belle turned back to Mac the Meat Man. "What I'm saying is that if you had an airship filled with hydrogen, you wouldn't expect it to blow up in a ball of flame just because someone happened to, say, completely unintentionally, discharge an assault rifle in the gondola of the airship and, you know, just happened to nick the hydrogen balloon with a few... a few... I suppose you'd call them *tracer* bullets, wouldn't you?"

"Tracer bullets?" said Mac. "Into a hydrogen balloon?" His face had gone pale.

"I mean," said Belle, "If the balloon happened to explode, you wouldn't think it was the tracer bullets would you? It's much more likely that the Judges used some secret weapon on us, isn't it? Something that had nothing to do with my tracer bullets. And therefore, at the end of the day, my firing through the balloon had nothing to do with it exploding."

"Ah, well," said Mac, still gamely looking for a way to agree with her. Streak wondered how he was going to wriggle out of this one. But a fiery hail of lead did tend to cause hydrogen to ignite, as Belle had so memorably demonstrated the other evening. Mind you, Streak didn't blame her for trying to find another explanation. It couldn't be easy to know you'd caused the death of your boyfriend and almost his entire gang.

If Streak hadn't managed to bundle Belle into the escape pod with him, a microsecond before detonation, the two of them would have been dead as well. He'd astonished himself by grabbing the girl and rescuing her. Many times since then, as their relationship followed its rocky course, he'd asked himself why he'd taken Belle with him into the pod. But the truth was that in the heat of the moment he hadn't even thought about it. He'd just done it, automatically, with an inevitability that was unquestionable and final.

Mac stared at Blue Belle, eyebrows wagging in bafflement, still trying to formulate a reply. But just then another voice spoke up and let him off the hook. "She fired into the canopy?" There was a whoop of laughter. "She blew you boys up?"

Streak turned and raised his gun. The blond Barkin brother, the one called Leo, was wide awake. He was grinning at them through a mouthful of bloody, broken teeth. Streak had smashed him in the face with rather more force than strictly necessary when they'd seized control of the control room. Still, Leo didn't seem to hold any ill will against his assailant. He sat up in the swivel chair in front of the control panel where they'd handcuffed him, checked his cuffs and winked cheerfully at Streak. "Your girlfriend isn't much of a shot, is she?"

"You shut up," said Belle, swinging round to aim her gun at Leo.

"Keep your gun on the other guy, sweetie," said Streak. "We need to keep all of our prisoners under our guns at the same time."

"How's my robot?" said Leo. "I hope you haven't damaged him." Leo scooted around in his swivel chair. His black-haired brother was lying limply in the seat beside him, his face also marked with blood, but Leo didn't pay any attention to him. Instead he stared over him, trying to get a better look at his robot, which was secured to the control panel about three metres away where Streak had fastened him with a bicycle lock through the convenient gap in his red metal neck. "Oh, there he is," sighed Leo when he spotted it. The bot rotated its bullet-shaped, red metal head and its circular white eyes flashed as if it was delighted to see its owner.

"Boyard-27 reporting for duty," said the robot. "Request permission to provide status report."

"Start with yourself, Boyo," said Leo. "Did you sustain any damage when these tattooed lovebirds busted in on us?"

"Negative, sir. I am fully operational except I seem to have a bicycle lock through my neck." The bot moved its head, causing a loud clanking sound as the bicycle lock struck against the zero gravity hand grip on the control panel which Streak had found to secure it on. "I am well and truly locked."

"But you didn't sustain any other damage?" said Leo anxiously.

"Not even chipped paint, sir."

"Thank grud for that," sighed Leo.

"Oh, would you listen to yourself?" said his brother,

suddenly looking up. Streak realised that both brothers must have been awake for some time, merely feigning unconsciousness in the hope of deceiving their captors. Sneaky bastards. But Streak didn't blame them as he would have done the same thing himself.

"Request permission for further status report, sir," said the robot.

"Permission denied!" barked the black-haired brother. Streak remembered that his name was Theo. He sat up, testing his handcuffs and glaring with hatred at Streak and Blue Belle. He then turned to the robot and glared at it with even more hatred. "Just keep your metal trap shut."

"Don't talk to him that way," said Leo.

"You know what I think?" said Theo. "You love that robot more than you do me."

"I rebuilt that robot myself, with my own hands," said Leo. "I restored him from junk yard scrap. I've got all that time and effort invested in him." He looked at his brother. "Whereas I've got damn all invested in you, bro," he said, and laughed nastily.

"I need to report urgently," said the robot. To Streak he sounded like a child who wanted to go to the bathroom.

"Permission denied!" snapped Theo.

"Don't talk to him like that," said Leo.

"Could you make all of them shut up for a moment?" said Blue Belle.

"Shut up, all of you," said Streak, brandishing his gun and trying to sound intimidating. "The lady has something to say."

Blue Belle stepped forward and cleared her throat. She stood over the two brothers and the robot. "Maybe it was indeed my small mistake that caused our airship to explode that night. But none of that would have happened, none of our comrades in arms or my boyfriend Big Blue would have been killed if not for you two." She pointed her gun first at Leo, then at Theo. The pink laser spot danced from one face to the other.

"If you two hadn't tried to double-cross us on the meat

deal," said Belle, "none of this would have happened." She thumbed the safety catch off. "It was your fault they died." Belle raised her gun.

"We were only following orders from Mac here," said Leo hastily. At the other end of the room the Meat Man twitched.

"Now boys," he blustered. "What's the use of pointing the finger of blame?" Belle looked at him and he fell silent.

"Request permission to report. Urgent," said the robot, sounding more than ever in need of the bathroom.

"Shut up," said Belle. She turned back to the brothers. They could clearly see the murderous look in her eyes.

"It's true. It was all Mac's idea. He wanted to corner the market in meat," said Theo.

"Boys, boys," said Mac. "That's all water under the bridge."

"He wanted to eliminate all his rivals," continued Theo, "which meant you. It was nothing personal."

"Oh, stop whining," said Leo disgustedly. Belle moved her furious gaze onto him. The pink laser spot danced onto the blond boy's forehead.

"You'd better start whining, too," said Belle. "And begging for your life."

"You're not going to shoot us," said Leo.

"No? Why not?"

Leo smiled. "Because you're going to have to take these handcuffs off us and beg for us to help you."

Belle glanced at Streak. "He's gone crazy," she said. "Fear has caused his mind to snap." Streak wasn't so sure. There was a disturbing note of confidence in Leo's voice. Belle swung back to Leo, pointing her gun at him. "You say you're going to help us," she said. "Help us with what?"

Leo nodded at the screens behind her. "Help you fight off those Judges who are hurrying along that slurry tunnel, on their way to this control room."

Belle, Streak, Mac and Theo all swung their heads to stare at the small Tri-D screen, which did indeed show a blurry black and white image of half a dozen heavily armed Judges hurrying along a tunnel, up to their knees in some dark liquid.

"Oh shit," said Belle.

"I was trying to tell you," said the robot.

"How the hell did they get in here?" asked Mac.

"Maybe they infiltrated," said Streak.

The smell of the slurry was appalling. Zandonella was in it up to her mid-thighs, wading through the thick, warm resistance of the fluid and trying not to breathe. Ahead of her was the pig, Porkditz, pluckily surging ahead even though his trotters couldn't touch the bottom. He didn't seem to mind swimming through the liquid filth. Indeed, after his initial reluctance to enter the factory farm, the pig had seemed relaxed and almost at home in his surroundings. Zandonella had seen a documentary about prisoners and she remembered that many of them, even the survivors of death camps, had espoused a strange nostalgia for the institutions where they had once been confined. I guess there's no place like home, she thought.

As far as Zandonella could determine, the slurry consisted of the waste matter from all the pig pens in the factory farm, combined with blood and entrails from the abattoirs, and a choice selection of garbage, including hospital waste, dredged from the smoking crater of the municipal dump below.

Beside her the tall figure of Dredd made his way through the slow-flowing muck. Behind her, Darrid, Carver and the Karst sisters followed. Dredd suddenly signalled for them to stop. "The tunnel branches here," he said. "We have to decide which way to go."

"Why don't we split up?" said Darrid. "I could take the sisters and–"

"Negative," said Dredd. "We stick together." He looked at Zandonella. "Which route does your friend suggest we follow?"

Zandonella looked at Porkditz floating in the filth. He gazed up at her with intelligent little eyes as if to ask her what she wanted. But how was she to convey her question to him? Zandonella pondered for a moment before moving forward.

She kept her eyes on his as she waded past him, to the point where the tunnel was divided by a thin vertical wall, turning it from one circular passage into two semi-circular ones. Zandonella set off down one tunnel and then came back, walking against the steady warm flow of the stinking ooze. She moved to the second tunnel, went down it a short distance, then came back again.

She looked at Porkditz. He looked at her. For a moment she had the eerie sensation that something passed between her and the animal, a sense of common understanding. And then Porkditz set off, swimming with energy down the tunnel to their left. Zandonella hesitated for a moment, looking at Judge Dredd.

"Right then," said Dredd. "Looks like we've got our answer. Everybody follow the pig." They all turned and started striding through the thick flow of muck once again, pursuing the twin pink ears of Porkditz.

In no time at all they came upon a structure bolted to the steel wall on their right. In a cylindrical cage a series of small jutting platforms rose upward at geometric intervals.

"Steps," said Zandonella. "A spiral staircase. Going up."

"Taking us to the control area," said Dredd. "Good. That's exactly what we wanted. This is where the perps will be. Everybody check their firearms."

Porkditz was already paddling eagerly towards the staircase. Zandonella wondered how he would manage to negotiate the structure, but the pig scrambled onto the bottom step with ease, and promptly began to ascend, shaking the slurry off him as he went. She waited for the shower of muddy droplets to stop and then followed, the filthy ooze flowing off her own boots and leggings. The metal steps clanked underfoot. Porkditz scampered ahead of her. They ascended up into the darkness of what had been an access shaft in the old space station. After a ten second ascent they came to a point where the shaft widened and a glowing panel was set in the wall. A metre below the panel the spiral steps broadened out to form a landing.

Dredd was following close behind Zandonella. "Don't touch anything," he said. The pig had hopped up on his hind trotters and pressed his front ones against the panel. There was pneumatic sigh from the wall, a flow of less tainted air, and a large rectangle of light appeared on the wall.

"Airlock," said Dredd. "I'm primary through it. Watch my back." He went through the door, moving like a panther. Zandonella went after him, followed by the pig and the other Judges.

The room that opened out before them was about twenty metres long but seemed smaller. It was cramped by the presence of two large space shuttles with Russian markings. Both vehicles were sitting on ramps that aimed them at large circular airlocks set in the outer wall of what had once been the space station.

"Escape craft," said Dredd. "This is the launch chamber. Darrid, you stay in here and stand guard."

"Why?"

"Because we don't want anyone escaping," growled Dredd impatiently. "The rest of you, we're going up that other staircase, over there. We're going to see what's above us. Be ready for anything." He moved swiftly up the spiral staircase, vanishing into the shadows above. Zandonella hurried after him, Porkditz trotting along at her heels. He seemed eager to reach their destination, whatever it might be.

Judge Dredd had reached the next landing above. Here was another illuminated panel with cryptic markings. Dredd reached out without hesitation and pressed the controls to open the airlock. Zandonella and Porkditz joined him just as it sighed open. Behind them, the other Judges clattered up the stairs. Porkditz gave a little squeal of anticipation.

As the airlock swung wide, Zandonella squinted into the space that was revealed. It was a large room lit with the ruddy red glare of heat lamps. A gust of warm air carried an overwhelming animal smell from within. Porkditz squealed again but now the sound was lost among countless similar squeals. The red glare was confusing.

They were standing on a small raised platform with a metal railing running around it. The platform overlooked a wide, open space like the interior of a giant shed with a ceiling that curved upwards. Hanging from the ceiling was a giant, luminous, pink plastic pig. The pig was depicted frozen in mid-scamper. He was smiling, licking his lips and wearing a napkin as though hurrying to a much-anticipated meal. On his sides, in bright purple lettering, were the words "Shop at Mac the Meat Man's!"

The floor beneath it was filled with a surging mass of life: faces, bellies, tails, ears. They were all in motion, all in upheaval, all shrilling in protest at the chaos of it all. Countless little pairs of eyes glowed eerily at Zandonella in the red light.

Zandonella stared back at them. Pigs. Thousands of them. Jammed together so close that none of them could lie down, or so much as turn around.

"Looks like we're not in the control section," said Dredd, turning to look at her. "I guess our informant gave us a bum steer." He looked down at Porkditz who waggled his tail uncertainly. Carver and the Karst sisters came puffing up the stairs and through the airlock out onto the platform.

"Turn around and head back down, Judges," said Dredd. "Looks like we've taken a wrong turn."

"Not back into that gunk again," said Carver.

"Move it, Judge," said Dredd.

Esma lifted her hand to point at something and said, "Hey, what's th−"

Zandonella turned to see what she was pointing at, but at that moment Esma's pointing hand exploded in a shower of blood.

"Down!" roared Dredd, shoving Zandonella and Carver to the floor. As they hit the deck Dredd swept over them and grabbed the Karst sisters, pulling them both down, just as the air above them came alive with angry motion and the vicious pinging of ricocheting bullets hitting the steel airlock door.

Gunfire, thought Zandonella foolishly. Someone was shooting at them. Esma's ruined hand was still spraying blood as she stared at it blankly, helplessly paralysed with shock. Her sister was equally stunned, but Judge Dredd already had a field dressing out and was slapping it over Esma's wound. As soon as this was done he drew his Law-giver and started returning fire.

FIVE

Bullets sizzled overhead. Zandonella lay on the platform beside Porkditz, his bristly snout pressed firmly against her cheek, seeking shelter and comfort. The pig didn't seem to have any problem understanding what was going on, or appreciating the keen need to keep his head down. There was a rattling blast of anti-personnel rounds from a Lawgiver as Dredd returned fire.

"Get off the platform!" he yelled. "We're sitting ducks."

Zandonella raised her head. There was a sudden string of pale green flashes of gunfire over the mass of pigs below. She ducked again as the bullets tore through the air above her. She felt a powerful hand gripping her arm, pulling her forward, under the railing and over the side of the platform. Dredd was diving over and taking her with him. Zandonella cried out as she fell, hitting the floor so hard it knocked the wind out of her. She looked up to see Dredd crouching beside her. The gunfire was constant now. They were lying on a floor that consisted of a metal grid with openings in it big enough to allow the pig droppings to fall through. Well, most of the pig droppings, thought Zandonella as she sat up and lifted her buttocks out of a soft repugnant mound. It didn't matter. She couldn't get any dirtier after her trek through the slurry tunnel.

Zandonella lifted her Lawgiver and turned to look at Judge Dredd for instructions. But Dredd had scrambled back onto the platform above her. There was a furious burst of gunfire in response to this move and she had to drop back down to floor level, this time landing with her chest in a soft pile of excrement.

A moment later there was a heavy thud and Carver landed beside her, face down in the mess on the floor, evidently shoved off the platform by Dredd. He was followed by Tykrist who landed on top of him and quickly squirmed off, fumbling with her gun, just as another shape hurtled off the platform. It was Dredd, cradling the wounded Esma in his arms. He landed lightly as a cat beside Zandonella, crouching coiled and ready to move. Zandonella helped him put Esma on the floor, her back against the raised section that formed the base of the platform. It was the safest place for them to be at that moment. Esma was clutching the bandaged ruin of what had once been her right hand, the white dressing soaked through with an angry red stain. Her eyes were glazed and Zandonella knew the woman was in shock. They'd have to get her to a med-unit quickly.

Now that her comrades were momentarily safe, Zandonella's thoughts immediately turned to Porkditz. She risked a quick look up at the platform and caught a glimpse of the little pig cowering there, out of the line of fire. Good boy, she thought, as Dredd seized her and pulled her back down.

"Stay down Zandonella," he snarled. "We have to make a move." He studied their position and Zandonella followed his gaze, trying to second-guess his thoughts.

In front of them was the long expanse of the shed-like room, crammed with pigs in a seemingly endless mass disappearing into the darkness beyond. The nearest pigs had backed fearfully away from the intruders, giving the Judges a little room at the base of the platform. But as frightened as the pigs were, they couldn't back up more than a tiny distance, because of the sheer number of their comrades behind them. There was commotion further back in the pig pack as another string of small pale explosions blossomed and Zandonella heard the pounding of another automatic weapon. The pigs shrieked and churned, trying to get away from the gunfire.

"They're hiding among the livestock," said Dredd. "There are two groups of them, one by the right wall, the other by the left. They're trying to pin us down in a cross fire."

As he spoke there was a second burst of gunfire and this time Zandonella caught sight of their assailants: a thin young man and half-naked girl, both of them covered with tattoos. The girl was feeding a bandolier of ammunition into some kind of heavy assault weapon that the young man was holding. A vicious stream of bullets ripped through the air. Dredd didn't need to tell Zandonella to duck. As soon as the tattooed couple stopped shooting, the other group of assailants opened up. They were crouching low amongst the writhing herd of pigs but Zandonella was able to see them now. There were two of them. No, three. Two men and a...

"Robot," said Dredd. "They must have removed its Asimov inhibitor chip. Watch out for it. It can probably shoot a hell of a lot more accurately than any of those other scumbags."

The robot was a gangly red metal skeleton with a barrel chest and a bullet-shaped head. It lurched up from among the frantic pigs and pointed a gun towards the cluster of Judges huddling by the platform. It never got a chance to fire, though. Dredd had his Lawgiver ready and squeezed off a round. There was a blast of noise and a sudden bright flare of explosion at the robot's midriff. The thing tottered and collapsed, falling apart in two distinct pieces separated at the waist.

"Armour piercing," said Dredd with grim satisfaction. "Remember that. These old-style robots are always vulnerable in their mid-section. Now their metal friend is officially out of action."

The pigs shrieked and churned as the two sections of the robot fell into their midst. But there was another shriek as well, a distinctly human sound. A man stood up out of the mass of pigs, screaming with rage and grief. He had blond hair and a black moustache and there was a flicker of recognition in Zandonella's mind. Where had she seen him before?

The blond man seemed to be freaking out at the destruction of the robot. Then a second man popped up, this one with black hair and a blond moustache, and Zandonella realised where she'd seen them both. The firefight in the rooftop funfair, on the night the airship had exploded. The blond man was still freaking out, presenting an easy target. Zandonella took aim at him just as his black-haired companion pulled him down amongst the herd of pigs. Zandonella fired and missed her target.

"They're pinned down," said Dredd. "Time to carry the fight to the enemy." He turned to the other Judges crouching under the platform. "Karst, you stay with your sister. Carver, you keep an eye on both of them, and on the exit. Zandonella, come with me."

The wounded sister suddenly sat up. The glazed expression had left her eyes. She raised her Lawgiver in her trembling left hand. "I've still got one good hand, Judge," said Esma in a strained, rasping voice. "I can give you covering fire."

"Stay down and wait for the Med-Squad. Don't try to be a hero," said Judge Dredd. "Leave that to your colleague here." He signalled to Zandonella and she followed Dredd into the squealing mass of pigs.

It was tough going. The pigs were terrified and wanted to get out of their way, but there was simply nowhere for them to move. Dredd and Zandonella pushed through the agonised tangle of shrieking, defecating life, constantly ducking and crouching as the perps fired at them. The gunfire was now only coming from one direction, near the left wall where the robot had gone down. And even that was becoming sporadic.

"Maybe they're running out of ammo," said Zandonella.

"Don't count on it," said Dredd. They were approaching the spot where the men and the robot had been firing and Zandonella braced herself for contact. She and Dredd were squeezing through the squirming mass of pigs, keeping low so as to present a minimum target for the perps. Zandonella's foot struck something on the floor and she looked down. A jointed length of metal glinted there in a puddle of dark liquid. The thing looked like two sections of pipe with a socket connecting them and a broad, flat suction pad was fastened on one end. There was an identical piece of metal lying strewn nearby also in a dark puddle.

"Legs," said Dredd, and Zandonella realised it was the robot's legs, blown off by Dredd, lying in pools of machine oil. "We're getting warmer," said Dredd, raising his Lawgiver. He started forward with Zandonella close at his side.

There was a staccato stutter of gunfire nearby, so close at hand it was deafening. Dredd and Zandonella dropped to the floor amongst the crowd of frantic pigs. A hot warm spray fell on them and Zandonella knew it was pig blood. Then the pigs themselves began tottering and collapsing on top of the Judges with high-pitched terminal squeaks and screams. Zandonella tried to slither out from under a bristly, twitching corpse but Dredd stopped her.

"Use it for cover," he said.

Zandonella fought with her disgust and overcame it. She crawled along the floor beside Dredd, both of them grotesquely pushing dead pigs along in front of them to use as shields against the incoming fire. Zandonella could hear bullets slamming into the pigs' corpses, flat meaty slapping sounds, and the small, still-warm body she held shuddered with each impact. The firing was very close now. They must almost be on top of their assailant. Abruptly Dredd reared up, throwing his dead pig aside as he fired his Lawgiver. Zandonella jerked out of concealment, raising her own weapon, just in time to see a bizarre shape blazing away at them with a machine gun.

The thing looked like a truncated scarecrow made of metal, but a scarecrow cut off at the waist. It was the remains of the robot, still active and still deadly. The thing consisted of a red metal abdomen shaped like an oil drum and two spindly arms clutching the rapid-firing weapon. The thing's grotesque appearance was considerably enhanced by the fact that its head was missing. The neck section of the robot terminated in a chaotic spray of torn wires, as did its severed torso, the latter leaking a thick black sludge of machine oil onto the floor. All around it, pigs were fighting to get clear of this hellish apparition.

Zandonella took all this in the instant before she ducked from the next burst of bullets, diving back among the panic-stricken porkers, trying to avoid their sharp little hooves as they danced in hysterical agitation on the resounding metal grid of the floor. She looked over at Judge Dredd.

"How can it shoot at us without a head?" she shouted. "It doesn't have a brain."

"Doesn't need one," snarled Dredd. "It's on auto, using its bootstrap operating system in its spinal area."

Another blast of gunfire flared from the robot's weapon. The pig nearest Zandonella dropped heavily to the floor, a sound like a sigh trickling from its mouth. It lay there inert and bleeding.

"But it doesn't have eyes," she said. "How can it see us?"

"Motion sensor in the chest area," said Dredd. He suddenly stood up and fired his Lawgiver, a single, carefully aimed round. The robot ceased firing. There was a grinding metallic sound and then the clatter of metal collapsing on metal. Zandonella risked a glance at the robot and saw that the robot torso was lying motionless on the floor, the weapon falling from its hands.

"Right about there," said Dredd, walking over to the robot and looking down at the neat bullet hole in the centre of its barrel chest.

Zandonella got to her feet, fighting the trembling sensation in her knees. All around them the pigs were still squealing at an ear-splitting volume, but because the gunfire had stopped the vast room seemed almost silent.

"Now that's what I call lucky shooting!" declared a familiar voice. Zandonella was shocked to see Judge Darrid standing behind them, knee deep in pigs, accompanied by Carver and Tykrist, both of whom were supporting the wounded Esma. Zandonella realised the four Judges must have crept up on her and Dredd when they'd been preoccupied with taking out the robot sniper. "You shot his robot ass off," said Darrid. "Must have hit it with a ricochet."

"Judge Darrid," said Dredd with dangerous deliberation, "what are you doing here?"

"I heard the shooting and came running. You can't keep old Darrid out of a good shoot-out. But I was too late. Looks like you've already got the situation well in hand." He beamed at Dredd, but the stoic Judge wasn't even looking at him. He was now scowling at Carver and the Karst sister.

"I told you to stay by the entrance and wait for medical assistance," he said.

"Leave the rookies alone," said Darrid. "I ordered them to follow me. You should thank us. We were providing valuable back-up."

At these words, Dredd swung back to Darrid. "And I told you stay and watch the shuttle craft," he said.

"What's the point of that?" said Darrid. At the moment he spoke, they all heard a low rumbling sound that seemed to be transmitting through the steel walls and ceiling and floor, and a moment later they felt a faint but distinct tremor that ran through the entire structure. With a sinking feeling, Zandonella recognised the signs of a shuttle craft being launched.

Darrid's eyes twitched guiltily. He looked at Dredd then quickly looked away. "Those shuttle craft are small. Even at a squeeze you can't get more than two or three people into them. How many perps are we after?"

"Not counting the robot, five," said Dredd. The roaring repeated itself, as did the tremor. "That will be the last of them leaving now."

The shuttle craft was extremely cramped with Theo, Leo, and Mac the Meat Man all jammed into it. The brothers sat in the twin bucket seats in front, facing the control panels in the cockpit. Mac the Meat Man's plump little self was crammed in the space immediately behind them in one of the two acceleration couches, so that neither brother could move his seat back more than a few centimetres.

But when Theo complained, Leo said, "You're lucky it isn't even more crowded. I would have brought all of Boyard-27 with us too, if I could."

"And I don't blame you, my boy," said Mac. "That robot was a fine and loyal companion."

Leo shook his head ruefully. "I know. It breaks my heart to leave his chassis behind. Poor old Boyard."

"If you like the damned robot so much," said Theo, "why don't you kiss him?"

"You're sick," said his brother.

"Me? Sick? Look who's talking. Look where you've got that robot's head."

Boyard-27's bullet-shaped red metal head, the only part of the robot that Leo had been able to salvage, was in fact on the shuttle seat nestling between Leo's thighs, jammed into his crotch.

"It looks like he's giving you a hummer," said Theo. "Now, that really is disgusting. Man-machine oral sex. Did you have to take out his Asimov chip before he'd do that for you?"

"Just shut your filthy mouth."

"Now boys," said Mac in a conciliatory tone. "Shouldn't we be keeping our eyes open for the other shuttle? Those tattooed freaks might try to ambush us or something. Our truce only lasted while we were joining forces to fight off the Judges and escape. Now we've left the farm, they could be planning to attack."

"How?" demanded Leo. "These cheap Russian shuttles aren't even armed." Nevertheless, he switched on the stern observation screen and they all saw the giant ball and doughnut of the helium balloon with the converted space station hanging below it. To the right of the screen was a diagonal streak of jet exhaust, glistening a bright white that contrasted with the rising brown smoke of the municipal dump. This was the vapour trail from their own craft. To the left of the screen there was another sharply angled white streak. That was the trail from the second shuttle.

"The tattooed kids are high-tailing it away from us, as fast as they can go," said Leo. "No need to worry about them."

"What about the Judges?"

"They can't follow us. We've taken both the shuttles. There's no vehicle they can use for pursuit."

"That only applies to the Judges we left back at the farm," said Theo. "But there will be others. Reinforcements. They won't have sent only five Judges after us."

"Why not?" said Leo cynically. "That's all it took to bring down our entire operation."

"They never would have infiltrated us if we hadn't been distracted by those tattooed thugs," bleated Mac.

"Who also infiltrated us," Leo pointed out.

"Nonetheless, there must be other Judges coming."

The robot suddenly spoke up, its voice muffled between Leo's powerful thighs. "Other Judges are currently arriving as reinforcements. Best estimate based on readings before we left the farm... Approximately sixty Judges."

"Sixty Judges? Pursuing us?"

"Negative to possibility of pursuit," said the robot. "All Judges are arriving on clandestine dump ships converted for the purpose."

"Dump ships? Those old crates? They'll never catch us. That's good news. Did you hear that, Mac? Did you hear the good news?"

Mac wasn't listening. He was looking at his floating factory farm shrinking in the distance, disappearing behind the dirty brown veil of burning garbage. "So long to the old farm," he said. A tear glistened in his eye.

Zandonella was relieved to find that, throughout the gun battle and the enemy escape, Porkditz had remained crouched on the platform by the airlock, out of harm's way. He was still there now, waiting for her, his bright little eyes gleaming up at her from the base of his snout. They seemed to be gleaming with some inner amusement. She crouched down beside him and scratched him behind one of his big floppy membranous ears, which folded back like a thick pink handkerchief. As she scratched, she looked over the railing. Below, the other Judges were approaching, making their way slowly back through the thousands of squealing pigs that filled the room, with Dredd in the lead.

"If you'd gone into that mass, you would have got lost and we would never have found you again," she told Porkditz, staring out at the heaving ocean of pig flesh. "I'm glad you stayed put." Dredd overheard her as he climbed up onto the platform and joined them.

"I only wish Darrid and the others had as much common sense as your pig," he said.

"I heard that," cried Darrid. "I heard it and I resent it."

Dredd continued to ignore him, turning instead to Carver. "Have you still got your backpack, Carver?"

Anxious to make amends, the young Judge hurried up onto the platform. "Yes sir. Right here, sir."

"Then take out the sniffer and get busy with it," said Dredd. Carver hastily opened his orange nylon backpack with a ripping of Velcro and delved into its black interior. He took out a sniffer; a forensic analysis unit modified to scoop in air with a small fan and sample it over a test membrane.

"What do we need the sniffer for?" said Darrid.

"Explosives."

Mac the Meat Man stared tearfully into the screen, watching his factory farm vanish into the distance behind the speeding shuttle craft. "I built that farm with my own hands," he sniffed. Then he cleared his throat shakily. "Well, all right, not literally. I built it with my own money. Other people used their hands. But it still breaks my heart to say goodbye to it."

Theo put a hand on his shoulder. "Take as long as you want saying goodbye."

"Don't take too long," said Leo, sitting at the controls of the shuttle. "We'll be out of range soon."

Dredd held the sniffer in the air, the gentle buzzing of its fan drowned out in the background noise of thousands of agitated pigs.

"I still don't understand why you're wasting time with that thing," complained Darrid. "We should be investigating the rest of this farm before the reinforcements arrive. Who knows what contraband we might uncover? We don't want those Johnnie-come-latelies getting credit for finding anything."

"We're staying put until I give you the all clear," said Dredd, studying the control panel on the sniffer.

Darrid frowned, twirling his moustache restlessly between his fingers. "What do you hope to achieve with that thing? Why are you looking for explosives? All the sniffer is going to sniff around here is pig shit."

"Tell him, Zandonella," said Dredd.

Zandonella looked at Darrid. The older Judge was seething with impatience. He wasn't going to listen to anything she said, but she decided to give it a try anyway. "The sniffer is an extremely sensitive device."

"I know that."

"It will detect the presence of any explosive compounds anywhere in this farm and indicate their location."

"But why all this gruddamned obsession with explosives?"

"Because obviously the perps might have rigged this place to self-destruct," said Zandonella, "now that someone has allowed them to get clean away."

"Self-destruct?" said Darrid.

Leo checked the control panel and made some adjustments. "Maximum signal range will be reached in approximately two and a half minutes," said the robot's head from between his thighs.

"That's all right, fellows," said Mac, turning away from the screen. "I've come to terms with the loss. We'll start over somewhere else. Somewhere new."

"That's the spirit," said Theo.

Mac nodded. "The people of this fair metropolis will still want to eat black market meat and we'll be back in business supplying them in no time. All we need is an empty building somewhere and some pigs to put in it."

"And some machinery to kill them with," said Leo.

"That's right, you boys and me will be back in business before you know it." Mac's eyes flicked to the screen and the dwindling shape of the balloon and space station. "We just have to accept that our old farm is gone."

"Not as gone as it's going to be in a minute," said Leo.

"Explosives?" said Darrid. Zandonella and the others had fallen silent. They were all watching Judge Dredd, who was studying the readout on the sniffer's screen.

"That's right," said Dredd. "About a thousand kilos of plastic explosives." He switched the sniffer off and handed it to Carver. "Put it away."

"Put it away?" shrilled Darrid. "But we need to know where the explosives are."

"We know where it is," said Dredd. "It's in here."

"In here?" Darrid and the other Judges exchanged looks and then stared around at the vast open metal room, packed with squirming, screeching pigs. "But there's nowhere in here to hide a thousand kilos of..."

Like all of the others, he was following the direction of Dredd's gaze. Up in the air. Straight up. At the giant, pink plastic pig hanging from the ceiling.

The escape shuttle bucked and jumped as it sped through the sky. Mac the Meat Man settled back in the acceleration couch and wiped his eyes. "All right, sentiment has its place, but so does action. Let's get even with those bastards who took away our beautiful farm."

"About time," said Leo.

Mac looked at Theo. "Did you make all the necessary arrangements, son?"

"You bet," said Theo.

"All right fellows, pull the plug," said Mac.

"Excellent," said Leo, making an adjustment to the control panel.

The robot head between his thighs said, "Space station auto-destruct protocol sent and received."

Leo chuckled. "We're in business."

His brother looked at Mac. "Are you sure you're ready, Mac?"

Mac the Meat Man took one last look at his farm on the screen and nodded brusquely. "Push the button," he said in a scratchy voice.

"Okey-dokey." Leo leaned towards the control panel, reaching out to push a large red button.

His brother slapped his hand away. "No, let me press it."

"No, me," said Leo.

"Boys, boys," said Mac.

Judge Dredd was ten metres above the floor on a thin line of carbon filament. He had fired a grappling hook onto the giant plastic pig and now he was using the line to winch himself up. Below, five Judges and countless thousands of pigs were watching his progress as he approached the distended pink belly above.

Zandonella stared up at him. Dredd was a tiny figure at this distance, dwarfed by the ludicrous cartoon pig. She watched as he reached the side of the pig, momentarily obscuring two of the purple letters of its slogan so it read, Shat Mac the Meat Man's! Dredd hauled himself up using the inertia effect of the winch and the strength of his powerful shoulders. He had now reached the sloping back of the pink plastic effigy and hauled himself onto it. For a moment he disappeared from view, examining the cluster of metal cables that kept the pig attached to the ceiling. Zandonella held her breath. Dredd was no longer attached to his safety line. If he put a foot wrong on the smooth slope of that plastic back and slipped...

Dredd came back into view and Zandonella started breathing again. He called down to them. "There was a receiver and a detonator. I've disconnected them." He took hold of the filament line and began to lower himself back towards the floor.

"He's such a show-off," said Darrid. "There was probably never any danger of them detonating that thing."

Mac, Theo and Leo all stared in consternation at the stern screen. The balloon and space station had long since disappeared from view, and the giant brown cloud above the dump was now also shrinking in the distance. "We should have been able to see the explosion from here," said Mac. He turned anxiously to Theo. "Shouldn't we?"

"A detonation of one thousand and twenty-three kilos of plastic composite explosive should be visible for approximately three hundred and fifty seven kilometres in line of sight," droned the robot's head from between Leo's thighs.

"Something must have gone wrong," said Theo.

"You must have screwed up the connection," said Leo.

"You must have screwed up the transmission," said Theo.

"Boys, boys," said Mac.

Behind them the municipal dump vanished in the distance as the shuttle craft thundered away over the Mega-City.

Once the reinforcements had arrived and the factory farm was secured, Zandonella led Carver and Darrid on a tour of the place using Porkditz as their guide. Tykrist had gone back to Justice Central with the medical team who were working on her sister. Unfortunately, it seemed unlikely they could save her hand. Dredd was busy with Psi-Judge O'Mannion discussing the report they would have to file on the raid, and all the other red tape necessary after the wounding of a Judge. Rather them than me, thought Zandonella.

Porkditz had led them safely through the maze of the abattoir, avoiding a tunnel full of whirring multi-toothed cutters, another tunnel lined with razor-edged hooks, a sharply sloping chute with back-curving disembowelling blades set in the floor ("I wouldn't want to slide down there with no pants on," said Carver), and an array of other grisly automated devices devoted to the slaughter of pigs.

The route Porkditz chose followed air ducts, access tunnels and some crawl spaces that were clearly part of the original space station and had never been adapted for use in the farm. Never again, thankfully, did he take them through anything as vile as the slurry tunnel. As they travelled they were getting a good overview of the layout of the farm, and were building an appreciation of the sheer scale

of the operation. They had encountered three more of the
giant shed-like rooms packed with pigs and Zandonella
suspected there were more to come. Her mind boggled at
the vast number of animals penned up between these steel
walls, and at the hellish existence they led before being fed
to the killing machines.

But Porkditz didn't seem to be taking them on a general
tour. It seemed to Zandonella that he was leading them to a
particular destination he had in mind. She mentioned this to
the others and instantly regretted it when Darrid burst into
laughter and Carver joined him.

"She thinks that pig's got brains," said Darrid.

"More than you," said Zandonella. But Carver and Darrid
continued to chortle. Porkditz glanced up at them in a
friendly fashion. He seemed to have no idea that they were
laughing at him. Maybe he's not so intelligent after all,
thought Zandonella.

They were moving through what was apparently an air
conditioning duct. It was circular in section and just big
enough inside for Zandonella to stand up erect. Dredd
would have had to stoop to move through it. Porkditz was
scampering ahead of the three Judges, his trotters making a
musical sound on the aluminium floor of the duct. Suddenly the music stopped as he came to a halt beside a trap
door.

"Looks like we've arrived at our destination," said Zandonella.

The trap door turned out to be in the ceiling of a long,
cool, shadowy room full of odd, spicy smells. The Judges
lowered themselves down one by one from the air duct and
onto a rectangular metal table. There didn't seem to be any
way to get Porkditz down, so they left him standing there,
peering at them through the circular trap door opening in
the ceiling with mysterious Russian instructions stencilled
beside it. The pig stared down, watching them.

"He doesn't seem bothered at being left behind," said Darrid.

"No," said Zandonella. "In fact, he seems relieved."

"Relieved," snorted Darrid as he fumbled along the wall and hit the light switch. The long room abruptly lit up around them.

"Holy grud," exclaimed Carver, staring at their surroundings. It was now obvious where the spicy smell was coming from. All across the ceiling were fitted long slender rods. Hanging from the rods on hooks were cylindrical red shapes of varying length and thickness.

"Sausages," said Darrid.

"Salami," said Carver, correcting him. It was the first time Zandonella had ever heard him contradict someone, or come up with a fact that was accurate. "It's a kind of special dried sausage."

"Is it?" said Darrid good-naturedly. "Well I'll bet this is more salami than you've ever seen in your life."

Carver reached up and took down one long thin salami with string wrapped around it in a diagonal diamond pattern. He sniffed its waxy red surface. "It sure smells good," he said. And as he spoke, a spurt of saliva jetted from his mouth. Zandonella stepped back hastily to avoid getting sprayed and shot Carver a furious look.

Darrid just laughed. "The boy's got an appetite," he said.

"They sure look tasty," said Carver, looking longingly at the salami as he turned it over in his hands.

Darrid took it from him and gave it a sniff. "Mmm, you're right. It does smell good."

Carver's stomach rumbled audibly in the quiet room. He looked at Zandonella. "Sorry," he said.

"Don't apologise to her," said Darrid. "It's perfectly natural, a man having an appetite after a daring operation like the one we've just been through. Danger makes a fellow hungry."

"You're both disgusting," said Zandonella. "I don't see how you can even think about eating that stuff."

"Listen to Miss High and Mighty," chuckled Darrid.

"You saw where it came from," said Zandonella. "You saw the stuff they were feeding to those pigs. Garbage from the dump! Rotting organic matter, radioactive sump oil, bird droppings, hospital waste... not to mention their own blood and excrement."

Darrid winked at Carver. "Our little Psi-Judge has a dainty constitution," he said. He handed the salami back to Carver. Carver turned it over and over in his fingers.

"It sure smells good," he repeated, mournfully.

"And besides, it's evidence," said Zandonella. She got back up onto the table and scrambled through the trap door to rejoin Porkditz.

SIX

When it was time to leave the farm, Judge Dredd rejoined them and led them to their point of entry, the giant oval air conditioning duct. They clambered through the angled steel shutters and once again found themselves outside on the lip of metal. The hover-chutes were lying where they'd left them, including the ones that Esma and Tykrist had used.

"I'll take the rigs used by the Karst sisters," said Dredd. "One of you can return them to the Armoury when we get back to Justice Central."

"I will," offered Darrid. It was unusual for Darrid to volunteer for any laborious minor errand but clearly he was eager to get back in Dredd's good books after the fiasco with the perps' escape. Dredd just grunted and clipped on his own chute, strapping the sisters' rigs to his chest. Zandonella fitted her own hover-chute and then coaxed Porkditz into his half of the tandem. The pig was cooperative, almost eager, and did not struggle as she strapped it onto him. Perhaps he had enjoyed the ride on the way in. Or maybe he was just glad to be leaving this place.

From the edge of the metal lip Zandonella could see the curving rim of the space station stretching away from them. A steady stream of dump ships, piloted by Judges, were ferrying back and forth to the station, using the docking ports designed for cargo transfer in space. The pigs from the farm were being loaded onto the dump ships and taken away like any other confiscated contraband. The squealing, squirming mass of animals was being piled into the dump ships as though they were garbage. None of the Judges seemed to be

brutalising them, but neither were they taking any great
pains to treat them well.

No one had said anything to Zandonella about Porkditz
and she had deliberately avoided asking. She was worried
that someone would give orders to leave the pig behind or
add him to the exodus of pink flesh on those dump ships.
She found that her fingers were trembling with eagerness as
she finished strapping on Porkditz's hover-chute. If she
could just get him out of here without anyone saying anything...

Darrid turned to Dredd and said, "What about Zandonella's little chum here?"

"I'll keep him at my place," said Zandonella quickly.

"At your place?"

"In case he's needed for any more exploratory visits to the
farm," said Zandonella, thinking fast. "It's still a dangerous
place and we may need a guide to lead us around it."

"Good thinking," said Dredd.

They floated away from the farm through the bitter brown
smoke of the municipal dump, the donut structure of the old
space station and the bloated sphere of its balloon receding
behind them like images in a dream. Porkditz hung patiently
and quietly in his harness as Zandonella guided them both
through the sky towards the weapons platform, still hover-
ing exactly where Dredd had left it. They climbed on board,
followed by the other Judges.

All of them unstrapped themselves from their chutes in
the rear of the FWP. Carver was staring out at the dump
ships powering through the sky, carrying their cargo of pig
flesh back to Justice Central.

"Why are we taking them?" Carver asked.

"Did you expect us to leave all that valuable black market
meat just floating there for anyone to take?" asked Darrid.

"The pigs are to be kept as evidence," said Dredd.

Carver kept his face pressed to the window, watching the
dump ships leaving vapour trails that were glowing pink as
the sun set over the Mega-City. The ships were stubby craft,
mostly painted white, with a small cockpit nestling over the

nose of the vehicle and a large, open rear section for the garbage containers. In the rear of them the pink heaving mass of the pigs could be clearly seen. Zandonella saw one pig drop off, a tiny figure, and fall twitching helplessly into the void. Then another fell. Then another, spilling hopelessly to its doom. She winced and looked away.

"Then what will they do with them?" Zandonella asked quietly.

"The Council will have to decide that," said Dredd. Zandonella released Porkditz from the harness of his hover-chute and the pig stepped daintily out of the rig, shaking himself as though he'd just had a bath. He needed a bath, thought Zandonella. So did she. They could both have a shower when they got back to the con-apt.

"Then what?" asked Carver. Zandonella wished they would stop talking about the fate of the pigs. It made her uneasy.

"Maybe we'll get to eat them," suggested Darrid, and Zandonella felt her stomach make a queasy somersault.

"I doubt it," said Dredd. "The whole reason for cracking down on the black market in meat is fear of the possible side-effects on public health. We have no idea what consuming that stuff might do to people. Look at what they were feeding those animals."

"That's what I said," said Zandonella.

"Possibly after due study the animals will be set free in the Cursed Earth," added Judge Dredd.

"What a waste," sighed Carver, apparently still remembering the fragrant salami he'd cradled in his hands. But Zandonella felt a fierce elation. Set them free? It had never occurred to her that such a benevolent fate might await the poor animals. After the hideous life and certain death of the factory farm, even the Cursed Earth would seem like a blessing. Life out there in the badlands would be tough, however, and short and dangerous. When she thought of Porkditz out there, fending for himself, Zandonella felt a strange pinching sensation in her heart. She quickly reached down and scratched the pig behind one of his large floppy ears.

Porkditz lolled his head back luxuriously and looked up at her with bright happy eyes.

"So that's what will happen to Zandonella's little buddy," said Darrid. "He'll have to go too, out into the Cursed Earth." Zandonella shot him an angry look. She could have killed him. Why was he so determined to nail down poor Porkditz's fate tonight? Couldn't he just be left in peace for a little while? But Darrid and Carver were staring at her. They seemed to be waiting for an answer.

"Of course I'll bring him in and put him with the others," she said. "When they are ready to be deported into the Cursed Earth."

Dredd said nothing. He climbed into the cockpit and started the FWP's powerful engines, steering them back towards Justice Central.

Zandonella got back to her con-apt and the exhaustion of the long day hit her as soon as she closed the door. She barely had the strength to undress, dump her soiled uniform in the cleaning unit and drag herself into the shower. Porkditz came into the washroom as she showered, lowering himself onto a bathmat and lying there quietly enjoying the warmth and perfumed steam that drifted out of the foamy, splashing shower stall. When she'd finished washing herself, Zandonella felt a little better, though it was still a struggle to stay awake. Without bothering to dress she climbed out of the stall and immediately coaxed Porkditz inside. Once he was in the stall she sprayed him thoroughly with the hand shower, then rubbed him with soap and showered him clean again. Nude in the shower with the cheerful pink animal, Zandonella ended up giving herself another wash too. Porkditz enjoyed the whole procedure, chortling contentedly under the gentle needling of the warm spray and driving his snout up against her hand to get a firmer rubbing.

"Given half a chance, you like being clean, don't you?" she said. Porkditz snorted good-naturedly and shook droplets of foamy water from his snout.

As she washed and dried the pig, Zandonella felt oddly maternal and contented. She padded into the kitchen barefoot, wearing her silk kimono with her hair tied up in a towel. In the refrigerator was half a bottle of good gin she had confiscated in a raid and smuggled home. Zandonella liked to think of it as her sole vice. She took it out along with some ice, a ripe lemon, and a miniature bottle of white vermouth and proceeded to mix herself a shaker full of very dry martini.

Porkditz came padding into the kitchen and watched the procedure with such rapt attention that she selected two glasses from the cupboard instead of one and filled them both from the frosted shaker. She took her glass into the living room and left the other one on the kitchen floor. Zandonella sat down on the couch and sipped and a moment later she heard some enthusiastic slurping noises from the kitchen. Porkditz eventually emerged, licking the corners of his mouth with evident satisfaction.

"Did you enjoy that?" said Zandonella. "Well, I guess you earned it." He came and nuzzled at her bare feet with his moist snout, as if he was trying to say thank you, and then flopped down on the floor and began to snore gently.

She left him sleeping in the living room in the spot that had lately become his own. As she drifted off to sleep she heard once again the sound of his delicate hooves on the floor and the flushing of the toilet. The pig had waited considerately until she went to bed before performing his bodily functions. He was not only smarter than Darrid, she decided, he was also better house-trained than Carver.

The raid on the factory farm took place on a Thursday. Zandonella wasn't back on duty until the following Monday, so she decided to take things easy and stay at home. Originally she'd planned to do some shopping and perhaps look up some old friends, but the comforting presence of Porkditz somehow made her want to just stay at home and be domestic. Besides, she would have felt guilty going out and leaving him on his own. As a result, Zandonella subsisted on food from the refrigerator and store cupboard, preparing meals for herself and her companion. The pig, unsurprisingly, seemed happy with whatever she offered him for a meal.

"Considering the terrible muck they were feeding you at that farm," said Zandonella, "I'd be awfully upset if you turned down anything from my kitchen." Porkditz nodded at her and chortled as if in appreciation of her wit, then returned to his feeding. He was eating chilli con tofu, three self-heating cans of it, out of a large aluminium salad bowl she had placed on the floor beside the kitchen table. Sitting at the table, Zandonella ate the fourth can of tofu from a rather smaller bowl with a spoon.

The rest of the day was spent watching the History Channel, curled up on the pale blue sofa in the living room with Porkditz curled up beside her. Finally, in late afternoon, Zandonella lifted the remote control, turned off the Tri-D, and succumbed to the urge to have a nap. She fell asleep beside the pig on a jumbled pile of purple and red silk cushions.

Two hours later she was jerked awake, confused and sweaty, trying to come out of deep sleep in response to the urgent clamour of her doorbell. Zandonella rose shakily from the sofa and tottered towards the door, her left leg clumsy and bloodless from being slept on. The bell jangled again, impatiently, as she opened the door.

Standing there, looking immaculate in a fresh uniform, was Judge O'Mannion, her silver hair impeccably arranged and styled. Zandonella, in contrast, was wearing a ratty old bathrobe and her own long, ink black hair looked like the nest of a particularly un-house proud bird.

"I hope I didn't wake you," said O'Mannion with no attempt at sincerity as she stepped across the threshold. She looked around the con-apt and gave a little sniff. "What a fascinating odour this place has. Not like an ordinary dwelling at all."

Zandonella rubbed her eyes and yawned, too tired to be insulted. "You seem to be making a habit of visiting me when I'm off duty."

"Not at all," said O'Mannion. "What I'm making a habit of is checking up on your roommate."

"My roommate?" Zandonella felt her mouth go dry. "Is there any word yet from the Council of Five?" O'Mannion looked at her sardonically and waited a moment before answering. Did she know how anxious Zandonella was about the outcome of the pig's fate? Was she deliberately tormenting her?

After what seemed an eternity, O'Mannion finally drawled, "No. Still awaiting a decision pending further tests." Zandonella released the breath she only now realised she'd been holding.

"Further tests?"

"Yes. They're having samples of the meat analysed to see about its toxicity versus nutritional value."

"Nutritional value?"

"Yes, and your friend Carver volunteered to be one of the guinea pigs in the experiment. Odd word that, isn't it? Guinea *pig*. You'd think 'laboratory rat' would be a more apt expression, especially for him. Anyway, your friend Carver–"

"I wouldn't exactly call him a friend."

"Your fellow Judge Carver, then," continued O'Mannion smoothly, "has courageously volunteered and has been eating some samples of the pork."

"The salami."

"Why yes. What an accurate guess. You really are very perceptive."

"Not really. I just saw his mouth watering over some samples of the stuff at the factory farm."

"Don't sell yourself short, Zandonella. You are perceptive. And that's far from being your only talent." Zandonella felt a cold chill at the base of her spine. Where was O'Mannion going with this?

The senior Judge smiled at her as though sensing her discomfort. "Don't think that I've forgotten that you're the finest example of a PNE we have ever had amongst our Psi-Judges. As a matter of fact, I think it's about time you exercised your special talent again."

"So soon?" said Zandonella. She knew that O'Mannion was teasing her, but she was unable to stop herself from rising to the bait. "But you remember what happened last time?"

O'Mannion smirked. "Indeed I do."

"I need more time to recover. I can't go back on assignment so soon."

"Oh, I think you're underestimating your powers of recuperation, Zandonella. You're a resilient young woman at the peak of her physical training and in the prime of her life. You're ready to go again. Plenty ready, I'd say."

"But I'm on assignment to Judge Dredd."

"Of course," said O'Mannion. "And no doubt this assignment is providing you with valuable insight into the workings of street Judges. But you're not destined to work the streets, Zandonella. You're a Psi-Judge and your job is to exercise your special powers, no matter how unpleasant or how debilitating they might be."

Zandonella sank back on the sofa, defeated. O'Mannion was right. The assignment with Judge Dredd was temporary. Her true work lay with her PNE powers. She would just have to come to terms with the raw, clawing horror that so often came with those powers. She had been hiding from the thought of dealing with them again, enjoying the carefree hours lolling around in her con-apt with Porkditz for company. But now O'Mannion had blown in like the cold wind of reality and forced her to remember what was in store for her. At the thought of returning to duty in the Psi-unit, Zandonella felt all the pleasure of the past day draining away. And the happy prospect of the coming weekend disappeared, too. Zandonella's leave had been ruined.

As if sensing this, O'Mannion rose to go. Her work here is done, thought Zandonella bitterly. "Sorry to love you and leave you," said O'Mannion blithely. "But I'd better be off." She turned towards the door and then turned back. "Just one word of warning."

"Warning?" said Zandonella dangerously. She'd just about had enough of O'Mannion.

"Just for your own good. I know you don't want to be the object of gossip. Nobody does. But some of the other Judges have been talking about you."

"You mean Darrid."

"I'm not naming names. Otherwise, what would I be but a gossip myself? But I thought you should know, there's been a lot of talk about you and that pig you've adopted." O'Mannion glanced at Porkditz, snoring contentedly on the deep red plush of the carpet.

"I haven't adopted him."

"Figure of speech. Don't take everything so literally. Anyway, most of this talk, this gossip, has been jocular. Poking harmless fun at the two of you. As a matter of fact, there was a very amusing cartoon someone drew in the toilets before it was erased by the cleaners. A pity you didn't get to see it." O'Mannion's eyes crinkled with nostalgic amusement. "Perhaps someone took a scan of it... Anyway, as I said, it's all good harmless fun. But some of the gossip hasn't been so harmless. Some has been downright malicious. There's even been some suggestion that the two of you are, how shall I put this... romantically linked."

"What?"

"You know, a little inter-species romance." O'Mannion smiled and delicately bumped her pelvis back and forth.

"That's disgusting!"

"Don't let it bother you." O'Mannion opened the door and stepped out of the con-apt. "It's just the way things are." As she shut the door, she glanced back at Zandonella and grinned wickedly. "Men are pigs."

That night, as if sensing something was wrong, Porkditz came in and slept on the floor near her bed. As he slept he emitted little snorting sounds that Zandonella found strangely comforting. The following morning she got up early, showered, breakfasted and set out a large tin bowl of fruit and nut muesli for Porkditz. As Porkditz chased the bowl around the kitchen floor with his snout, munching contentedly, she went into the bedroom and got dressed, putting on her Judge's uniform.

She'd decided to go back on duty. She might as well. Her leave had been ruined by O'Mannion's visit. The moment she thought of O'Mannion, the doorbell rang. Zandonella went and answered it, expecting O'Mannion to be there in the flesh.

She was. But so was Judge Dredd. He followed O'Mannion into the con-apt, stooping to get through the front door. The living room, which had previously seemed like a generous space even with Zandonella, the pig and O'Mannion in it, suddenly seemed to shrink into a small cramped room when Dredd was present.

"Sit down, please," said Zandonella. Dredd shook his head.

O'Mannion smiled. "She never invites me to sit down. She must like you."

"Sit down if you like," said Zandonella.

O'Mannion settled comfortably among the cushions on the sofa. "Why thank you. You're all dressed for duty. Did you have some kind of premonition?"

"No, I just decided I didn't need a weekend sitting around here doing nothing."

"Oh, but what about your little friend with a corkscrew tail? Surely looking after him doesn't count as *nothing*."

Zandonella tried to ignore her. "I've decided to go back to work," she said, not offering any further explanation.

"Good," said Dredd. "Because I came to get you. I need you on a detail I've been assigned to command."

"Before you tell her about the detail, let me give her the news," said O'Mannion from the sofa. She was still sprawled luxuriously among the cushions, but her voice had lost its customary playful tone. She sounded serious for a change and Zandonella felt her stomach sink. The room had suddenly gone quiet. Even Porkditz, who had been busy scraping his bowl of muesli around the floor of the kitchen, fell silent as if listening.

"What news?" said Zandonella.

For once O'Mannion wasn't smiling. She looked Zandonella in the eye and said, "The Council of Five has made its ruling. The scientists have now given them all the facts. Item number one: those pigs are some kind of mutant strain."

"Well, obviously," said Zandonella. "That's clear just from the intelligence they're exhibiting," she tried hard to sound sarcastic, but there was a sick feeling of dread in the pit of her stomach.

O'Mannion didn't respond to her sarcasm or her anger. In fact, O'Mannion seemed thoroughly subdued. Her vulpine face showed no trace of its usual malicious wit. She continued soberly. "Scientists have determined that, despite the lethal swill on which it was fed, the mutant pork..."

Zandonella noticed how O'Mannion was saying "pork" instead of pigs. It was clever. By talking about the animals as if they were a mere commodity, it was suddenly possible to begin to allow all sorts of things, to excuse the most awful predations towards the pigs, who after all were fellow creatures on this troubled planet.

O'Mannion's silver eyebrows, usually sharply angled for sardonic malice, were for once softened into curves of sympathy. But her voice remained calm and official as she went on passing sentence. "It transpires that the mutant pork from those factory farmed pigs is nutritious."

"Nutritious?" said Zandonella, her voice thick with disgust. "Did you see the toxic filth they were eating?"

Dredd spoke up. "Maybe so. But the meat from those pigs still turns out to have a higher nutritional value than munce and other synthetics."

"What doesn't?" demanded Zandonella. She turned to O'Mannion. "You should get a whiff of Judge Carver after he puts a load of that stuff in his guts. You'd never eat it again."

"I never eat it anyway," said O'Mannion with a shade of her old asperity. "But this isn't about Judge Carver. It's about the Law. And the Law is founded on scientific fact. Like the fact that the pork from these animals..."

At least she had the good grace to call them animals.

"... has more nutritional value than many other foodstuffs. It seems one of the mutations in these pigs has given rise to a unique digestive system."

"They don't just have mutant stomachs," said Zandonella. "They also have mutant brains. And those brains are intelligent."

"Unfortunately, it's not the brains we're concerned about. Their unique digestive system allows them to process even that toxic filth, as you called it, into wholesome meat."

"Wholesome?"

"Well, relatively speaking. Wholesome compared to munce. It even compares well with the genetically modified stuff like the produce from Sausage Tree Farm."

"And the Council doesn't want us to be too dependent on the produce from Sausage Tree Farm," said Dredd. "They think it would be a good thing to have a secondary supply of meat available right here in the Mega-City."

"A good thing," said Zandonella with audible bitterness.

"Of course, what this means," said O'Mannion, "is that all those factory farms we've been busting, like that old space station hanging over the municipal dump, are suddenly going to become legal. In fact they already are."

"Already?" Zandonella couldn't believe her ears.

"Certainly. Licensed meat dealers have sprung up overnight. And retail outlets of Wiggly Little Piggly..."

"Wiggly Little Piggly?" Zandonella felt as if she was caught in a nightmare.

"A new fast food franchise specialising in pork products. Their first branches opened this morning to an enthusiastic and almost rapturous reception from our citizens," O'Mannion grimaced, "who are, after all, hardly gourmets. They've been mobbing every branch as it comes on stream. There's even been rioting at a few locations when supplies of their special spicy spare ribs ran out."

Again Zandonella felt a chill, but this time it had less to do with Porkditz and more to do with policing. By the sound of it, the populace's sudden hunger for pork was going to create some problems for the Judges.

As if he'd read her mind, Dredd said, "It looks like it's turning into a full-blown Mega-City craze."

O'Mannion suddenly became impatient. She rose from the sofa in a single supple movement and tossed back her mane of silver hair. "Anyway, the long and short of it is, the trade in this meat is now legal and the pigs must be returned."

"To face captivity in factory farms?"

"That's right," said O'Mannion coolly. "Including your little friend." She glanced towards the doorway of the kitchen where Porkditz was standing silently, snout lifted attentively from his muesli bowl as if he was listening. O'Mannion turned abruptly and walked out without saying another word.

Dredd and Zandonella were alone in the con-apt. He looked at her. "Tough break, Judge, but the Law is the Law. The pig can stay with you until the end of the week. If you don't bring him in after that, I'll be forced to bring him in for you."

Zandonella fought back the tears welling up in her eyes. Her voice only contained the tiniest tremor as she said, "You mentioned a detail you wanted me on."

"Correct," said Dredd. "We're helping to police the arrival of the Cetacean Ambassador."

Normally, Zandonella would have been proud to be requested by Dredd for an assignment. But on this Saturday morning as she rolled through the Mega-City on her Lawmaster, motorcycle she was so depressed she felt as if she was moving through a pall of gloom. Dredd was immediately ahead of her and Carver rode at her side. Darrid had apparently not been selected by Dredd for this detail. It was somewhat surprising that Carver had, after the fiasco at the factory farm. More surprising still was the presence behind them of not only Tykrist, but also her wounded sister Esma, each on their own bikes. Esma seemed perfectly in control of her powerful Lawmaster. She must have spotted Zandonella looking at her because she smiled and waved with a streak of glinting metal.

The Med-Judges had amputated the shattered remains of Esma's hand and had replaced it with a stainless steel prosthetic while they tried to grow her a new one in the tanks, a lengthy and unreliable business. The steel hand shined at Zandonella in a sardonic little flutter. Was Esma giving her the finger? Zandonella studied the girl's face in the rear view mirror and saw Esma was smiling at her. She certainly seemed in good spirits. Maybe it was the medication, still swirling around her system. Zandonella hoped it wouldn't dull her reactions. She had a feeling that all the Judges would need to be operating at full efficiency today.

On this ride alone Zandonella had already seen two Wiggly Little Piggly fast food outlets in flames, the result of a shortage of spare ribs combined with a volatile populace in the grip of the latest craze. Dredd and his patrol hadn't stopped to help because other Judges were already roaring to the scene. Carver had stared fretfully at the bright pink plastic of the burning buildings. The fast food joints' facades consisted of the cute pink curves of a pig's rear end with a huge spiral of pink neon representing the animal's tail. The positioning of a large serving window directly beneath the tail indicated to Zandonella what quality of food emanated from the establishments. But the Big Meg's citizens had been bitten by the bug. They were jostling in lines that extended back for entire city blocks, waiting interminably for their turn at the pig's backside serving windows – except for those unfortunate branches where food shortages had sparked rioting.

As they drove past these places Carver wore a fretful expression entirely due to worry that all supplies of Wiggly Little Piggly products would be sold out by the time he got off duty. "I've been looking forward to some ribs ever since they were legalised this morning," he'd told Zandonella when she met him at the motor pool.

"At midnight, to be more precise," said Tykrist.

"At midnight plus one, to be even more precise," said her sister, flexing her new metal hand as she tested the throttle on her Lawmaster.

"I thought you wanted salami," said Zandonella, as she checked out her own motorcycle.

Carver shook his head. "I had my fill of that during the toxicity versus nutrition tests." She remembered that the young Judge had volunteered to be a guinea pig. Carver smiled. "Now what I want to try is the ribs."

Now he was casting worried looks around as they drove down an access ramp past Sofia Coppola Heights. Zandonella realised the reason for his concern. They were passing the flagship branch of the Wiggly Little Piggly fast food chain, a giant pink pig's rump which had been hastily constructed on a cantilevered plateau, a slab of steel jutting horizontally from the surrounding structures. Sometimes the only way for expansion in the Mega-City was by using such retrofitted developments. This platform was strung from the side of the Carmine and Francis Ford Coppola Block and abutted onto Nicolas Cage Block. The three buildings formed a tripod of supports for the restaurant and the rectangular slab on which it sat. The fourth side of the slab faced out onto a three hundred-metre drop, the drop that Zandonella and the other Judges were now negotiating by way of the long, sloping access ramp on their Lawmasters. Above them, crowds of eager citizens were converging on the restaurant from all three of the buildings joined to the platform. It seemed Carver was nervously estimating their numbers. Zandonella eased back on her bike so she was riding beside him.

"Trying to guess whether they'll be sold out by this evening?" she said.

Carver flicked his worried eyes at her. "That's the biggest Wiggly in the whole of Mega-City. If they sell out there, there won't be any hope."

"There'll always be tomorrow," said Zandonella.

"But I want it today," moaned Carver, unsuspectingly giving voice to the mantra of the Mega-City millions who were stampeding along in the mania of this latest craze.

"Well, I hope you manage to get hold of some."

Carver blinked at her. "Really?"

"Sure," said Zandonella. She didn't add that she was thinking that maybe some good would even come of it, if it led to less catastrophic flatulence from her comrade in arms. She sighed and touched the accelerator on her Lawmaster, speeding away from Carver again and dropping back into formation immediately behind Judge Dredd.

While she'd been talking to Carver she'd tried to keep from making the connection between the greasy takeaway treat Carver was longing to try, and the living flesh on the animal she'd left snoring soundly on the carpet in her living room. But it was impossible. She couldn't get Porkditz and his fate out of her mind. That's why she'd been hoping to go back on the job today. She couldn't sit in the con-apt with the poor innocent pig, watching him sleeping peacefully, unaware of his fate. Or maybe he would have become aware of his fate, somehow picking up some subtle subliminal clues from her, at a level deeper and more ancient than spoken language. He certainly seemed to sense that they'd been talking about him this morning...

"Too bad," said Dredd. Zandonella looked up, startled, to see that he'd dropped back from his point position to ride beside her.

"What's too bad, sir?"

"That your new friend is going to end up as additional protein for the Mega Citizens." Zandonella stared into his face, searching in vain for some flicker of emotion to go with those words.

"But how can we hurt them?" she said. "All those pigs. How can we eat them? They're intelligent, like us."

A sudden sound of a small explosion interrupted their conversation. Dredd's Lawgiver leapt into his hand from the holster fitted to the side of his bike. Zandonella found that she was gripping her own gun, drawn and levelled without conscious thought. They glanced back towards the source of the explosion, just in time to hear another one and to see that the cause was an empty plastic bottle, one of several that some thoughtless litterbug had tossed from overhead. Carver had driven right over it, causing the sealed bottle to burst with a gunshot sound. Carver looked at them sheepishly as he fought with his bike, trying to avoid the other bottles. Behind him, the Karst sisters manoeuvred around the bottles effortlessly. Carver hit a third bottle and his face began to glow a bright red.

"Intelligent like *some* of us," said Dredd, and sped off ahead of her again.

As they merged with the traffic on the Diana Krall Skedway, Zandonella caught sight of the entourage following the Cetacean Ambassador, a trio of stretch limousines. The lead limousine was painted a glaring shade of pale blue, and the two trailing behind it were basic black. The black cars contained assorted Mega-City dignitaries and their wives on their way to the ambassador's reception. The blue limo contained the ambassador himself, or rather served as a platform for his tank.

The Cetacean Ambassador was a dolphin. His tank was a transparent plastic, bulletproof cylinder three metres high and four metres in diameter, full of sloshing water and sealed at the top. Zandonella assumed it was bulletproof. At least, she hoped it was. The stretch limo had been adapted to accommodate the tank by cutting the back of the vehicle open, removing the roof and turning it into the kind of flatbed you got on one of those old-fashioned pickup trucks. The Cetacean Ambassador seemed oddly dignified, motoring along the skedway in his tank of slopping water. Occasionally he would adjust his position, turning smoothly in the tank to peer out at the passing Mega-City landscape.

There were already five Judges escorting the ambassador's limousine, one at each corner and one in front, all on Lawmasters. As Dredd roared up, the five Judges dropped back to make way for him and his detail. Dredd took point and Zandonella settled into position on the left of the limo's front bumper. She was amused to see that the driver's compartment was concealed behind smoked glass, so that the chauffeur could remain anonymous while his famous passenger was on display in a transparent tank for the whole city to see. Carver buzzed up on his bike to take position to the right front of the limo. The Karst sisters settled in at the two rear corners. The other Judges placed themselves on either side of the black limos behind with the fifth man taking up the rear.

Everyone was in place. Easy and smooth, thought Zandonella. This is going to be a piece of cake. Just then a bottle bounced off the roof of the ambassador's limousine and landed on the road in front of her. Zandonella steered her bike around it with ease, but four more bottles hit the road on either side of her and then half a dozen brightly coloured fast food takeaway cartons glanced off the limo. Zandonella recognised the colours on the cartons as being those of the Wiggly Little Piggly franchise. Greasy remnants of barbecued pork spilled out of the containers and spattered on her visor. Zandonella wiped it clear in time to see a further shower of bottles and food containers spilling from the sky.

Where the sneck were they coming from? She looked up to see a steady stream of debris spilling down from the cantilevered platform high above with the Wiggly Little Piggly restaurant perched on it. Zandonella's first thought was that some kind of anti-dolphin faction was deliberately dumping debris on the ambassador's motorcade. Stranger things had happened in the Mega-City. Then she heard a thin distant scream and saw that it wasn't just rubbish that was being dropped. A plump young man with long, flowing red hair was also tumbling through the sky.

Zandonella looked back to see the man hit the road behind her with a messy *splat*. The Judges driving beside the black limos had to take swift evasive action to dodge the body. One of the limo drivers panicked, swerved, and almost took out the Judge beside him. There was more screaming, a lot more screaming, from high above. Zandonella looked up to see people falling from the rim of the platform. There were maybe five or six of them, it was hard to tell with their bodies writhing through the air on the long fall down. Zandonella heard motorcycle brakes squeal and then the powerful revving of an engine as Dredd dropped back from point position to fall in beside her. She looked over at him, desperate for an order or an explanation. There were bodies falling all around them. One hit the roof of the black limo in the rear and bounced messily off, leaving a huge dent. The limo's brakes screamed abruptly as rubber burned.

"What's happening?" she said to Dredd. He was gazing up at the platform above them, people and debris now spilling off the edge of it in a continuous stream.

"The platform," said Judge Dredd. "Too many people on it. The supports are giving way."

"The supports?" Zandonella remembered the steeply angled concrete pillars that ran from the surrounding sky-scrapers to the platform. If they were to collapse...

"Follow me," said Dredd. "We have to do something or they're all dead."

SEVEN

Zandonella followed Dredd, who was powering back up the access ramp, engine gunning as he raced towards Sofia Coppola Heights and the concrete shelf on which the restaurant sat. She had initially obeyed his command without question, but as they screamed back up the ramp, she found herself doubting Dredd's assessment of the situation. The concrete platform was a massive structure. How could it just begin to give way?

But as they climbed higher, Zandonella started to get a better view of the structure and she saw that Dredd was absolutely right. The shelf was a giant circular slab of stone supported on three tubular sloping concrete supports, like a table with three legs. Each leg was attached to a different building and the triangular arrangement should have provided a strong and stable structure. But one of the legs, the one attached to Nicolas Cage Block, had begun to buckle. Jagged black splinter lines were running through the grey concrete and they were growing and spreading as Zandonella watched.

The concrete platform began to tip sickeningly. On it were crowded several thousand citizens who a moment earlier had had only one thought in their minds: to get to the Wiggly Little Piggly restaurant that occupied the centre of the platform. Now those citizens had a new single thought. Survival. As the support trembled, the giant concrete slab tipped forward and several dozen junk food fans went slipping down the slope, spilled over the guardrail at the rim and tumbled helplessly over the side towards the streets far below. Zandonella was suddenly reminded of the sight of pigs spilling off the dump ships...

Brakes screeched and Dredd pulled to a stop at the side of the access ramp. Zandonella slowed down and rolled to a halt beside him. They were opposite Nic Cage Block, directly over the damaged support. It slanted up past them, a concrete tube as big in diameter as a sewer pipe and at least two hundred metres long. The damaged section of the support was about fifty metres below them and now Zandonella could see that the cracks in it were opening up into dark hollows like pockmarks in the grey surface. Dust and concrete fragments spilled out with a crunching sound like big bones breaking. The support trembled and the platform above lurched as though shaken by an earthquake. Dozens more people fell off, screaming and writhing. Zandonella realised that it wasn't just the crowd around the restaurant that was in danger. If the supports collapsed, the whole platform would drop like a giant bomb into the streets below, destroying everything in its path.

She turned to Dredd. "We have to do something." The words sounded ridiculous even as she spoke. What could they do?

Dredd looked at her. "Do you have a grappling hook round in your Lawgiver?"

"Of course. But–"

"Fire it at that," Dredd pointed at the crumbling concrete support below them. "As close to the breaking section as you can get it."

"But what good will that do?" The flimsy line paid out by the grappling hook would barely support a Judge's weight, let alone the millions of kilos of trembling concrete above.

"Just do it," snarled Dredd.

Without further thought, Zandonella raised her Lawgiver, took aim, and fired. The expanding grappling hook glinted briefly in the sunlight as it sped down at a steep angle towards the fragmenting section of the support. Behind it the filament line paid out in a thin gossamer loop. The grappling hook hit the concrete and bit into it in a fine spray of dust just above the crumbling hole, which was now big enough to hide a man in. The bigger the hole got, the more unstable the support became, ready to hinge in on itself and snap. What they needed to do was spray some kind of quick setting cement into the hole to plug the gap and stabilise it. Only no cement could set that quickly, and they didn't have any, anyway.

"Good shot," said Dredd. "Now secure the line to your bike."

Zandonella obediently tied off the line to her Lawmaster. "What are you going to–"

"Stand back," said Dredd. He backed up his bike, revved the engine, switched to turbo boost and shot forward, the bike growling like a savage creature. Dredd drove past Zandonella, right off the edge of the access ramp, and straight into the void.

Zandonella wouldn't have believed it if she hadn't seen it with her own eyes. Dredd used the turbo boost facility to jump his bike off the ramp and send it out into thin air like a bird taking wing. But as soon as the bike left the ramp, it began to fall like the thousand kilos of inert metal it actually was. Yet it was a controlled fall, Dredd steering – or more accurately, wrestling – the bike into position as it dropped through the air. As he did so Zandonella began to realise what he was up to.

The fragmenting concrete had taken a bite out of the thick cylindrical support and the open edges of the bite looked like they were going to snap down onto each other, causing the entire support to bend beyond a critical limit and snap in two. But Dredd was aiming for that bite in the concrete. As the bike descended towards the support, Dredd kicked free and launched himself into freefall. Zandonella understood, belatedly, the vital importance of the grappling line she had fired. Dredd grabbed for the line as he fell past it. For one heart-stopping moment she thought he'd missed it, but then the line tightened, jerking her bike towards the edge of the ramp. Zandonella automatically threw the parking brakes on and the skidding stopped. Dredd was holding onto the grappling line with both hands, hanging there, his weight supported by her bike like a big fish on a line.

While he swung there, his own bike hit the support, slamming neatly into the hole just as the gaping concrete jaws of the hole snapped together. But instead of closing on empty space and causing the rest of the pillar to break, the edges of the hole snapped shut on the Lawmaster, crunching the metal mass of it into a tight deformed bundle with a sound like a giant hand crushing a huge beer can. Dredd had filled the gap. The concrete support pillar was stable... for the moment.

Zandonella was still gaping in astonishment at this feat when she heard Dredd yelling at her. She realised he'd been yelling for some time as he hauled himself hand over hand up the grappling line, back towards Zandonella and her bike, and the safety of the access ramp.

"Evacuate those citizens," he bellowed. Zandonella looked up at the crowd surrounding the Wiggly Little Piggly on the platform above. The screaming had stopped now they realised they were safe. Some of them had even begun to applaud Dredd's manoeuvre. Others were hurrying back to the restaurant to resume their clamouring for pork.

Zandonella understood the urgency in Dredd's voice. The Lawmaster had plugged the hole but it was just a stopgap measure. The support pillar was fundamentally unsound and it could give way at any moment.

She got on her communicator and ordered more Judges to the scene to oversee an evacuation as Dredd approached the rim of the access ramp, swinging hand over hand with smooth athletic skill. Above them the applause was growing as more and more of the crowd realised what Judge Dredd had done for them. Not everyone was pleased, though. Zandonella saw a small child chuck the contents of his Wiggly Little Piggly bucket over the edge of the guardrail, sending down a spill of half-chewed, greasy ribs to drop with fiendish accuracy right on top of Dredd. He shouldered his way through the shower of oily pork fragments and seized the edge of the access ramp.

"Help me up, Zandonella," he snarled.

Zandonella jumped off her Lawmaster and ran to help drag Dredd back onto solid ground. He accepted her assistance and for a moment they were wrapped into an embrace like any two lovers, but then Dredd got his feet planted and quickly let go of her, standing up straight and stable and calm. Zandonella was amazed. If it had been her, her knees would have turned to jelly at this point and she would have needed to sit down, if not lie down. Dredd merely brushed the remains of the bright red spare ribs off his uniform.

"Let's cite that little creep for littering," he said, looking up at the platform where the child with his empty spare rib bucket was waving at them.

Zandonella's communicator buzzed in her ear and she heard Carver's excited voice gabbling at her. She only listened for an instant before she turned to Dredd. "We'd better get down on the skedway, sir. There's a problem with the Cetacean Ambassador."

"Problem is an understatement," said Dredd, staring at Carver, who was standing white-faced beside the tangled wreckage of what had once been his Lawmaster.

"Yes sir," muttered Carver, his voice hardly audible but filled with embarrassment and shame.

"What you're telling me," continued Dredd relentlessly, "is that you've lost the Cetacean Ambassador."

"He's not exactly lost, sir," stuttered Carver. "He's still in his tank in his official limo."

"But you have no idea where that might be," said Dredd coldly. Carver shook his head.

Dredd turned away in disgust. "How is she doing, Zandonella?"

Zandonella looked up at him from the street where she was kneeling beside the Karst sisters. She was crouching between the wreckage of the two black limousines, helping Tykrist wrap a tourniquet around Esma's hand, or rather the bloody stump of what had once been her hand. They were sitting in a stretch of road that had been sealed off with roadblocks at both ends. Between the roadblocks lay the wreckage of the two limos, three Lawmaster bikes and one wounded Judge. There was broken glass on the road surface and dark stains from spilled motor oil and blood.

"We've got the bleeding under control," said Zandonella.

"What exactly happened?" demanded Dredd. Carver opened his mouth and started to answer, but Dredd held out a hand, cutting him off. "Let her tell me."

Tykrist looked away from the spreading red stain on her sister's clean, white bandage. Esma's eyes were shut but Zandonella could see the girl's lids trembling with pain. Zandonella couldn't tell if she was conscious or not. Hopefully by now the painkillers had knocked her into some comfortable twilight zone.

Tykrist cleared her throat. "The driver of the blue limousine–"

"You mean the dolphin's driver?"

"Yes, the driver of the Cetacean Ambassador, he just seemed to go nuts sir."

"Exactly what kind of nuts, Judge Karst?"

"He began to veer his vehicle wildly."

"Do you think he lost control? Maybe he was injured?"

"We thought so at first, sir. He hit Judge Carver's bike and knocked him off, so I went to help Carver while Esma – Judge Karst – went after the blue limo to see if she could help. But then the limo hit the brakes and stopped directly in the path of the other two limousines. It forced both of them off the road. One of them smashed into a streetlamp and the other one into a side barrier. They were both write-offs."

"What about the passengers?" said Dredd.

"The VIPs? Shaken but not apparently injured. We got the other Judges to take them away from the scene. They're being checked out at hospital now and–"

"What about the blue limo?"

"Well, by now it was pretty evident that the driver was deliberately trying to damage the other vehicles."

"Pretty evident?" said Dredd. "Yes, I'd say so. And also trying to take out all the Judges in the escort."

"That's right, sir. Like I said, I stopped to help Judge Carver. Before I realised what was happening, I'd got off my bike and the blue limo drove straight into it, totalling it."

"So Carver's bike was down, your bike was down, and your sister's..."

"My sister went after the blue limo like a bat out of hell, sir," said Tykrist, looking up at Dredd. There were tears in her eyes and a note of pride in her voice. "She stayed right on his tail as he headed for the off-ramp."

"What was the dolphin doing all this time?"

"The ambassador? Well he looked pretty shook up, too, sir. The water in his tank was bubbling and frothy after all the crashes and impacts and so on."

"But he was still alive and well?"

"Yes, sir. He was splashing about, a bit agitated and all. But he looked fine. Water is a pretty good shock absorber, sir. He would have been insulated from the worst of the impacts."

"So he was driven away towards the off-ramp with your sister in pursuit?"

"Yes."

"What went wrong?"

"When the bastard – I mean the driver of the blue limo realised he was being followed, he jammed on the brakes."

"And she went straight into the back of him."

"Yes, sir," said Tykrist. "Her bike went into the back of the blue limo at high speed. And she came right off. But that didn't stop Esma. Not her. She grabbed on."

"Grabbed on?" said Zandonella. It was a hot day and she could smell the spicy tarmac of the road surface and the toxic sweetness of the spilled oil.

"Yes, onto the back of the blue limo. She used her new metal hand." At this point Tykrist's voice became unsteady, but she managed to keep control of her feelings and continue to report. Dredd listened impassively with no flicker of emotion on his face as she went on.

"She grabbed on to the rear bumper of the limo and held on for dear life. The driver must have known she was there because he began to accelerate in an attempt to shake her off. She was being dragged along the road, but her uniform and her Judge's helmet protected her. The blue limo continued to accelerate but it also began to swerve. Esma was hanging on like a cyborg bulldog. She wouldn't let go. But unfortunately her hand did: her metal hand. The limo hit top speed and pulled it clean off." Tykrist began to cry. "She was left lying there in the road with nothing left but a bloody stump."

"Your sister did a good job," said Dredd in a cool, level voice. "She was brave and I'll see she gets a citation for attempting to stop the abduction." He looked around at the wreckage and the roadblocks. "But that doesn't alter the fact that we were supposed to protect the dolphin and we didn't. Now we have to find him." He turned and walked away towards the cavalcade of Judges that had just arrived to help clean up the mess.

Zandonella looked down at Tykrist who was trying to wipe away her own tears while she cradled her sister in her arms. "Don't worry," said Zandonella. "They'll be able to fit her with a new hand."

At that moment, as if she'd been listening all along, Esma opened her eyes. She looked at Zandonella and said, "Where did they take the ambassador?"

"We don't know," said Zandonella. But she had a hollow feeling in the pit of her stomach that they were going to find out. And in doing so, she would have to call upon her special psi capabilities.

"Kidnapped?" said Blue Streak.

"Or dolphin-napped," said Mac the Meat Man. "If you prefer."

"But why?" said Blue Belle. The tattooed girl's voice, demanding and strident at the best of times, rose above the sound of trickling water and echoed harshly off the tiles that lined the walls of the swimming pool room. The tiles were pale green in colour, the ceiling lustrous panels of bronze, and the floor and the pool itself were painted white and had perhaps once been spotless and not as dirty as they were now. The pool was part of an underground health spa in what had once been a luxury hotel. Now it smelled of mildew and mouse droppings.

Mac smiled at Belle. "All will be explained when we get the ambassador here and hear what he has to say."

"Say?" said Belle. "You mean this fish can talk?"

"Strictly speaking he's a mammal, not a fish." Mac adjusted his tie; a black shoelace affair that secured the collar of a bright red shirt of the sort cowboys wore in movies. Very bad and very old movies, thought Streak. Mac was also wearing a white suit, buttoned tight over his little round paunch. He had obviously made an effort to dress up and he looked quite the dandy. Streak wondered if this was in honour of the Cetacean Ambassador or because Mac knew he was going to see Blue Belle again. He felt a small hot flash of jealousy.

Belle was dressed to fight rather than to impress, wearing camouflage combat trousers, steel-toed boots and a tank top. But her flimsy and frankly minuscule tank top did nothing to conceal the abundant and shapely tattooed breasts swelling beneath it, and Streak was convinced that Mac was using every possible opportunity to try and peer down at her cleavage. Streak decided that if he caught the little man in the act he would grab him and strangle him slowly with the thick, red rubber hose that snaked across the floor, feeding a steady flow of water from a tap in the wall into the kidney-shaped swimming pool that filled two thirds of the room.

"And this mammal," continued Mac, "is a highly intelligent creature. Otherwise they would never have made him ambassador, I guess." He smiled and twinkled at Belle. Streak thought maybe he'd stuff the hose up one of his orifices and turn the water on full blast...

"How does he talk?" said Belle. "He's under water, isn't he?"

"There's a translation device fitted to his tank. It converts cetacean chirps and grunts into English. We'll be able to talk to him just fine when he arrives, don't worry."

"We aren't worried," said Streak. "Maybe you're the one who should be worried."

"Why?" said Mac, his disgustingly huge, white eyebrows doing a little dance of innocent puzzlement on his face. Streak wondered how Mac would respond to having those eyebrows torn off his face.

"You invited us here," said Streak. "We're your sworn enemies and you decided you wanted to meet us here, all alone, just you and both of us. Don't you think you should be worried?" Streak patted his waistband under his billowing black T-shirt, feeling for the reassuring hard shape of the pistol he had tucked there.

"Let me take your points one at a time," said Mac, smiling cheerfully and raising his chubby fingers so he could count on them. "Number one..." He extended one little pink finger. "We aren't sworn enemies."

"Oh no?" said Streak.

"Certainly not. We're just competitors. Competitors in the same business."

"The meat business," said Belle, who obviously felt she had been left out of the conversation for too long. Streak reflected that she was never one to fail to point out the obvious.

"That's right," said Mac. "That's exactly right, young lady." He extended a second fat, pink finger and Streak indulged himself in a sadistic fantasy of lopping those fingers off with some kind of heavy-duty cutting tool. Shears, bolt cutters... Anything would do, really.

"Number two: there may be two of you and only one of me, so to speak, at the moment, but the boys are due here any second."

"The boys?" said Belle.

Mac bobbed his head jovially. "The Barkin brothers. You remember? Theo and Leo, plus Leo's faithful robot companion. The three of them will be arriving shortly, with our guest the ambassador."

There was a sudden grumbling and squeaking of machinery that had apparently been left unused for a long time.

"What's that?" said Streak, reaching under his shirt for his pistol.

"Cool your jets, son," said Mac with an infuriating note of condescension in his voice. "It's just the elevator. Sounds like the boys are here already."

"What kind of place is this, with an elevator and a swimming pool?" said Belle, who could always be relied upon to ask the most irrelevant questions.

"It used to be a four-star hotel," said Mac. "But now it's a no-star flop-house. They've closed down their sub-basement, subsequently mothballing a sports centre and, as you can see, this nice little swimming pool. But old Mac managed to get access to it." He twinkled and put one fat finger alongside his nose in a gesture of self-congratulatory slyness. "It's very handy because the boys can get to it through an equally disused basement garage that once served the hotel. No one will see them coming in with our cetacean friend."

A rusty screeching sound filled the room as the grumbling elevator came to a halt. A rectangular section of the green tiled wall opposite the pool lurched open to reveal smooth, featureless bronze doors that in turn slid open to reveal the brightly lit interior of the elevator. Inside were two men, a robot, and a large, cylindrical water tank sitting on a low, motorised platform of the kind used in hotels to carry around piles of luggage.

Inside the tank was the Cetacean Ambassador, a large, dark and streamlined blue shape hanging alertly in the water, his smiling face pressed to the glass. "Why is he smiling like that?" said Streak.

"He isn't. That's just the way dolphin's faces look. Their mouths are in a smiling shape. Like a cat's."

The dark-haired Barkin brother stepped out of the elevator. He had a gun in his hand. "What the hell is going on?" he demanded, looking at Mac. "What are these two doing here?"

"I like cats," said Belle. "I had a cyborg cat, but it broke." Her voice was nonchalant, but Streak saw how she turned slightly away from the elevator so the Barkin brothers couldn't see her hand slide down the side of her combat trousers and take hold of the chrome Peaceful World automatic pistol sagging in her pocket.

Neither of the brothers, nor Mac, noticed what she was doing. But the red metal robot suddenly stepped out from beside the dolphin's tank and announced, "Female intruder reaching for hand weapon."

"Intruder?" said Belle, bringing the gun into view. "That's not very nice. I was invited."

"Put it down or I'll shoot," said the blond brother stepping out of the elevator, raising his own gun.

"Now boys," said Mac the Meat Man, stepping between the two opposing parties. "Let's everybody calm down and put those guns away. I asked our tattooed friends here because we're all in the same business, aren't we? Which got me to thinking, why shouldn't we be in business together?"

"Together?" echoed the Barkin brothers simultaneously.

"Certainly," said Mac. "Partners."

"Why do we need partners?" asked Leo.

Mac gave a patient, tolerant smile. "Because the meat trade is a tough racket and we need all the help we can get."

"Are you going senile?" said the other brother, Theo. "Our mutant pork has just been legalised. You know that. You helped us sell a full warehouse to Wiggly Little Piggly Enterprises. Have you forgotten that?"

"I am neither forgetful, nor senile," said Mac. "As for the legality of the meat trade, I fear our cetacean friend here will have something to say about that."

The brothers glanced at the dolphin in his tank. "Him?" they said with simultaneous scepticism.

"Certainly," said Mac. "That's why we brought him here. Now if you would be so good as to switch on the ambassador's translation device..."

"What translation device?" asked Leo.

"Allow me, sir," said the robot, and pressed some buttons on a band of metal that circled the base of the dolphin's tank. As if responding to the pressing of the buttons, the dolphin swung around to face the humans, alert and calm. There was a sizzle of static as a loudspeaker came to life in the base of the cylinder, and then some strange clicking noises, rapid and sharp. After a moment, the clicking faded into the background and a synthesised voice murmured at them.

"Is that water for me?" he said.

The humans all looked at each other. Mac the Meat Man beamed at Blue Belle. "See? I told you he was smart." Mac glanced at the level of the water in the swimming pool. The hose was now floating three or four metres above the floor of the pool. He hurried over, pulled the hose out of the water and went to the wall and turned the tap off. He wiped his hands and turned to the dolphin's tank, smiling and bowing. "Yes, Ambassador, it is indeed for you."

"I am pleased to hear it," said the voice from the tank. "I would appreciate a change of water, or better yet, to leave this tank altogether. It is filled with an uncomfortable quantity of my own excrement after that high-speed chase."

Zandonella knew what was coming as soon as they called her to the morgue. She went without delay but there was a constant, sickly tremor in her solar plexus. The morgue was a gleaming circular room with walls and floors of polished steel. A shallow trough ran all along the circumference of the burnished walls. The entire place was designed for easy cleaning.

A number of metal autopsy tables stood in the middle of the floor. Only one was occupied at the moment, and Judge Dredd and Judge O'Mannion stood beside it. Zandonella approached with trepidation. The corpse on the table was of a middle-aged man with a muscular build and long, black hair combed carefully to try to conceal a large bald spot at the top of his head. This vestige of vanity seemed heart-rendingly pathetic on the naked corpse. He had a livid gunshot wound just below his sternum, the burn marks and powder residue indicating a mortal wound made at extremely close range. Someone had simply put the gun to his chest and fired.

"This is Delbert Tance," said Dredd. "Licensed chauffeur and light vehicle operator. He does a lot of work for visiting diplomats. Today he was supposed to be driving the Cetacean Ambassador."

"Until somebody put a bullet in him and took his place," said O'Mannion. Zandonella remembered the smoked glass on the blue limousine. Behind that glass had been an assassin, hijacker and kidnapper.

"The way we've pieced it together," said Dredd, "he was killed at the limo company's garage and his body concealed in a locker. Whoever did it then proceeded to steal his vehicle and collect the ambassador from the airport. There, they were met by the other limos and the preliminary escort of Judges. From the airport they drove to the rendezvous point, where we joined them."

"Which is also the point where the platform began to collapse," said Zandonella, remembering the crumbling support pillar and Dredd's unbelievable feat in rescuing thousands of people. "That's quite a coincidence," she said.

"It was no coincidence," said O'Mannion, who seemed immune to anyone's irony except her own.

"They wanted a diversion to disrupt the escort," said Zandonella.

"Correct," said Dredd. "Forensics has determined that a charge of plastic explosive was placed on the support pillar to be remotely detonated when they saw us drive underneath."

"A neat plan," said O'Mannion. "And they probably think they've got clean away, with the ambassador as their captive." She smiled her witchy smile and looked at Zandonella. "But they weren't reckoning on the likes of you."

Zandonella swallowed and tried hard to settle the queasy feeling in her stomach. Here it comes, she thought.

O'Mannion turned to Dredd. "We Psi-Judges have all kinds of skills, but Zandonella here is really something special."

"I understand she can help us trace the perps," said Dredd. "Thanks to her ESP."

O'Mannion smiled. "Not ESP but PNE. And this is a scenario perfectly suited for her. A PNE is a possessive necro-empath. This means that if she touches human remains, say a murder victim," O'Mannion nodded at the body on the table, "then she can project her consciousness into the person physically closest to them at the time of death. Usually the killer."

O'Mannion turned and looked at Zandonella. Dredd was looking at her, too. "Well, get started," said O'Mannion.

Zandonella stepped forward and put her hands on the cold flesh of the corpse...

The Cetacean Ambassador splashed from one end of the swimming pool to the other half a dozen times in quick succession before rearing up with his cheerfully smiling bottle-nosed face above the surface and crashing down, splashing the humans who were all standing beside the pool watching the show.

Leo looked furiously at the water dripping off him. "Try that again, Flipper, and we're going to turn you into sushi..."

"He can't hear you," said Theo.

"In point of fact, he can," said the robot. "Not only can he hear you, he can understand you and also reply." Even to Blue Streak, the robot seemed to possess a pain-in-the-ass, know-it-all tone.

Theo turned on the robot and said, "But his translation device is attached to his..."

"Tank thingy," supplied Blue Belle.

Theo nodded. "That's right. And he isn't in the tank thingy any more."

The robot managed to sound almost smug as it replied. "The cetacean has a translation receiver and transmitter surgically implanted in his body."

"In other words," said a voice from behind them, "I can hear you and you can hear me." Streak and the others spun around, startled.

"It's coming from the empty tank," said Streak.

"Or rather, from the control panel at its base," said Mac.

"The tank isn't empty," said Belle pedantically. "It's full of water. And dolphin shit."

"And I am over here," said the voice from the speaker at the base of the tank. They all turned to stare again at the smiling dolphin that was looking at them from the swimming pool. "You might say I am throwing my voice."

"The cetacean is making a pun about ventriloquism," said the robot.

"Shut your metal face," said Theo. "And somebody explain to me why we've got this dolphin here."

"Touching on that matter," said the cetacean, via his remote speaker, "could you kindly explain the circumstances of my abduction? I am somewhat confused. I was expecting to be at an embassy reception right about now, eating considerable quantities of snow crab."

"The circumstances?" said Theo. "I killed your chauffeur and hijacked your limo and brought you here."

"But why?"

"It's quite simple, boys," said Mac. He glanced at Belle and made a little bow. "And girl." Streak could have killed him right then. "We're all in the meat business. And our friend splashing in the pool here has come to the Mega-City on a mission of vital importance to that business."

"You don't mean the dolphins are going to muscle in on our trade?" said Streak.

"On the contrary," said the voice from the empty tank. "My people would never sully their fins or snouts with that bloody, filthy criminal commerce."

"Ha! That shows how much you know," said Leo. "It's not criminal any more. The mutant pig business is entirely legit now. The Council of Five says so. The Judges even have to protect pork vendors instead of closing them down."

"That may be so," said Mac gravely. "But boys – and girl – that may all be about to change."

"What do you mean, change?" asked Belle.

"I mean no sooner have we become legitimate tradesmen – and women – than our dolphin friend here has come to the Mega-City to try and put us out of business."

"What the hell?" said Streak. "I'm only just getting used to not being a criminal, and now you tell me I'm going to be one again?"

"Pretty much," said Mac. "If our dolphin chum here has his way."

"Well, I don't like it," said Streak. "I don't like it at all. Let's gut the fish."

"The mammal," corrected Belle.

"No need to get hot under the collar, son," said Mac. "We're doing everything in our considerable power to stop it happening. That's why I had Theo here kidnap the ambassador."

"Theo kidnap him?" said Leo. "You make it sound like he did it all by himself. Who set the explosives on the pillar? Who detonated it? Who distracted the Judges?"

"A much needed distraction at a critical moment," said the robot in a whining, prissy voice. Streak was getting annoyed just listening to it, and he had nothing to do with the damned thing. So he was hardly surprised that the other brother turned to the robot, his face turning red.

"Who asked you, metal face?" he said.

"Leave Boyard-27 alone," said Leo.

Theo's face grew redder still. "Why don't you just–" Suddenly, he fell silent.

A sensation of falling. Like walking down a staircase and putting out your foot for the bottom step, but the bottom step isn't there.

Instead you find yourself plunging down through endless darkness, disorientated and experiencing fear, the most profound fear possible. The fear that comes with utter loss of self. The fear that has forgotten who is feeling the fear. A fear without centre, without reference or context.

A moment before, there had been a person with emotions and memories and a personal history. Someone called Belinda Zandonella reached out her hands in a brightly lit morgue and touched the cold flesh of a corpse.

Then there was nothing. No step at the bottom of the stairs. No person called Zandonella. Just darkness.

Just darkness and loss of identity and a sensation of falling and sudden cold...

And then the falling stopped and she felt the hot sensation of connection.

Suddenly, Zandonella was standing in an echoing tiled room with a swimming pool at one end. Splashing in the water was a strange inhuman shape. A dolphin. She had found the Cetacean Ambassador. Her heart leapt in her chest.

Except it wasn't her heart. It wasn't her chest.

She was in a new body, looking out through new eyes. There were people standing around her: three men, a woman, and a robot.

They were all staring at her.

EIGHT

Her strange heart thudded violently in her strange chest. Sweat flowed out copiously over a body that wasn't hers, yet was. It was a man's body. Zandonella looked down at her hands: large, powerful male hands with scars and dark hairs writhing over the thick knuckles. She took a deep breath. She had to calm down. It was always like this after a jump. It was the most dangerous time because of the utter disorientation. Who was she? Where was she?

Zandonella had jumped into a new body, subverting and displacing the mind of its owner, like a bird taking possession of a strange nest. The personality of her victim was still here, but buried deep in the electrochemical processes of the brain, overwhelmed and dominated by her own personality.

This was the most dangerous time.

She mustn't let the others suspect anything. She had to act normally. But what was normal for this new body, this new person? She had to fight off the urge to panic. Be calm and take control. She looked at the ugly, gnarled male hands that now belonged to her. She told herself that the others wouldn't notice anything. She wouldn't let them.

Zandonella looked up at the men and the woman and the robot. She recognised them now. They were the perps from the factory farm over the municipal dump: Mac the Meat Man, the tattooed couple, the robot and the blond brother.

Which suggested, by process of elimination, that she was the other brother, the black-haired one. She wouldn't know for sure, though. Not until she got a look in a mirror. She couldn't worry about that now. They were all staring at her.

They were all expecting her to say something.

Zandonella realised that there were words waiting to be said. At the tip of her tongue, as the saying went. She spoke the first words that came to mind.

"You don't just *like* that robot," she said. She had no idea who she was saying it to or why she was saying it, but the phrase hung in the forefront of her mind, inherited from the personality she had just displaced.

"You *love* it," she said in an unfamiliar, ugly voice. "Why don't you kiss its metal ass?"

Then the words ran out, like a buffer in a computer emptying. She had nothing more to say. That was all the dark-haired brother had left behind for her. She had used up his thoughts. Now his head was full of her thoughts.

But it was enough. The others all relaxed.

She was one of them. They had accepted her. They were ignoring her. The tattooed girl was turning to Mac the Meat Man. "How do you know all this?" she said. "How do you know what the dolphin plans to do?"

"Yes, that is an interesting question," said a disembodied voice. Zandonella turned around to see the empty cylindrical tank from the limousine. There was a loud speaker fitted to the base of it. It was the translation unit, of course. It was the Cetacean Ambassador talking. "How did you know of my diplomatic mission?"

"I pay off the right people," said Mac proudly. "They keep me informed. I knew all about your visit and the topics you planned to discuss because they impacted on my business." He looked at the other humans. "*Our* business," he corrected. "And now that that business has become legal, it was more urgent than ever that we stopped you."

"Why not just kill him?" said Zandonella. It was a risk asking a question like that. But she had to start talking sooner or later, and she wanted to know the answer. She just prayed that it was something the dark-haired brother might legitimately ask. "Why kidnap him?"

"Dolphin-nap," giggled the tattooed girl.

"That's a damned stupid question," said the blond brother, with a thick note of contempt in his voice.

"Not at all," said Mac. He turned to look at Zandonella. She tried not to flinch under that bright beady gaze. No matter how many times she did this, she always felt that someone would spot the impostor, see her lurking there in a stolen body. But Mac just smiled at Zandonella hidden deep in the black-haired brother, and suspected nothing. "That's a good question, Theo."

Theo. Good. At least she knew what her name was now.

"Another question that also interests myself," said the disembodied voice from the tank. Mac turned and glanced at the dolphin frolicking in the pool.

"I try to avoid killing," said Mac.

"Ha!" snorted the tattooed man.

"Except where absolutely necessary," said Mac. "It's wasteful. I hate waste. At my factory farms I don't waste the pigs. Not a particle of them. I use everything but the squeal, as the saying goes. And I'm working on voice-activated slaughter technology that will make good use of the squeal, too. So I thought if we had a chance to talk to our aquatic friend here, we might be able to come to some sort of arrangement."

"I still say we should just kill him," said the blond brother. "Kill him and chop him up. We could do a side line in fish meat."

"The thing is, Leo, if we do that," said Mac, "the cetacean community will just send another representative."

"So what?" said Leo. "They'll send him, we'll get him, and turn *him* into fish meat, too. It'll become a thriving side business."

Zandonella had heard enough. She'd checked her pockets and found a vid-phone. She began moving away from the others and surreptitiously slid it out, activating the picture messaging and text facilities. She worked quickly and smoothly. No one was taking any notice of her...

Except for brother Leo. He was staring at her. "Who are you texting?"

"None of your damned business," said Zandonella. She was getting the hang of the brothers' relationship.

O'Mannion was in the med-unit at Justice Central with Zandonella's comatose body when Dredd came in.

"We've got a signal from Judge Zandonella," he said.

O'Mannion couldn't help glancing at the sleeping body lying in the med-bed at her feet. Of course, that wasn't Zandonella, even though it looked like her. It was just an empty shell, a vessel into which Zandonella's mind and personality could be poured, and from which it could be drained away again at command – at O'Mannion's command.

O'Mannion suppressed a pang of primitive fear. She was a hardened and experienced Psi-Judge, but even she found PNE a little spooky. But she faked a casual smile and kept her voice sardonic and unconcerned as she spoke to Dredd. "Really? Already? Good for her. What has she got for us?"

"Sent an image from a vid-phone, along with a text message. From the image we've managed to identify the location where they're holding the Cetacean Ambassador." Dredd checked his Lawgiver. He was clearly eager to start shooting at something. Dredd was reliable and got results, but his approach tended towards the linear.

As if sensing O'Mannion's sardonic assessment of him, Dredd looked up from his weapon. "I came here because I thought you would want to join us for the bust."

"It's not a matter of wanting to," said O'Mannion. "It's a matter of having to. Unless you want to look after this vegetable yourself." She nodded at Zandonella's comatose form lying on the med-bed at their feet.

"What do you mean?" said Dredd. "She's not coming with us."

"She is. Zandonella's body has to be brought into physical contact with the person she's jumped into. That's the only way she can get back into her own skin. Of course, we could wait until you bring all the perps back here and then do the transfer." O'Mannion smiled. "But things have been known to go wrong in the past. It's better to do the switch as soon as possible. Did she send an image of herself – of the body she's in?"

"Affirmative," said Dredd. "A three-time loser called Theo Barkin."

"Good. Circulate the picture to all of the Judges who are coming on the raid. Tell them that despite all appearances, that knuckle-dragging thug is actually our own delightful Judge Zandonella and must be treated as such."

Dredd nodded. "I'll instruct them not to shoot her."

"That would be nice," said O'Mannion.

Mac the Meat Man stood at the edge of the swimming pool looking down at the dolphin lolling in the water, sleek belly upwards, smiling its fixed smile at him. "You can see our position," said Mac.

"Indeed," said the disembodied voice from the dolphin's tank.

"We've only just put our business on a legal footing and then you come along, threatening everything."

"That is indeed an accurate summary of events."

Mac got down on his knees so he could be closer to the dolphin floating happily in the pool. "Please," said Mac.

"Don't beg," snarled Leo. "It's not dignified." He had his revolver in his hand and he was clearly twitching to use it.

Zandonella checked her own weapon, a sawn-off pump action shotgun. It was no Lawgiver, but it would do and she'd use it if she had to. She wondered what it would be like to shoot her own "brother". But of course, the shooting wouldn't stop there. She glanced covertly at the tattooed couple. They were equally armed and dangerous. And the robot: she'd seen what he was capable of, blasting away at them in the pig farm even though he'd been cut in half. Now here he was, rebuilt as though nothing had ever happened to him, and looking more deadly than ever.

Zandonella prayed that Dredd would arrive soon.

"I am not begging," said Mac, on his knees by the pool. "I am merely trying to get our point across to our friend here. As one businessman to another."

"I am not a man, nor do I do what you call business," said the dolphin.

"Then why are you interfering with it?" persisted Mac. "What do these pigs matter to you? If you just promise to keep your mouth shut – I mean promise to say nothing about the meat trade – we can let you go." Mac beamed hopefully. "You'll be back snapping snow crab at the ambassador's reception in no time."

"If it will clarify the situation," said the dolphin, "I will outline my position on this matter."

"Please do."

"I will in no way, now or ever, through any action or inaction on my part, allow your bloody and evil trade to continue. I will do everything in my power to put a stop to it, and to bring you and your red-handed fellows to justice. You have been guilty of unimaginable atrocities but at last they are at an end."

The dolphin's words rang in the tiled room with unmistakable authority and conviction. The hairs on the back of Zandonella's neck stirred in response and she felt a ludicrous impulse to applaud. But she knew there was no cause for celebration. The Cetacean Ambassador had just signed his own death warrant.

"Hmm," said Mac. "That's pretty clear, I suppose."

"I told you we were wasting time," said Leo. He started towards the swimming pool, pistol in hand.

"Never mind," sighed Mac. "It was worth a try. Say goodbye to the ambassador, folks." He rose slowly from his kneeling position, an old man with rusty joints.

"Wait," said Zandonella, moving quickly and getting between Leo and the dolphin. Everyone was staring at her. It was now or never. Once again she felt sweat breaking out on the body that was not hers.

"Get out of the way, Theo," said Leo.

"No, wait."

Leo grinned crookedly. "Suddenly become a fish lover? Maybe you'd like to climb in the pool and swim around with your new boyfriend? That might be fun for you. I understand they have unfeasibly huge willies."

"Actually, that's true," said the Cetacean Ambassador modestly.

"Let *me* do it," said Zandonella quickly. "Let me kill him." She held up her own shotgun.

"I don't care which of you boys do it, just so long as it gets done," said Mac gloomily. He seemed depressed at his failure to win over the dolphin.

"Leave it to me," said Zandonella. "The rest of you get out of here and I'll follow."

Leo's eyes narrowed with suspicion. "What's the sudden rush?"

"We've been hanging around here too long. The Judges could be arriving any second." As she said these words, Zandonella was praying that they were true.

"Theo's right," said Mac. "There's no point in us staying here." He looked at the dolphin still floating calmly in the pool, as serene as a smiling Buddha. "Not now that our offer has been so peremptorily spurned," he added bitterly. He turned to the tattooed couple. "Let's get out of here and go somewhere convivial to discuss the terms of our new partnership."

"Who says there's going to be any partnership?" said the tattooed man.

"That's exactly what we need to discuss," beamed Mac. He had recovered his usual bonhomie. He put his hands on the shoulders of the tattooed pair and steered them towards the elevator. "I'm sure we can come to some agreement." He looked back over his shoulder. "Theo and Leo, you follow just as soon as you get rid of that uncooperative sea creature once and for all."

"I'll see to it," said Zandonella quickly. "Leo, you take that robot you love so much and go with them." That seemed to hit an authentic note of sibling insult. "I'll catch up with you."

"No," said Leo stubbornly. "I want to kill the dolphin."

"Why?" said Zandonella through Theo's lips. Her exasperation was unfeigned.

"I just want to. You got to do the abduction. You get to have all the fun."

"Oh, for grud's sake."

"Boys, boys," Mac called back to them.

"I want to shoot the dolphin," said Leo petulantly. He raised his revolver and clicked the safety off. Zandonella could see that he wouldn't be swayed. She thought quickly.

"I'll flip you for it."

"Flip me?"

"Sure. Have you got a coin or something?" asked Zandonella. Leo lowered his gun and began to look in his pockets. She relaxed a fraction. Now at least she had a fifty-fifty chance. As the blond moron dug out an old relic – a coin – from his pocket, his eyes gleamed meanly. She had judged the rivalry between the two brothers correctly.

"Funnily enough, I keep this antique with me as a lucky charm. Heads or tails?" said Leo.

"Heads," said Zandonella. Leo flipped the silver dollar coin and it sailed up in the air, glinting. She held her breath. Fifty-fifty. If it was tails, she was going to have to start shooting. First Leo. Then who? Both of the tattooed kids were dangerous, but so was the robot. She'd have to make the right decision and she'd only get one chance. She had to get it right. The robot would have faster reflexes than any human. So first Leo, then the robot, then the tattooed couple. By then there'd be no element of surprise and they'd be firing back. So after she took out the robot, she'd jump into the pool. It would make her a more difficult target. They'd have to approach the pool and she'd have the advantage. She could duck under water. Also, she'd be in position to protect the ambassador...

All these thoughts flashed through her borrowed brain as the coin spun in the air. Leo held out the back of his hand and the coin landed on it. Leo covered it with his other hand with a slapping sound. He looked under his hand and then looked at Zandonella. Zandonella felt her throat go hollow, her whole body weightless with a rush of adrenaline, the shotgun heavy in her hand.

"Heads," said Leo sourly. He pocketed the coin and walked away, following Mac and the tattooed couple to the elevator.

The robot hurriedly clanked after him. They crowded inside, the elevator doors closed and they were gone with a rumble of ageing machinery. As simple as that.

Zandonella dropped her shotgun and sat down on the floor. Her legs wouldn't support her any more. She laughed, quietly at first, and then at such wild volume that her laughter rang off the tiled walls. It was the bass laughter of a big man but it carried an erratic quiver of hysteria. Zandonella didn't care. She laughed until she felt utterly drained and her face was wet with tears. Then she cried for a while. It was always like this when the pressure was off after a dangerous mission.

"Do you mind telling me what is so amusing?" said the dolphin via his voice box. Zandonella dragged herself to the edge of the pool. She was still so weak with relief she could hardly move. She sat down on the rim of the pool and let her legs dangle over into the cool water. Theo Barkin's shoes were getting soaked but she didn't care. The dolphin stared up at her with its bright intelligent eyes.

"I'll tell you," said Zandonella. "I am not actually Theo Barkin. I'm a Psi-Judge who has jumped into his body to come to your aid. My name is Zandonella."

"Delighted to make your acquaintance," said the dolphin with a preternatural calm that was only enhanced by the synthetic tone of the voice box. "You seem to have done your job very well."

"Not that well," said an even more inhuman voice.

Zandonella turned to see the robot standing there. Astonishment and disbelief pulsed through her borrowed brain. The robot had departed in the elevator and the elevator hadn't returned. She would have heard it. Then Zandonella noticed another door in the far corner of the room; a door that led to the stairway. She hadn't heard its approach but it had heard everything she had said.

All these thoughts and more flickered through Zandonella's mind as she turned and saw the robot standing behind her. The robot was holding a streamlined riot gun with a circular magazine that looked like it held a lot of ammunition. One of the other thoughts that came to Zandonella in that instant was just how far away her own gun was, lying there on the floor halfway between her and the robot. Exactly where she'd dropped it in her moment of relief. Bad move.

Time for a different move.

Zandonella threw herself forward, towards her gun. The robot began to open fire at the same time. Zandonella heard bullets sizzle overhead and drill into the far wall, shattering tile and sending fragments splashing into the swimming pool. Zandonella hit the floor, rolling. The robot adjusted its aim. Again bullets burned overhead, but closer now. She heard them plop into the swimming pool and as she rolled across the floor her mind flared with fear for the safety of the Cetacean Ambassador.

She stopped rolling and picked up her shotgun. She could still hear the tiles at the far end of the room fragmenting and falling into the pool. The robot changed its aim, its reaction time faster than a human's, and kept firing at her. Bullets whispered past her head, chewing into the floor instead of hitting the water in the swimming pool. Good. The dolphin was safe. Zandonella raised her shotgun and took aim at the robot. The red metal skeleton swelled out at the hip, chest and head. Pick a target. Zandonella could still hear the shattering tiles spilling into the pool at the far end of the room. The noise was increasing, as though the tiles were shattering ever faster. That didn't make sense. It didn't matter. No time for that now. The robot was correcting its aim again. Now the riot gun was pointed straight at Zandonella. She aimed at the robot's chest and fired.

The robot lurched back as it took the hit of buckshot. It hinged on its knees, its head and torso dropping backwards while its feet remained firmly planted, like a toy bending in half. Zandonella pumped her shotgun and fired again. She missed. The robot was still falling backwards. Her shot went cleanly between its spread legs and over its chest and head as they bent back to touch the floor. Behind her Zandonella could hear tiles breaking and falling into the pool along with

what sounded like larger blocks of concrete. The whole wall
was falling apart by the sound of it but she couldn't turn to
see what was happening.

The robot was getting back up, its head and torso rising
from the floor by the force of its firmly planted legs, like a
bouncy toy springing back into position. It was still clutching the riot gun. Zandonella pumped her shotgun again. Try
for the head or the chest. She'd hit the chest last time and
that hadn't done her much good. The robot's head was
already rising back into view. That made her decision easy.
She fired. The robot took the blast of shotgun pellets right in
its head. The head bounced back down to the floor like a
metal basketball, but it remained connected to its neck, and
its neck remained connected to its shoulders, and the entire
robot, solid and intact, began to rise inexorably back up.
Zandonella pumped her shotgun again while a flood of cold
feeling began rising up her spine. The shotgun was the
wrong weapon for the job. Its barrel had been shortened
which meant it lost accuracy and the pellets began to spread
as soon as they left the barrel. By the time they hit the robot
there wasn't enough payload to do any permanent damage.
She had to get closer.

Zandonella stepped forward. Behind her there came an
almighty splash as what must have been a huge section of
wall toppled into the deep end of the pool. What was happening? A few stray bullets couldn't cause damage like that.
The entire wall was falling apart. No time to think of that
now. The robot was bouncing back up from the floor. It was
coming up with its gun first this time. Zandonella had to fire
now. The shotgun blast hit the robot low in the chest box
and slammed it back down. Zandonella kept moving forward. She had to get closer if she was going to deliver a
killshot. Behind her there was a thunderous noise as the
entire wall began to give away. Zandonella couldn't help herself. She had to look.

As she turned around she felt a rush of cold air on her
face, bringing a smell of diesel fuel with it. The air was rushing in through a hole in the wall at the far end of the room.

Tiles were spinning off in all directions and large chunks of concrete were falling free. The debris spilled into the deep end of the swimming pool. The Cetacean Ambassador had fled to the shallow end and was sheltering at the bottom of the pool. A piece of wall the size of a door fell into the pool with a thunderous splash. The hole in the wall was growing, enveloped in a cloud of smoke and dust. Then a gust of air dispersed the cloud and Zandonella saw the yellow shape of the Mk 4 Pat-Wagon.

The Mk 4 Pat-Wagon was a special penetration unit used for busting into dwellings on raids by Judges. It was a modified anti-grav bulldozer with armoured plating and turret-mounted street cannons. Normally it had seven Judges riding in it. This one had six. Judge Dredd was at the controls, the Karst sisters and Darrid sitting to his left in the gun bays. To his right sat O'Mannion and Carver. The sixth position was filled with a med-bed containing an unmoving figure.

With a queasy dislocating shock, Zandonella recognised her own body. It wasn't a new experience, but seeing herself this way was always like a premonition of death. She turned away from the spectacle of the collapsing wall to face the robot once again. She had only looked away for a fraction of a second, but it had been too long. The robot was back on its feet and aiming at her.

Zandonella fired. The robot fired. She saw the robot's head part company with its shoulders. A lucky shot. That should slow the bastard down. But the robot kept firing as the head bounced away across the floor. Zandonella felt bullets hit her on the arm, the shoulder and in the head.

The world tilted and everything faded to a deep, blood-coloured haze a moment before it was swallowed by blackness.

"Zandonella's been hit!" shouted O'Mannion as she jumped down from the perpdozer. She landed in the now muddy grey water of the swimming pool. She was standing on a jagged tangle of wreckage in the deep end of the pool: concrete blocks and twisted bars of rust-red iron from the wall. Fragments of pale green tile were scattered everywhere like leaves shed in autumn. O'Mannion dived off the mound of rubble into the murky water and started swimming across the pool, chopping through the water with desperate speed. There was a vast splash and the water in front of her frothed in a fury of bubbles. Someone else had dived in, landing in front of her. It was Dredd. He was carrying something, something as big as he was: the med-bed, with Zandonella in it. Dredd had realised the urgency of the situation.

Zandonella, in the perp's body, was seriously wounded. They had to get her body to her and make contact before the perp's body died. Dredd was dragging the med-bed behind him as he cut through the water with powerful strokes. A blue shadow flashed up from the depths of the water, a lithe streamlined shape. It was the Cetacean Ambassador. The dolphin swam under the med-bed and pressed its head against it, propelling it through the water.

The dolphin was pushing Zandonella's body for Dredd.

Dredd and the dolphin reached the shallow end of the pool. Dredd scrambled out, shedding water in a spray of speed, taking the dripping med-bed with him. O'Mannion stroked desperately to catch up. As she reached the shallow end, the dolphin swam around her, ghostly and agile, grazing her with a gentle passing caress. O'Mannion reached the far end of the pool and erupted from the water, running after Dredd. He'd reached the perp's body; the black-haired Barkin brother. He was shot in the head, his skull a grisly ruin. Dredd shoved the med-bed down so that Zandonella was next to Theo Barkin.

O'Mannion joined him, grabbed Zandonella's wet, unmoving hand and pressed it onto Barkin's body.

"Contact," she said.

After a PNE jump, a Psi-Judge normally received a statutory ten days off duty to recover.

Zandonella spent the first two days asleep. She was profoundly exhausted and beyond the reach of ordinary

consciousness, but she would nevertheless awake occasionally from jangled fragments of a nightmare to see the pig,
Porkditz, standing in the doorway of her bedroom peering at
her with every sign of concern. She found his presence reassuring and went quickly back to sleep.

On the third and fourth days she still slept, but less
deeply. She was no longer shielded by utter exhaustion and
the noises of the Mega-City kept her awake. The usual
urban din had been supplemented by a constant boisterous
haranguing of the advertising dirigibles that floated outside
her window, exhorting her to come down to her local Wiggly Little Piggly outlet and take advantage of the special
offer on all pork products, "Including Crunchy Bacon
Wunchies, Down-home Dracula Cajun Blood Sausages,
Offal Lot of Fun Buckets of Offal and Sweetbreads and, for
this week only, special edition Spicy Ricey Chinese-Style
Ribs!"

Half a dozen other competing pork franchises were also
advertising in an attempt to win themselves a slice of the
obviously huge and hugely lucrative market. Zandonella had
hoped the fad would have peaked by now. But if anything,
the mania for the new food seemed to be on the increase.
"The citizens of Mega-City One are eating Mr Piggy in a
bun," as a maddening jingle from Wiggly's leading competitor, Pork Lane PLC, put it.

On the fifth day Zandonella had recovered sufficiently
enough to make some vegetarian meals for herself and
Porkditz, and to watch the History Channel. Zandonella sub-
scribed to an expensive premium pay per view channel so
she only had to suffer through an ad break every five minutes or so. Virtually all the ads were for competing pig meat
franchises. Wiggly Little Piggly had struck back against Pork
Lane with an even more annoyingly catchy jingle: "Get some
fast pork on your fork", which was so hypnotically upbeat
and joyous that even Zandonella found herself humming it
in unguarded moments.

In between ads she and the pig sat through documentaries
about Louis XIV, trench warfare and doomed polar explorers

with handlebar moustaches. But even during these fascinating snippets of ancient history, the noise from the dirigibles
outside, all advertising pork products in a cacophony of
nifty slogans and jazzy jingles, was so deafening that Zandonella could hardly hear her Tri-D set. So she dug out a pair
of headphones that provided the soundtrack in 17.1 sur-
round sound while blissfully shutting out all external noise.

Then, after a moment's guilty reflection, she dug out a second pair and fitted them carefully over Porkditz's large,
delicate pink ears. He seemed to appreciate the high fidelity
sound, grunting cheerfully along to the Wiggly Little Piggly
jingle whenever it played. Zandonella went into the kitchen
and mixed them both a large dry martini. Porkditz liked his
with extra lemon rind.

That night Zandonella had vivid, endless, sweaty night-
mares. In them Porkditz was eternally squealing and
spurting blood as he was dismembered and eviscerated in
vivid, full-colour detail to provide the Meg's madcap citi-
zenry with its Crunchy Bacon Wunchies, Chinese-Style Ribs
and Offal Lot of Fun Buckets of Offal.

On the sixth day Judge Dredd arrived. He stood, filling the
doorway and looking down at Zandonella without expression. He might have been there to give her an official
reprimand and take away her badge and gun. Equally he
might have been about to issue a commendation and pin a
medal on her.

Instead, he said, "You've got a visitor. You don't have to see
him, but he asked to meet you again."

"Again?" Zandonella was about to ask who the sneck this
visitor was when Dredd stepped away from the door to allow
O'Mannion to approach with the Cetacean Ambassador's
tank.

The tank – this time a slim-size version for special visits –
was floating on a hover platform that O'Mannion steered
using a control line. She looked like the girl at the circus
leading an elephant. "The ambassador asked to see the
Judge who saved his life," said O'Mannion with a note in her
voice of what might almost have been pride.

"I offer greetings and thanks and the gratitude of my entire pod," said the dolphin diplomat, smiling in his cylindrical tank. His synthesised voice boomed from the base of the tank. "If you are ever swimming in the Magellan Vortex of the South Indian Current please do drop in on us. We shall splash in your honour."

"Uh, thank you," said Zandonella. "You are welcome. But I was only doing my duty." Just then Porkditz poked his head in to see what was going on. He took one look at Dredd and O'Mannion and the Cetacean Ambassador, floating there in his tank on its hover platform, and he scooted off back down the hall to the bedroom, his trotters rattling on the floor.

"I seem to have startled your friend."

"He's probably nervous because he senses he's scheduled for execution. Or slaughter, as people prefer to call it. He was given a week before being turned into food." Zandonella turned to O'Mannion and Dredd. "Is it time? Did you come here to take him away?"

"We came here because the ambassador wanted to see you," said Dredd. "Why don't you stop talking and listen to him?"

"There is new hope for your friend," said the ambassador, smiling in his tank.

Zandonella hardly dared to believe what she'd heard. "What do you mean?"

"In a sense, he is the reason I left my mother the ocean and came into the Mega-City. He and others like him. A new breed of mutant pigs with extremely high intelligence."

"I said he was intelligent," said Zandonella. "I tried to tell people." She shot an accusing look at O'Mannion.

O'Mannion smiled at her and said, "This sudden rise in pig IQ, combined with a steady drop in IQ among the Mega-City couch-potato human citizens, means that pigs are now adjudged to have an intellect close enough to humans to merit citizens' rights."

"Citizens' rights?" said Zandonella.

"Like myself and other cetaceans," added the dolphin.

"That was the reason for the kidnapping and assassination attempts," said Dredd. "The meat lobby desperately wanted to sabotage the ambassador's mission."

"But what you're saying is that Porkditz can live."

The ambassador flipped himself over playfully in his tank. "Porkditz can live. Just as I, thanks to you, still live. I present my gratitude, and now, sadly, my farewell. I must return to my mother, the sea."

"Goodbye," said Zandonella. "And thank you. For saving my friend's, er, bacon."

"No need to thank me," said the dolphin's voice box as O'Mannion guided his tank out through the door. It was a tight squeeze. Once she'd steered the tank through it, O'Mannion glanced back.

"You got out of Theo Barkin's body just in time," O'Mannion said. "A few seconds later he was brain-dead; in a comatose state. If your consciousness had still been inside him, we have no idea what would have happened to you."

With this cheery thought, she left. Dredd remained standing in the living room, looking down at Zandonella. "You realise what this means, don't you?"

"A change in the Law," said Zandonella. "And Porkditz gets to live." Dredd stared at her in grim silence. His face was lit for a moment by the sweeping coloured searchlight of an advertising dirigible outside the window, peering in, looking for someone to beam its message at. The Wiggly Little Piggly tune blared.

"Think," said Dredd.

Zandonella looked at him. The advertising jingle made it hard to think. Then she realised what he meant. "Oh my grud."

"That's right," said Dredd. "The Mega-City is now hooked on pork. When this new Law makes their favourite fast food illegal, millions of citizens are going to be very snecked off." He went to the window and stared out at the darkening streets.

Zandonella's happiness ebbed away and she felt a rising chill. "Get ready," said Dredd. "It's going to be a war zone out there."

NINE

A flaming bottle sailed through the dark night sky. It arced brightly, rising in a graceful curve before it began its swift descent, flame flickering through the air, glowing ever brighter as it grew ever larger, falling from the sky to finally shatter with a brilliant crash and a blazing spatter. The flame exploded on Zandonella's riot shield.

The riot shield was a curved rectangle of shatterproof plastic approximately a metre and a half tall. It was held by means of a strap that the Judges clasped in their left hands, or their right, whichever hand didn't grasp their daysticks – large lightweight clubs that could smash any miscreant to the ground in a compliant, uncomplaining heap. "Every citizen is a model citizen once he's been tapped," was the saying amongst the Judges.

Zandonella held her shield in her left hand, tilting it up toward the sky at a gentle angle. The mess of broken glass and burning grease slid harmlessly onto the ground. On either side of her, the Karst sisters held up their own riot shields, Esma using her bright new steel hand to hold onto hers. Behind Zandonella, Carver fumbled with his shield, struggling to get the strap over his hand. "It keeps slipping off!" he whined.

Meanwhile, more bottle bombs sailed through the night sky. Zandonella and the Karst sisters closed ranks, Carver huddling behind them. Glass smashed on the concrete around them and several puddles of fire blazed up.

Esma looked over at Zandonella. "What's in those things? Gasoline?"

"Pork fat," said Carver.

"Pork fat?"

"Maybe mixed with a little gasoline," conceded Carver. "They get the pork fat from the restaurants."

"No drokkin' kidding," said Esma.

The Judges were crouched in the middle of a large grey concrete parking lot painted with radiating yellow lines. It was situated outside the Sylvia Plath Shoplex and Fun Centre. There was normally space enough in the parking lot for six thousand vehicles, but tonight the concrete expanse was covered with crowds of rioting citizens. The rioters were typical Mega-City dwellers of all ages, from infants to senior citizens, and they formed a turbulent howling mass that swept back and forth in front of the shoplex, swarming over shopping trolleys, concrete planters full of shrubs, and any vehicles unlucky enough to still be parked in the lot.

The neon lights from the block made the eyes of the rioters glow, wide and ferocious, as the cits were swept up in the mob emotion of the moment. The flames of banned cigarette lighters gleamed as the rags of bottle bombs were ignited, and then the flaming missiles themselves rose up into the air.

The rioters had by now been contained into half of the parking lot and were gradually being forced into an even smaller area. The shoplex was an imposing pentagonal building that once had been used as government offices. Zandonella remembered vaguely that it had something to do with national security. Now it had been taken over and resanctified to the religion of shopping. Retail outlets sprouted on each of its long high walls and the pentagonal space at its centre had been turned into a giant illuminated fountain with a glowing hologram that blossomed at regular intervals to read, "Shop at Sylvia's – Formerly the Pentagon" in rotating letters of fire as high as a house.

The shops all around the perimeter, with one exception, had been locked up to prevent any of the rioters getting inside. However, this was a relatively futile measure since the one exception was the huge, lurid Wiggly Little Piggly's that was the cause of the trouble. The fast food outlet jutted from the wall facing Zandonella. Like other WLPs, its frontage consisted of a massive pink pig's ass with a neon curly tail. The riot had begun here and the restaurant remained the epicentre of the storm.

The crowd, despite its variety in terms of age, sex and physical types, did have certain unifying traits. Approximately half of the rioters were wearing pink T-shirts or pink baseball caps while the other half were wearing blue T-shirts or blue top hats. The pink and blue factions were savagely tearing into each other, with grim results. Bleeding and groaning casualties were lying all over the parking lot, those on the fringes of the violence being removed by Med-Judges to med-wagons, after being judged and sentenced for affray, disorderly conduct, creating a public disturbance, bleeding on civic property and littering. Many of those carried off didn't look like they'd live long enough to pay their debt to society. Other than the bottle bombs, the rioters weren't wielding any weapons more sophisticated than a lead pipe or the occasional knife. Most of them were using their bare hands, but that was quite enough.

"I don't understand what they're rioting about," said Zandonella.

"Do you ever?" said Esma. "I don't."

"I mean, they're ripping each other apart. They hate each other. But why? They basically agree. They're on the same side."

"The same side?" said Carver, still fumbling with the wrist strap on his riot shield.

"Yes. They all eat pork."

"But the ones in pink eat at Wiggly Little Piggly." There was a certain note of approval in Carver's voice, which turned into disdain as he added, "and the ones in blue eat at Pork Lane." Carver shook his head. "That's a big difference."

"A big enough difference to kill each other?"

"They're like mega-ball hooligans," offered Tykrist, raising her shield to fend off a flaming bottle bomb. "Or religious fanatics."

"I thought I told you to drive the rioters back towards the shoplex," grated a voice behind them. They turned to see Judge Dredd standing there with Judge Darrid at his side. Neither of the men carried riot shields. Instead, Dredd held what looked like a bazooka with glandular problems – evidently a missile launcher of some kind – and Darrid had a sophisticated-looking megaphone.

"I'm sorry, sir," said Zandonella. "But we can't move forward and engage the crowd until Carver has his riot shield fitted."

"So why isn't it fitted?" demanded Dredd.

"It's this damned wrist strap, sir," said Carver. "It won't stay on my wrist."

"Here. Give it here," said Dredd impatiently. He grabbed the shield and strapped it onto Carver. To Zandonella it seemed absurdly like a parent buttoning a child up in foul weather gear before sending him out into the rain. "Now get down to business."

"Yes, sir."

"Try to contain them in the area immediately in front of Wiggly Little Piggly's," said Dredd. "Darrid and I are going to get onto the roof of the restaurant and see if we can use sedative gas on them." Dredd held up the rocket launcher. "Have you all got your nose filters in?"

"Yes," chimed Zandonella and the others.

"Good. Just make sure you don't breathe through your mouths. Especially you, Carver." Zandonella saw his point. Carver was a natural mouth breather. Dredd turned to go, but Darrid insisted on staying a moment longer.

He lifted up his megaphone. "And if the gas doesn't work I'll use the public address system," he said happily.

"Come on, Darrid." Dredd dragged the smaller man away and they vanished into the night.

By the time the pair appeared on the roof of Wiggly Little Piggly's, Zandonella and the others had fought their way to within fifty metres of the fast food outlet. The crowd of rioters had been squeezed into a dense mass by the inexorable advance of the Judges on all sides, holding their shields high and wielding their clubs with enthusiasm.

Yet the rioters still seemed largely unaware of the presence of the Judges. They were obsessed instead with attacking each other, the Wiggly Little Piggly adherents trying to brutally murder the Pork Laners, and vice versa.

"Here we go," said Esma, pointing up at the sign over the Wiggly Little Piggly. There under the pink neon corkscrew of tail, Dredd and Darrid stood. Dredd took aim with his rocket launcher.

"Everyone got their nose plugs in?" said Zandonella. "Carver, close your mouth." She was glad that Dredd was in position. Her left arm was tired from holding the shield and her right one was tired from clubbing rioters into submission. Dredd fired; a pale lilac flame flared at the nozzle of the launcher and a gas projectile sailed out over the crowd, spraying gas in all directions in a glowing milky cloud. The sinister cloud settled rapidly towards the milling heads of the rioters below.

"This is more like it," said Esma. "In thirty seconds all we'll have to do is start stacking the sleeping beauties and shipping them off to cells."

"Make sure you stack them in the recovery position," said Zandonella.

"Why?" said Carver.

"Because if you don't they'll suffocate, you bozo," said Esma.

But at that moment, as though at the whim of a sardonic fate, the mild breeze strengthened into a brisk wind that danced around, shifting quarters and vigorously blowing the gas away to disperse harmlessly into the night.

"That's that," said Zandonella.

"Damn," said Esma regretfully. "It would have been an easy way of putting a stop to this rumble."

"Can't he just fire another one?" said Carver, looking up at Dredd standing tall under the neon pig's tail.

"What's the point?" said Zandonella. "The wind isn't dropping." Indeed, the wind seemed to be picking up strength and speed, blowing away with it all hope of deploying riot control gas.

"What are we going to do now?" moaned Carver.

"Just keep on swinging," said Esma jauntily, bringing her club down on the head of a portly and pugnacious Pork Lane supporter wearing nothing but a blue top hat and blue jock strap with the initials PL on it. There was the sizzle of electricity and the rioter fell to his knees, then toppled slowly forward, unconscious from the blow, his fat, hairy white buttocks jutting up in the air in obscene entreaty.

"Wait a minute," said Carver. "Judge Darrid's stepping forward. He's going to do something." Zandonella looked up to see that Darrid had moved into the position vacated a moment earlier by Dredd under the Wiggly Little Piggly sign. He was raising his omniphone to his lips.

"Switch on your noise-cancelling earphones," said Zandonella quickly. She reached up and made the adjustments on her own helmet. The dense, ghostly sizzle of white noise filled her ears. The headphones were designed to block out external sounds using active audio control by profiling the unwanted signal and echoing it out of phase so as to cancel it.

Even so, Zandonella could still hear a tinny insect echo of Darrid's voice as it boomed from the public address system on the roof above. Like the sleep gas, it was an approved means of crowd control. Zandonella could hear the faint echo of Darrid saying, in his most unctuous voice, "Citizens, there's no point in you fighting."

The crowd in front of the Wiggly Little Piggly paused for a moment in its battle and looked up at the tiny figure of Darrid standing underneath the neon corkscrew of the tail. Zandonella was startled that they had stopped fighting; all of them, at once.

"They've stopped fighting each other," said Carver.

Maybe Darrid was going to pull this one off after all.

"You're fighting tonight to show your love and support for your favourite fast food pork provider," continued Darrid, "but there's no point in that. Not anymore."

"Oh no," said Zandonella. "He isn't–"

"Isn't what?" said Carver.

"That's right. No point. Because both restaurant chains are being closed down," said Darrid brightly. The crowd below him had fallen dangerously silent and now it gave a collective gasp. "That's right," chirped Darrid, "in a few short hours pork in all its forms will be completely and utterly illegal."

Zandonella winced. The old fool knew nothing about crowd psychology. The collective gasp from the crowd was like the sighing of dying wind that signalled the onset of a tropical storm. A hurricane, in fact. There was an agonising moment as the message penetrated sluggishly into the collective mind of the rioters with its full implications, and then as comprehension dawned, a tumultuous roar of insane rage rose from the crowd. The two factions forgot all about combat with each other and instead turned as one to face the Judges, murder in their eyes.

Zandonella, Carver and the Karst sisters fell back as the bottle bombs and other missiles smashed against their shields, arriving a few seconds ahead of the howling mob itself, hurling itself forward in a bloodthirsty fury, adroitly united by Darrid's little speech.

Judge Carver sat in the canteen. There were tears in his eyes. Real tears. Sitting opposite him, Zandonella stared in disbelief. It was nearly midnight, but both of them were still in their riot gear which stank from the smoke of the riot at the Sylvia Plath Shoplex. The smell of burning pork fat was sunk deep in their uniforms. It had taken a further three hours to quell the crowd after Darrid's little speech had invigorated the mob and sent them on a unified rampage. Now both blue and pink clad partisans were all languishing in cells or in secure med-units, recovering from their wounds. The rest were in the morgue.

On the plate in front of Carver was a jumbo-sized Wiggly Little Piggly pink plastic bucket of spicy spare ribs. WLP didn't have an outlet inside Justice Central, but Carver had purchased a large selection of food from the outlet in the Plath Shoplex after the riot. The restaurant had remained open throughout the violence and had actually taken in a lot of business that night. Carver religiously brought in such takeaway meals from outside to eat in the canteen, but since the new Law had been announced, he knew his pork eating days were soon to end.

Carver was eating from the bucket with one hand, bright red grease on his face from the ribs, while looking at the wrist of his other hand on which was strapped a chunky chronometer. Carver was stuffing his face, keeping an eye on the time, and weeping. Big fat tears were oozing down his cheeks, cutting a path through the red grease.

"I can't believe it, Carver."

"I know, I know."

"You're crying. You're actually crying."

"I know."

"How childish can you get?"

Carver paused and wiped his mouth with the back of his hand, smearing the grease around but doing nothing to remove any of it. "I'm sorry."

"Don't apologise to me. Just stop it."

"It's just that I'll be so sorry to see all this go." He swept his greasy hand over the table to indicate the half-full bucket of ribs in front of him as well as the empty containers scattered nearby which had recently contained salami sandwiches, a bacon bun and sausages with chips. "I just love it so much," blubbered Carver.

"Pull yourself together. And stop using words like 'love' in connection with a junk food addiction."

"Don't call it junk food. Munce was junk food. This isn't junk. This is great. It's *pork*." Carver's voice was tremulous with emotion.

Zandonella sighed. "It used to be intelligent creatures, before they were butchered and cooked for you to eat."

"I know, I know," said Carver. "But they were so tasty. Why did they have to be so intelligent?"

"Learn to live with it," declared Zandonella with satisfaction. "At one minute after midnight the new Law comes into effect."

"Don't remind me."

"All this," Zandonella gestured at the junk food cartons, "becomes illegal."

"I know, I know."

"That's why we're here. That's why I came off leave early, yet again."

"I know."

"Because all hell is going to break loose in the Mega-City when pork addicts like you are forced to comply with the new legislation."

"I am not an addict!"

"No? You're weeping because you're being forced to give up your favourite snack."

"It's not a snack, it's the backbone of my diet."

"Speaking of backbones, do you know what they put into those sausages?"

"I don't care. They are so tasty. I mean they were."

"We're all pulling extra shifts on riot duty because people like you think this stuff is so damned tasty."

"Not people like me. I'm a Judge."

"Then act like one, instead of like a deranged fast food junkie."

Carver sighed a tearful, liquid sigh. "I'm going to miss it so much. All these wonderful forms of pork." He stuck his face into the pink plastic bucket full of ribs and his voice reverberated from within. "I can't believe I'll never taste it again."

"It's just as well." Zandonella pointed at his bulging waist-line, pushed tight against his Judge's belt. "You're getting as fat as a..."

She stopped herself just in time. Carver didn't notice. The alarm on his wrist went off at that moment. He stared at the chronometer in horror. "No. It can't be. You distracted me. It's–"

"Midnight plus one."

"But I haven't finished my ribs."

"Too bad. It's past the deadline. It's now a felony to touch anything in that bucket."

"It's not fair. You distracted me." Carver clutched the bucket to his chest protectively. Then he leaned forward and whispered to Zandonella. "You wouldn't tell on me, would you? I mean, it's only just past the deadline." His big schoolboy eyes glinted. "Just a teeny bit, a teeny weenie bit past. Don't tell anyone. No one need know. Just let me finish my ribs."

Before Zandonella could reply, a hand reached over Carver's shoulder and seized the bucket. Carver resisted for an instant before he looked up and saw that it was Judge Dredd. He immediately let go of the bucket.

Dredd looked down at the glistening red mess of ribs with distaste. "I'll take this down to the incinerator, Judge."

"Yes, sir," said Carver meekly.

"And if I find any more pork in this canteen it will be confiscated and logged as evidence of a crime, with full punishment for any Judges involved. Do I make myself clear?"

"Yes, sir. Absolutely clear, sir."

"Then get your riot shields and clubs. We're going out on patrol again now. The fun's really begun."

The fun referred to by Dredd was, of course, the rioting that erupted in the wake of the new legislation. The very moment that pork became illegal, the violence began.

"Is it another rumble between Wiggly Little Piggly fans and Pork Lane supporters?" asked Zandonella as they climbed into the rear of the FWP that would carry them back into the Mega-City night.

"Not any more," said Dredd. "But there's just as much mob violence. We're moving in and shutting down all the fast food outlets still selling pork."

"But they were supposed to close themselves down automatically at midnight plus one."

"Unfortunately, no one is complying with the new legislation."

"But it's the Law," said Carver.

"If everyone obeyed the Law, Judges would have an easy time of it," said Dredd. He moved through the passenger section of the FWP, stooping as he climbed into the cockpit.

"But it's not easy to obey the Law," said Carver. He turned to look at Zandonella, who was strapping herself in beside the Karst sisters. Darrid wasn't with them on this patrol. Evidently he was still in disgrace after his snafu with the omniphone. Dredd had probably demoted him to traffic control.

"Not easy?" said Dredd over the intercom in a menacing growl.

"They keep changing it, they keep changing the Law," said Carver, hastily justifying himself. "First pork was illegal, then it was legal, now it's illegal again."

"That's illegal two times out of three," said Zandonella. "I think the general thrust of the Law-making process is easy to discern."

The FWP undocked and they went flying out over the Mega-City, its dark streets dotted with the cheerful flames of burning fast food restaurants. On one rooftop there was the incongruous pale gleam of water. Zandonella looked down and recognised the Neverland Fun Fair that had been the scene of her first encounter and shoot-out with the Barkin brothers. Except it wasn't the Neverland Fun Fair any more. Construction work seemed to be nearing completion on a new consumer Mecca, something that announced itself on a brightly illuminated sign as the "Aquatomic Fun Pool and Fission Reactor Complex."

"They use waste heat from the atomic piles to warm the water in the lagoon pool," explained Esma, looking over Zandonella's shoulder. She stared wistfully down at the pool as it receded in the distance. "I'm looking forward to having a swim there, as soon as it opens. Having a swim and relaxing..." Her voice took on a nostalgic note. "When this is all over."

"Fasten your seatbelts," snarled Dredd over the intercom. "Anti-aircraft fire ahead." Bright spheres of blue flame blossomed in the night ahead of them, illuminating the glass and steel skyscrapers on either side of their craft, a glinting canyon receding into the distance.

"That anti-aircraft fire sure looks pretty, doesn't it?" declared Esma. The vehicle bucked with the turbulence of air displaced by the explosions.

Zandonella had a feeling it was going to be a long night, and she wasn't wrong.

It was six in the morning with red traces of dawn smearing the sky before she was able to stumble back to her con-apt. She unlocked the door, swiping her card key with trembling hands, and stepped over the threshold.

Porkditz came scampering in to greet her from the bedroom. He stood there staring at her with his happy gleaming eyes peering up and his little curly tail jauntily twitching.

"Don't look so cheerful," said Zandonella, bending down to pat the pig. "Next time I go out, you're going with me."

"Timber!" shouted Judge Darrid, trying to make himself heard over the banshee scream of the chainsaw that dominated the communication band in the Judges' helmets like jagged yowling static.

"What does that mean?" yelled Zandonella into her own helmet microphone. It was noon of the day after the first big pork riots and she was back on duty after a couple of hours in a sleep machine. She had never heard the word before. Timber?

"Watch out for the falling tree," said Darrid's voice as the chainsaw noise diminished. At that same moment a powerful hand grabbed Zandonella by the shoulder and dragged her back. Zandonella was a full-grown woman, but the hand moved her like a child being scooped up by an adult. The hand belonged to Judge Dredd. As he pulled her to safety, there was a scream of rending wood and a thin, dark shadow swept across Zandonella's face with stroboscopic speed. The tree came toppling towards her and crashed to the ground, shaking the entire rooftop. The topmost branches gently lapped at the toes of Zandonella's boots.

The tree had missed her by millimetres. Zandonella turned around to look at Dredd. He had pulled her out of danger at the last possible instant. "Thank you," she stammered.

"Be more careful in the future, Zandonella," was all Dredd said. He turned to Darrid. "And you. Watch how you handle that chainsaw."

Darrid shrugged apologetically as he set the saw aside. "All finished anyway," he declared. "We can go in now." He gestured at the space he'd cleared in the tight cluster of trees that filled the dome.

The dome was a transparent plastic bubble that occupied most of the huge expanse of the rooftop of Lobsong Rampa Villas Block, a skyscraper that stood overlooking one of the Mega-City's more elite districts. Dredd hadn't offered any explanation as to why they were here and Zandonella knew better than to ask him. Dredd might seem like some kind of unstoppable automaton, but in reality he was as human as any other Judge and the night of rioting had left him short-tempered and irritable. Zandonella had kept her mouth shut as they'd landed on the roof, opened the steel airlock door that sealed the dome from the city's polluted air, and gone in with guns and chainsaws.

The air in the dome was extraordinary. Zandonella had never experienced anything like it. It tasted clean and moist, and had a smell that reminded her of certain synthetic bath-room cleaners, although it was subtly different. She assumed the smell of the air must have something to do with the tall skinny trees covered with green needles that grew in the soil that had been dumped on the rooftop to form a floor a metre deep. The trees filled the dome, growing so closely together that almost as soon as they'd entered the airlock Darrid had been compelled to get busy with his chainsaw. Zandonella and Dredd had followed, with Carver bringing up the rear. He too was carrying a chainsaw, but unfortu-nately this piece of saw-toothed technology had malfunctioned. Zandonella wondered why Carver insisted on carrying the heavy saw when it was clearly useless, but she'd decided not to humiliate the young Judge by saying anything about it; he'd work it out soon enough.

"All right, we're going in," said Dredd. "Be careful and have your weapons ready."

The gap Darrid had created in the trees gave access to a circular clearing. Lush green grass, longer and shaggier than the synthetic turf Zandonella was accustomed to, covered the clearing. In the centre of the grass was a large tent made of white fabric drawn up in high, fanciful crescent shapes. Coloured lights glowed inside the tent and Zandonella thought she could hear the sound of a voice from within, raised in song.

"Leave your chainsaws here," said Dredd. "You too, Carver." He set off into the clearing and the others followed.

Their footsteps were silent as they crossed the grass towards the tent, although any attempt at stealth was pointless now, after the prolonged ear-splitting shriek of the chainsaw. Any perp who hadn't heard that must be so stone deaf that the explosion of a tactical nuke wouldn't tip him off. They neared the tent. There was an opening in its side, covered by a billowing sheet of opaque white fabric. It didn't appear to be secured in any way.

"I guess you don't need a lock on your door when you live in a dome," said Zandonella.

"Quiet," said Dredd. "I'm going in first. Cover my back." He stepped through the door of the tent, lifting the white fabric over his head and disappearing inside. The voice from within the tent continued in a monotonous tune. Zandonella, Darrid and Carver looked at each other for a moment before following Dredd.

Inside the tent there was a spicy perfumed smell coming from the coiling oily smoke of incense that burned in a large brass bowl studded with green gemstones. The brass bowl sat on a low gleaming circular table of dark polished wood that occupied the centre of the tent. Other than the table, the only piece of furniture visible was a large, state-of-the-art Tri-D screen that stood at the far end of the room. The floor of the tent was covered with rugs woven with strange geometric designs in black, red and white.

Sitting on a pile of brightly coloured cushions in front of the table was a thin man with a long, lustrous braid of dark hair that curled down his naked back like a black snake. The man's only garment was a baggy loincloth of red and black silk, which Zandonella thought looked like fancy diapers. The man's naked torso was skinny, but not starved, with smooth, lean muscles cladding his ribs. Carefully walking from behind him to his side, Zandonella could see that his eyes were shut as he sat on the cushions, chanting. Spherical coloured lights hung from the ceiling like illuminated balloons and their glow showed on the man's oiled skin.

The man's chants seemed to rise towards the ceiling of the tent along with the smoke of the incense. Dredd stood looking down at the man with an expression of patient disgust on his face. "Come on, Featherman," he said. "The show's over."

The small man stopped chanting, opened his eyes and looked at Dredd. His eyes were cool and blue and amused. "I hope you didn't chop down too many of my pine trees when you barged your way in here."

"We have a standing search warrant for these premises."

"For what crime, pray tell?" The man smiled politely.

"You know perfectly well what crime," grated Dredd. "Running a black market pork operation."

"Black market pork? There must be some kind of administrative error." He offered no resistance as Zandonella fixed pneumatic cuffs on him, adjusting them to fit snugly on his thin wrists with a sigh of compressed air. The small man looked her in the eye and winked. "Not an entirely unknown phenomenon at Justice Central, I might add."

"No error," grated Dredd. "Just a major crime. And you're going down for it."

"I know where the source of confusion might lie," said Featherman, studying the handcuffs. "I was indeed a licensed pork wholesaler, but only when it was legal. Only during that brief window of mercantile opportunity that was opened to us honest business folk before it was slammed shut by the Council of Five – in their infinite wisdom, of course." He smiled at Dredd. "Naturally, as soon as dealing in pork was made illegal, I divested myself of all business interests in that area. I sold my last shares shortly before midnight on the day preceding that fateful day, which I like to call P-Day, when the Law so precipitately changed."

"Sure, you sold *some* of your holdings," said Dredd.

"All of them," corrected Featherman patiently.

"You sold them to hollow corporate shells and fronts and holding companies, all of which can be traced back to you. It was a flimsy attempt at a paper trail that kept our fraud team busy for all of half an hour."

"Well, I hope they were entertained," said Featherman.

"They ran you through their computers and got the answer. You're still the owner of a vast illegal pork syndicate."

"Am I? Pork syndicate. Vast. Illegal. You know, I rather like the sound of that."

"And you're going to do time for it."

"That, I like the sound of rather less. But all this sounds very theoretical, you know. Where's your hard evidence?"

"You want hard evidence?" Dredd turned to Zandonella. "Go and get the special deputy."

Zandonella was back in less than two minutes, accompanied by the scampering Porkditz, who had been snoring contentedly on the rooftop in the shade of the FWP that had brought him here. She had the pig on a retractable plastic lead, more for his own safety than any other reason.

"Is that the special deputy?" said Featherman. "I must say I'm impressed. It seems that recruitment for the Judges has reached a new high standard."

"Keep making jokes, Featherman," said Dredd in a dangerously rumbling monotone. "Zandonella, see what he can do."

Zandonella took the lead off Porkditz. The pig shook himself happily then trotted out of the tent and back into the stand of pine trees. The Judges and the prisoner followed. They came to a clearing in the woods and Zandonella noticed that Featherman was no longer making any jokes. When Porkditz began to dig, his face went pale. Dredd turned to look at their prisoner.

"You see, our science department worked out that pigs have extremely sensitive noses; more sensitive than even our best equipment. And one of the things they're extremely good at detecting is other pigs." Dredd looked at the hole Porkditz was excavating in the thick, dark loam. "Or the remains of other pigs."

In the hole, amidst the dark, black earth and green shreds of pine needles, was the unmistakable red gleam of meat. Porkditz stood back from his work and looked happily at Zandonella.

"Looks like pork to me," said Darrid, twirling his moustache.

Featherman sighed and shrugged. "I don't suppose you'd believe me if I told you that's organic fertiliser," he said.

"It's organic fertiliser, all right," said Dredd. "It's also a ten-year sentence."

They led the handcuffed man back through the wreckage of his forest, out the airlock of his atmosphere dome and back onto the baking tarmac of the rooftop. The Karst sisters were waiting for them there and guarding the open airlock as Porkditz came trotting out ahead of the Judges.

"You got him," said Esma.

"Porkditz found the evidence," said Zandonella.

Dredd nodded. "He couldn't bring himself to destroy it. They never can."

"That's right," said Carver. "Dirty pork seller."

"You've certainly changed your tune," said Zandonella.

"When it was legal I liked eating it, but now that it's illegal I can see the error of my ways," said Carver. He sounded like he was reciting something that he had memorised slowly and painfully. Which was probably the only way Carver could memorise anything, reflected Zandonella.

"Oh," said Featherman. "Were you occasionally fond of a spot of tasty pork, Judge?"

"Occasionally?" said Esma. "He was forever stuffing his face with the vile stuff."

"It was vile stuff," said Carver dutifully. "I can see that now. I can see the error of my ways and–"

"What sort of pork, Judge?" asked Featherman. "Chops? Cutlets? Bacon and sausages? Ham? Ribs? Black pudding?"

"Unh," said Carver indistinctly. Zandonella suspected he was salivating so vociferously that he couldn't speak. She felt ashamed of letting Porkditz hear this kind of talk, although of course he couldn't understand any of it. Carver swallowed audibly then said, "Salami at first but then mostly ribs."

"Ah, ribs."

"And bacon sandwiches and sausages," said Carver, his voice beginning to garble again as he drooled uncontrollably.

"Carver, button it," said Dredd. "And you Featherman, shut up."

"Just trying to pass the day pleasantly," said their prisoner. Dredd grabbed him by the handcuffs and dragged him along so quickly that his feet could only touch the ground in a rapid skipping dance.

"Pleasant enough for you?" said Dredd.

Their FWP was waiting at the edge of the roof where they had landed, the sun gleaming on it. "Snazzy vehicle," said Featherman. "Is that what I'll be riding in as you take me to pay my debt to society?"

"Enjoy it while you can, creep," said Dredd. He was walking directly in front of Featherman and Zandonella was behind the prisoner as they escorted him towards their vehicle. The Karst sisters followed and Carver and Darrid were bringing up the rear. Dredd suddenly turned and looked at them.

"What are you doing?" he demanded.

Darrid twitched visibly. He was still understandably sensitive about the fiasco at Sylvia Plath Block. He shared a worried glance with Carver. "What do you mean?" he said. "We're following you, escorting the prisoner in. We're not doing anything."

"Exactly," said Dredd. "You're not doing anything. You're leaving the airlock open." They all turned back to look at the atmosphere dome with the green blur of pine trees inside it.

"Get back there and secure it. This is a crime scene. We don't want any of this creep's friends getting in and tampering with evidence."

"Yes," said Featherman. "Who knows what tantalising, damning and fiendishly incriminating items I might have left scattered around my modest domicile?"

"Shut it, creep," said Dredd. He turned to watch Carver and Darrid hurry back to the airlock and begin struggling with the cumbersome mechanism. Dredd watched them for a moment and then shook his head. "I'd better show them what to do. Zandonella, take the prisoner to the vehicle and put him in restraints."

"Aren't these restraints enough?" said Featherman, holding up his skinny wrists with the massive cuffs hanging from them. Dredd ignored him as he strode back to the dome's airlock.

"Come on, creep," said Zandonella, giving Featherman a nudge to get him moving again. As they started for the FWP, now only a few paces away, she stepped in front of the prisoner, leaving the Karst sisters to watch him from behind.

Looking back on it, Zandonella would realise that that was her big mistake.

No sooner was her back turned than she heard a rapid stutter of gunfire. She spun around to see that Featherman had broken away and was running for the edge of the roof. Both the Karst sisters had their Lawgivers drawn and were firing what sounded like non-lethal interception rounds at the fleeing fugitive.

"Hold your fire," shouted Zandonella, diving in pursuit. The rounds might be non-lethal but she had no desire to take one in her back. She ran after Featherman, who had darted to the left of the FWP and was running along the edge of the roof. Zandonella was gaining on him swiftly and she wasn't even trying very hard. After all, there was nowhere for the prisoner to go. The rooftop had a waist-high, black and yellow striped safety railing running along it. On the other side was a drop of approximately one kilometre, straight down. It was ludicrous that he'd even attempted to run.

"He's not going anywhere," shouted Zandonella as she closed in on him.

That was when Featherman stepped over the railing and jumped.

Zandonella flung herself onto the railing but it was too late. The Karst sisters joined her, followed by Dredd, Darrid and Carver soon after. Finally, Porkditz came and took a careful peek.

"Should we get in the FWP and follow?" said Darrid helpfully.

"Too late," said Dredd. "He's gone."

They watched the tiny black and red speck that was Featherman's parachute as he steered it like a hang-glider between blocks. He disappeared into a vast, shadowed canyon of steel and glass.

"Where did he have the parachute hidden?" said Esma.

Zandonella shrugged ruefully. "In his haute couture diapers."

TEN

Three weeks passed and Porkditz became quite adept at sniffing out caches of contraband meat and illegal pork dens. He began to enjoy going out on patrol with Zandonella and the other Judges. The discovery of the dismembered and cooked remains of his fellow pigs didn't seem to disturb the otherwise acutely sensitive creature. Indeed, Zandonella and Dredd had on several occasions been obliged to drag Porkditz off a pile of seized meat before he enthusiastically devoured the evidence.

"He isn't too choosy what he eats, is he?" observed Carver.

"Look who's talking," said Zandonella.

"At least I'm not a cannibal."

"You are if you adopt the assumption that all living creatures are one," said Tykrist.

"Not that *we* adopt that assumption," said her sister Esma hastily, holding up her metal hand with the middle finger jutting obscenely at Tykrist. "Sometimes you sound like one of those radical vegetarian nuts."

"Vegetables and nuts go together," said Tykrist, and both the sisters giggled.

"Quiet back there," said Dredd.

The five Judges were walking along the upper level of a two-story shoplex on Ben Franklin Skedway. It was a medium-sized shoplex with approximately seven hundred and fifty businesses in it. There was nothing distinctive about the place. It was merely the next one on their search pattern.

In front of the five Judges walked Porkditz.

The pig occasionally paused to sniff the air or the ground. But for the most part he maintained a brisk pace which the humans were hard pressed to keep up with. They passed the elaborate shop front of a Chinese restaurant. The name Fu Man Chew was emblazoned in gleaming red lacquer letters set over green, faux jade panels. Between the jade panels were glass doors. The doors opened and a little old Chinese lady in a red and black dress ran out to greet them. She held a white bowl with a blue dragon decoration around the rim.

Inside the bowl were milky green cubes which glistened like slime. "No pork here," said the old lady. "Just pure synthetics!" She produced a pair of chopsticks from a hidden pocket on her dress and delved into the bowl with them, deftly capturing one of the green cubes and holding it up. "You try?" The green cube dripped at the end of the chopsticks.

"No thanks," said Zandonella. Judge Dredd ignored the question and the Karst sisters quickly shook their heads. Even Carver declined.

"No pork here," repeated the old lady, shaking her little head. Porkditz sniffed at the hem of her robe and then turned away.

"Evidently you're telling the truth, ma'am," said Zandonella. Porkditz trotted away from restaurant towards the next unit in the shoplex and the Judges followed him.

The next unit was a MPEG52-DVD rental outlet that boasted "Ten acres of viewing pleasure!" Porkditz hesitated at the door before going in. Zandonella went after him. They made their way between the endless racks of video discs. There were action movies and sport and music promos but she soon began to get the impression that nine of those ten acres of the store were devoted to pornography.

At the back of the store was a counter with a cash register manned, if that was the word, by a teenage boy and girl. They were both wearing baggy white T-shirts with large black lettering on them. The boy's T-shirt read "Will work for bandwidth." The girl's read "Don't just stare – buy me a drink." The couple looked up apprehensively at the group of

Judges approaching them, their advance spearheaded by the merrily scampering pig.

Porkditz went straight past the counter, past a low table piled high with discount MPEG52-DVDs, including *My Big Fat Greek Orgy*, *Justice Academy 37: Juves on Patrol*, *From East Meg One with Love* and the complete films of Chuck Norris. There were two more tables of execrable DVDs and beyond them a large wire mesh rubbish receptacle. Here Porkditz paused, sniffing.

Zandonella approached, snapping on a pair of latex gloves. "What are you doing?" said the boy, who had hurried out from behind the counter.

"Don't want to contaminate the crime scene," said Zandonella breezily.

Porkditz had got his snout in the brimming trashcan and was now nosing through the pile of discarded fast food cartons and soft drink containers. He emerged from the pile with a pyramid-shaped tin clutched in his mouth. He dropped it with a clatter at Zandonella's feet. She turned to look at the boy. The girl had come out from behind the counter now to join him. She took his hand and stood behind him, sheltering there from Zandonella's sardonic gaze.

"What's that?" said the boy.

"We'll ask the questions," said Dredd. Carver and the Karst sisters followed him as he went behind the counter. While the Judges searched there, Porkditz returned to the waste bin and ferreted out another pyramid-shaped tin.

"Some kids put them in there," said the boy. "They were browsing in the store and eating something."

"It sure smelled bad," said the girl.

"It sure did," agreed the boy quickly. "They were eating from those tins and they just chucked them in the bin when they were finished. I've been meaning to take the garbage out."

"Do you know what these tins had in them?" said Zandonella.

"No," said the boy and girl, shaking their heads.

"They contained Sputam."

"Never heard of it," said the boy.

Zandonella smiled at him to let him know she didn't believe him for a moment. "Sputam is mutant ham. It consists of pork products heavily processed into a toxic pink sludge and then sold in these distinctive tins." She kicked the empty, pyramidal tins that Porkditz had piled at her feet.

"Well if we see those kids in here again we'll call you," said the boy.

Dredd stepped forward. "You know what they put into Sputam?" he snarled.

"No," said the boy in a small voice. The girl just shook her head.

Dredd proceeded to tell them, in great and grisly detail, and a moment later the boy and girl were white-faced and trembling, hands to mouths in an attempt not to vomit. The description was substantially accurate, Zandonella knew, but recent investigations had left her so inured to the horrors of the black market meat trade that her stomach barely heaved. They cautioned the kids, bagged the tins for evidence, then left the DVD store.

The next unit in the shoplex was a tattoo parlour called Lucky Jack's. Porkditz stood on the threshold, staring into the brightly lit shop. He turned and looked at Zandonella as she approached with the other Judges.

She could have sworn there was excitement in his little piggy eyes.

"We need to irradiate the Sputam," said Mac.

"What do you mean, irradiate it?" said Blue Belle.

"I mean blast it with radiation, zap it."

They were sitting in the control room of the factory farm. It was exactly the same control room and the same factory farm that the Judges had raided a few weeks earlier; the converted Russian space station that hung suspended by a balloon over the Trinny and Susannah Municipal Dump.

It wasn't hanging there now, but being back here freaked Blue Belle out a little nonetheless. After the raid, during the brief period of legitimacy for the pork business, Mac had bought the farm at a police auction at a competitive price. He had gone straight back into business, taking the precaution of concealing the farm in a new and secret location. This precaution paid off as soon as pork became illegal again. Belle had to concede that behind that cheerful, fat little face, there was a sharp brain. She was even beginning to like his fluffy white eyebrows.

"You want radioactive meat?" said Belle.

"Not radioactive, just germ free," said Mac.

"It's a wise precaution," said the robot sitting beside Leo Barkin at the control panels. "The whole slaughter process is one vast cloaca."

"What's that in plain English?" said Leo testily.

"What's with the attitude?" said Blue Belle. "I thought you and that robot loved each other."

"That's what Theo used to say," said Leo, his voice suddenly thick with emotion. "That's the joke he used to make when we were kidding around together."

"Kidding around? You were deadly serious. You guys hated each other," said Blue Belle.

"Appearances can be deceptive," said Mac the Meat Man gently. Blue Belle was astonished to see that there were tears in Leo's eyes. Or maybe not so astonished. Leo hadn't been the same since his brother had been shot by the Judges and put away in medical lock-up. The rumour on the street was that Theo's head wound had left him completely brain-dead. As far as Belle was concerned, that wouldn't be much different from before.

There was an uncomfortable silence in the narrow control room which was finally broken by the robot. "A cloaca is the lower part of the digestive system found in reptiles, amphibians, birds and some fish. I was trying to make an analogical point that our abattoir is a breeding ground for harmful bacteria."

"So what?" snarled Leo, wiping his face. "Since when are we concerned about food hygiene?"

"Since our customers started getting sick," said Mac.

"Since when did we care about *that*?" said Blue Belle.

"Killing our customer base is simply a bad idea. Trust me. That's why I'm using the nuclear plant at my Aquatomic Pool Complex to irradiate our Sputam and other pork products."

"I thought that was supposed to be a legit operation, the Aquatomic thing."

"It is indeed. The leisure pool complex and the nuclear power business are completely legitimate and above board. It's an ideal way for us to launder our black market pork profits. You should visit the place. Our customers come for a swim or buy our electric power off the grid. It's a truly wonderful operation. You really must come and see it. We heat the water with our nuclear reactor to create steam to turn the turbines that generate the electricity. Then we recycle the heat to warm our swimming pool to a pleasant tropical temperature that the kids love. And we use waste water from the pool to feed the power plant. It's a wonder. It's a miracle."

Belle smiled sardonically. "But you still can't resist smuggling a shitload of illegal pork in and out the back door?"

Mac the Meat Man shrugged. "It's a cost-effective solution." He stroked Belle's arm and purred like a big fat cat. "You must allow me to take you on a guided tour. You can go for a swim. Free of course. No charge." Belle thought about telling Mac to take his pudgy hand off her, but she didn't. She kind of liked it.

"Where's Blue Streak?" said Leo suddenly.

"He's gone over to Lucky Jack's to make arrangements for the next delivery of pork," said Belle.

Mac's fat white eyebrows wiggled in puzzlement. "He's gone there in person? He could have done that over the phone."

Belle sighed and rolled her eyes. "He's trying to score a free tattoo."

Lucky Jack had four small tattoos on his forehead: a four leaf clover, a swastika, a black cat and a small, stumpy white object which Jack had become so sick of explaining that he had tattooed the words "Rabbit's Foot" underneath it. He had done all this work in a mirror, wielding his tattoo needles while under a local anaesthetic from the eyes up. He had done a pretty good job as far as Streak was concerned.

Streak liked coming to visit Lucky Jack. There were usually some fascinating women hanging around the tattoo parlour and Jack was always a good sport about providing free tattoos for business partners. Now Streak was in the chair receiving the full benefit of this largesse. The needles were buzzing and Lucky Jack's sweaty, bald head was bent intently over Streak's chest.

Jack was a big man with a wrestler's build, a neatly trimmed black beard and a shaven head. He wore khaki trousers, sandals and a navy blue tank top which revealed the expertly executed tattoos that writhed over his powerful biceps. Those biceps jumped and shifted as Jack manipulated the needle, its insect song varying in pitch as he worked on Streak, turning away now and then to consult the photograph of Blue Belle's face which he had pinned up beside the closed-circuit Tri-D screen which offered him shifting views of the front of his shop.

Lucky Jack was in the process of transferring that photo with great fidelity to the area just below Streak's sternum, a blank spot Streak had been saving for something special. There was a mirror over the chair which allowed Streak to see what was happening, and it was clear that Jack was doing a magnificent job. The face he was tattooing on Streak's flesh was both beautiful and recognisably Belle's. Streak had every reason to be happy, but he wasn't.

"Pretty girl," said Lionel Featherman, examining the photograph.

"Don't touch it," said Streak. Featherman was the reason he wasn't happy. He hadn't expected to find a competitor here at Lucky Jack's, but the little man with his ridiculous long braid had been sitting comfortably sipping a cup of tea when Streak had arrived. Featherman was dressed in white robes that looked like some kind of judo outfit and seemed quite at home. How could Jack do it? How could he even be talking to a rival black market meat provider? And Featherman, the little creep, didn't even have any tattoos.

"Touchy," said Featherman, turning away from the photo. He loomed over Streak, who was reclining helplessly in a red leather chair which had once been used at a dentist's surgery, accommodating people receiving a different sort of voluntary torment. Featherman smiled at Streak. "He's doing a dandy job, isn't he?"

Streak turned away from Featherman's grinning face. He tried to catch Lucky Jack's eye. "What is this creep doing here, Jack? Letting people like this into your joint only lowers the tone of the place."

"That's not very nice, is it?" said Featherman, shaking his head mournfully. "I merely dropped by to discuss with Jack the possibility of adopting a new supplier who might be able to offer him improved service and a superior product at a lower price."

"Superior product," sputtered Streak. "Jack, this scumbag sells the skankiest, most diseased–"

"Diseased?" said Featherman. "Now that really is the tea pot calling the kettle black. From what I've heard, your canned pig products have to be zapped with so much radiation that you can eat them in the dark. Combination main course and table lamp. Just open the tin and cover your eyes."

"Guys," said Jack in his gentle lisping voice, "no arguing in the shop please. Arguments bring bad vibes and bad vibes make for bad tattoos." The way he said it, it sounded like "bad tattooth". Streak always found the contrast between Jack's rugged appearance and his soft lisp puzzling. But maybe there was no puzzle. The poor guy probably had to become a body builder and develop all those muscles to stop people bullying him over his absurd lisp.

"Of course, Jack," said Featherman silkily. "Sorry. I'd only like to note that the vibe was perfectly serviceable before our friend in the chair here arrived."

"Wait 'til I'm finished with Streak's picture of his lady here and then we can all have a cup of coffee and discuss business in a civilised fashion," said Jack.

"In my case, a cup of tea," said Featherman. "Perhaps that rather nice mint concoction you offered the last time we..."

As grateful as Streak was for the sudden silence, he wanted to know why Featherman had stopped talking. He looked over at the man. Featherman was staring at the closed circuit Tri-D screen. But only for a moment. Then he flashed a quick glance back at Jack and Streak before he turned with a sudden swirl of white judo robes, and was gone, fleeing out the back door without a word.

"What the sneck?" said Jack, looking up from the tattoo.

Streak was staring at the Tri-D screen and seeing what Featherman had seen. Judges. Judges pouring into the front of the store. Judges and a pig, scuttling in, sniffing. Leading the Judges right behind the pig was Dredd himself. Streak leapt up from the chair, painfully grazing himself on Jack's needle as he did so.

"Hey, Streak. Watch it," said Jack.

But Streak was already snatching up his shirt from the chair where it hung. He fled through the back door, clutching the shirt to his bleeding chest.

"I don't know anything about any illegal pork operation," said Lucky Jack. Zandonella felt sorry for the big tattooed man, standing there lisping his way through such obvious lies.

Judge Dredd shook his head ominously. "Our deputy here says different." Lucky Jack looked down at Porkditz who was sitting on the floor, peacefully curled up at Zandonella's feet.

"That's your deputy?" said Lucky Jack.

Zandonella frowned. "What of it?"

"Nothing, nothing," said Jack. "He's a very nice-looking pig. But I'm afraid I can't help you out with this black market pork thing. I don't sell any kind of food here. It's a tattoo parlour, for grud's sake." The way he said it, it sounded like "for grudth thake".

"What about downstairs?" demanded Dredd.

"Downstairs?" said Jack nervously.

"Your basement." Dredd crossed the room to a trapdoor in the middle of the bare wooden floor. "According to schematics on file at Justice Central, the basement area of your business is twice the size of the upstairs rooms."

"Ah, the basement," said Lucky Jack. "Actually, you see, that's nothing to do with me. I rent it out."

"Rent it out to who?"

"Some kind of religious group. They hold their meetings down there and..." Jack fell silent as Dredd reached down and tugged the trapdoor open. From the basement below came the clatter of cutlery, the cheerful babble of happy diners and the warm steamy smell of cooking pork.

Dredd turned to the other Judges. "Get ready for a mass arrest." He swung down into the opening in the floor. An instant later, the happy voices and tinkle of cutlery ceased, to be replaced by shrieks and screams as the perps tried to flee the scene.

Carver and the Karst sisters quickly followed Dredd into the hole. Zandonella stayed upstairs with Porkditz and their prisoner. Lucky Jack looked at her and said, "My grud. They're running some kind of restaurant down there. I had no idea."

"Save it," she said.

It took the rest of the afternoon to process the arrests of the fifty or so pork eaters who were caught red-handed in the basement of Lucky Jack's, plus of course the tattooed owner himself. By the time the processing was complete, Zandonella's shift was over and she took Porkditz home for a well-earned rest. But as soon as she stepped into her conapt, she knew something was wrong.

She could smell a tart, floral fragrance in the air: a trace of expensive perfume, an all too familiar perfume. Porkditz was sniffing too, trying to identify the odour with his ultra-sensitive nose. But Zandonella already knew where it was coming from. Or rather, *who* it was coming from.

Psi-Judge O'Mannion was sitting on the pale blue sofa in the middle of Zandonella's living room, looking perfectly comfortable and at home. She didn't even get up as

Zandonella and Porkditz came in. She smiled instead and said, "Hard day at the office?"

"Isn't this called breaking and entering?"

"Not when I use the copy of the domiciliary key card you're required to file at Justice Central." O'Mannion held up the card. "Hope you don't mind me making myself at home, but I got bored waiting outside."

Zandonella sighed and sank into an armchair piled with pale blue cushions beside the window. It was the second best seat in the room. O'Mannion was sitting in the best. Porkditz came and settled at Zandonella's feet. "What is it this time?" she said.

"You don't sound particularly enthusiastic."

"I'm not."

"Is that because you regard me as being invariably the harbinger of bad news?"

"Harbinger?" said Zandonella.

"Sort of a messenger."

"I got it."

"In any case, I wouldn't say it was bad news this time. In fact it could be very good news, both for you and the department."

"Really?" said Zandonella cautiously.

"Really. The Council of Five has devised a new strategy for the war against pork."

"The war against pork?"

"That's what they're calling it. Like the war against drugs."

"I got that, too. So how do I feature in this strategy?"

"Not as prominently as your roommate here." O'Mannion smiled at Porkditz. "You see, we've decided that Porkditz could use his nose to detect living pigs as easily as he does dead pork."

"I suppose that's true. So what?"

"So it would be a vastly more effective deployment of resources. Don't you see? Instead of busting all these little pork parlours one by one, like Lucky Jack's today, we can go to the source of supply and root out the problem once and for all."

"You want to go after the factory farms."

"That's right." O'Mannion rose from the sofa and came over to crouch beside Porkditz. She scratched him behind the ear and the pig grunted contentedly, accepting the attention. Zandonella felt an irrational flash of jealousy. O'Mannion looked up at her and smiled as if sensing this.

"He's going to sniff them out for us."

"I'm telling you, we've got to do something about that pig," said Blue Streak. His voice rang out loudly in the control room. Mac the Meat Man was busy scrutinising something on one of the screens and he didn't reply. Blue Belle glanced up at Streak but she didn't say anything either. She was still sulking. He scratched the bandage on his chest. Why was she giving him the silent treatment? He was the one who'd suffered. It wasn't his fault and the damned thing still itched like hell.

No one said anything for a long moment. There were just the three of them here at the factory farm today – along with tens of thousands of pigs, of course. Leo and his beloved robot were off on some mission. Streak cleared his throat, feeling uncomfortable in the silence.

Belle pulled on latex gloves then took a syringe and a sealed sterile bottle of antibiotics out of the medical supplies kit which lay open on one of the folding tables. Mac kept staring at the screens high on the wall above them. Most of the screens featured silent, monochrome images of pigs. Pigs waiting in masses in the waiting areas, breeding in the breeding rooms, and being killed in the killing chutes. But the particular screen Mac was watching showed a different image, a coloured map of the Mega-City. Mac zoomed in on a certain neighbourhood and studied it for a moment in frowning concentration, his furry white eyebrows pressing together like kissing caterpillars. He then turned to Streak and said politely, "Sorry?"

"We have to do something about that pig," repeated Streak.

"I'm doing something," said Belle impatiently. She finished filling the syringe, put the bottle back into the med-kit, and turned to the big slumbering shape that seemed to fill half the room. Lying there on the floor, snoring from time to time with a soft, almost human sound, was a full grown female pig with a brass ring in her nose and the words "Satan's Sow" tattooed on her back in large letters. Streak had done the tattooing to make her easier to identify. On the screens, all pigs tended to look the same, and they didn't want this one going down the killing chutes by accident. Giving her the markings made her distinctive. Streak had borrowed Lucky Jack's tattooing needles for the job. Now he felt a hot flush of shame thinking about Jack and remembering how he had abandoned him that day, leaving him to face the Judges. He forced the memory from his mind.

"Not *that* pig," he said. "The one the Judges are using to sniff out illegal pork rings."

"Mmm, pork rings," said Mac jovially. "Sounds like a delicious new snack." He turned away from the screens and smiled at Streak and Belle. If he keeps smiling at her like that, thought Streak, I'm going to kill him.

"Who cares if the Judges are using this pig?" said Belle. She went to the sleeping pig and stuck the syringe into its back, pushing the plunger down to send the antibiotics racing into the animal's bloodstream. The sow snorted in her anaesthetised slumber. "There, as good as new." Belle threw the disposable syringe into a bin and snapped off her latex gloves. "What does it matter if a few crappy little pork joints get busted?"

Mac shook his head. "As it happens, my dear, Streak is correct. We should be concerned about this pig the Judges are using."

"Why?"

"Because it's no longer just a 'few crappy little pork joints,' as you put it, which he is sniffing out. In the week since Lucky Jack was arrested, the Judges have changed their tactics. They've been using the pig to detect larger operations. Supply operations. In a word, pork farms."

"Like us?" said Belle.

"Precisely like us."

"That's what I've been saying," said Streak. "We should do something about that pig. I've been saying so ever since they took down poor Jack."

"Poor Jack?" said Belle, a rising note of fury in her voice. She strode over to Streak and, before he could do anything to stop her, she tore the bandage off his chest. Streak started to cover it with his hands, but what was the point? He let his hands drop to his sides and let them both stare at the tattoo.

After a moment Mac said, "Uh, it's a very... a very fine likeness. Jack did a fine job." Belle said nothing.

Streak stared down at the tattoo. It was indeed a very fine likeness of Belle's face, exactly as Lucky Jack had done it just before the Judges busted in.

"Except for the, uh..."

"Except for the moustache," snapped Belle.

Streak felt himself redden with shame. There was indeed what *looked* like a moustache, a bold curving blue line, across the upper lip of Belle's tattooed face. It was the mark made by Lucky Jack's needle when Streak had jumped from the chair and fled. He put the bandage back on his chest, covering this permanent memento of his cowardice. It was like a moustache on the Mona Lisa. Belle hated it.

Mac broke the awkward silence. "You're quite right, Streak. You have been saying we should do something about the Judges' pig. But we don't want to act too soon."

"Why not?" asked Streak. His face was still burning with embarrassment.

"Because all the factory farms they've detected so far have been run by our rivals. Mostly by Featherman."

"That bastard," said Streak.

"Right, my boy. So you see, it's been good business practise to let the Judges close them down. Allows us a bigger share of the market. But now..." Mac turned back to the screen with the map glowing on it. Streak saw that it was a street map of the municipal swamp area. "Now they're getting too close for comfort."

"Then why don't we do something about it?" demanded Streak. There was a sudden buzzing noise and a series of red lights flashed on the control panel. It was the sound of the airlock being activated.

Mac turned and smiled at Streak. "We are, son, we are. That's exactly what Leo and his metallic friend have been doing. And now they're back." He turned to Belle. "Is she ready, our prize sow?"

Belle smacked the pig on its rump. The pig trembled and opened its eyes, groggily coming out of its anaesthetic daze. "She's fine," said Belle. "She's got enough antibiotics in her to keep her going another month or two."

"That's just grand," said Mac. "We wouldn't want her picking up an infection. She's our number one Judas pig. Take her back to the holding sheds, would you, my dear?"

"Come on, fatty," said Belle, tying a length of cord to the pig's nose ring and pulling on it. The pig tottered to her feet and followed Belle towards the door, still moving a little unsteadily from the after effects of the dope. But before Belle could push the door control, someone opened it from the other side.

Standing in the doorway were Leo and his robot. At their feet was a little pink pig who wore a miniature replica of a Judge's badge on a ribbon around his neck. The badge read "Porkditz". The little pig and the big sow stared at each other.

Leo grinned and said, "Porkditz, meet Satan's Sow."

The little pig lowered his head and squealed forlornly.

"What?" said Zandonella.

"Look, just calm down," said O'Mannion.

"He's been *kidnapped*?"

"No, of course he hasn't been kidnapped. Only human beings can be kidnapped. He's been stolen, technically speaking."

"He is an intelligent creature. He has been kidnapped."

"All right, all right. Just calm down." O'Mannion paused to look at Zandonella. Both Judges were standing in the corridor outside the briefing room in Justice Central. There was no one else in sight. For a moment it seemed as if O'Mannion might drop her sardonic façade and offer some sympathy. But the moment passed.

"What's happening to him now?" Zandonella tried to control her trembling voice.

"We can't know and there's no point in trying to guess. But they didn't kill him outright. They took him alive. There's hope in that."

"He looked so cute, with his little badge..."

"Pull yourself together, Judge," said O'Mannion in a cold, cutting voice.

Zandonella looked at her, blinking away tears. "I should have never agreed to him going out on patrol without me."

"Don't be ridiculous. You had other duties to attend to. Porkditz was a valuable resource who had to be shared throughout the department."

"I should never have let him go out with those idiots Carver and Darrid."

"There you may have a point," said O'Mannion. "But don't say anything when we go inside. It's unprofessional for one Judge to publicly criticise other Judges." There was a glint of humour in her foxy eyes. "Or physically attack them."

They stepped into the briefing room. Carver and Darrid were sitting waiting for them at the table; a cylindrical ebony slab made of shining black wood. They shot Zandonella identical guilty glances. At least Carver had the good grace to try and stammer out an apology. "We're sorry about what happ–"

"Exactly what did happen?" Zandonella interrupted.

"There was nothing we could have done," blustered Darrid. "There was nothing anybody could have done."

"I doubt that," said O'Mannion. "Where was Judge Dredd?"

"We'd just supervised a big bust at one of Featherman's factory farms in Baden Powell Park. It was a combined operation: farm, farm shop and restaurant."

"Farm shop?"

"They were selling salamis," said Carver. His voice had a certain nostalgic tremor, but when he saw the way Zandonella was looking at him, he quickly added, "It was disgusting."

"The point is," said Darrid, "we had numerous perps to process; several hundred in fact. So Judge Dredd was busy supervising that. But we didn't have anything else to do and we..."

"Decided to act on your own initiative," said O'Mannion acidly.

"Yes. That's right. We took Porkditz out to see if he could sniff out any further black market meat operations in the area. He seemed to pick up a trail right away. In fact, he took off so quickly that we had trouble keeping up with him."

"He ran away from you," said Zandonella bluntly.

Darrid frowned at her. "You should have trained that pig better. It's your own damned fault."

"Judge Darrid," said Dredd in a dangerous voice. Zandonella looked up with a start. She hadn't seen him enter the room.

"We were hurrying after him," said Carver. "And we were about to catch up with him."

"But then there was this explosion," said Darrid. "The gruddamned Peace Pagoda in the middle of the park was blown to pieces."

"A diversionary explosion," said Dredd. "Exactly the same ploy they used when they kidnapped the Cetacean Ambassador." He didn't bother to disguise the contempt in his voice.

"When we got back from investigating the explosion Porkditz had disappeared," said Darrid, refusing to look anyone in the eye.

"We found out how they lured him away," said Dredd. He held up a small bottle in a plastic evidence bag.

"What's that?"

"Truffle oil."

O'Mannion shot Zandonella a puzzled look. "Pigs can't resist truffles," explained Zandonella.

Dredd slapped something down on the table. It was a sealed package; a squat cylinder wrapped in the characteristic blue plastic of the Justice Central evidence lock-up.

"Dredd," said Darrid. "There was no way we could have prevent–"

"Button it, Darrid," said Dredd. He began to unwrap the package. "The Council of Five is extremely unhappy at losing Special Deputy Porkditz. We've been deprived of our best means of finding the illegal pork farms at a time when we're under increasing political pressure to settle this situation once and for all."

"It's the Cetacean Ambassador, isn't it?" said Darrid. "Those damned dolph–"

"Darrid, shut your trap," said Dredd. "The Council is determined to go on bringing down those farms. We mustn't slow down our arrest campaign. Immediate results are required." He pulled the last of the blue wrapping off the cylindrical package to reveal a Wiggly Little Piggly bargain bucket.

Everyone at the table stared at it. From the carton came the greasy aroma of cooked pork.

"What's that doing here?" said Zandonella. She felt a queasy squirming in her stomach.

"We've lost your friend, the pig," said Dredd. "But we still have to track down the factory farms."

"Yes, I got that. But–"

"So we've decided to use your special ability, Psi-Judge Zandonella."

"My ability?" said Zandonella. "But I'm a PNE. I jump into the body of someone who was nearby at the time of a killing."

Dredd watched her, grim and unmoved. "I know that, Judge."

"I deal with murder victims," said Zandonella.

Dredd tipped the bucket over and Piggly Little Wiggly barbecue ribs spilled out on the table, bright red and glistening.

"Here's your murder victim," said Dredd.

ELEVEN

Zandonella focused on her subject, the greasy bucket of Wiggly Little Piggly spicy ribs. Her PNE powers had never failed her before, but for a moment it seemed like nothing was going to happen.

There was no sound in the briefing room except the distant background hum of the air conditioning. The five Judges sat around the circular black table. Its surface was as shiny and smooth as the lid of a grand piano. Zandonella stared into the gleaming ebony depths, trying not to look directly at the grisly bucket of junk food in front of her. She didn't need to *look* at it. The stink of it slithered into her nose, an oily slaughterhouse fetor.

Judge Dredd was sitting to her right. Next to him sat Psi-Judge O'Mannion. On the other side of the table were Carver and Darrid, who were watching her with twin stares of bafflement. Zandonella looked into the bucket of ribs. The bright red mess had once been a living creature. She felt her stomach heave briefly. She looked up at O'Mannion.

"Well?" said Dredd.

"Nothing," said Zandonella.

"Nothing?" echoed O'Mannion. Zandonella shook her head. She looked down at the bucket again. It was a vile shade of green with the violently pink Wiggly Little Piggly logo embossed on it. She peered over its rim into the pile of ribs. Dredd had poured them on the table but she'd scooped the remains, as she thought of them, back into the bucket. Zandonella regarded it as a kind of fast food funeral urn. The cremated remains of the dear deceased. She could feel the grease from the ribs still sticky on her fingers.

"Keep trying," said Dredd.

Zandonella nodded. She could feel the sticky grease on her fingers...

There was a sensation of falling.

Like walking down a staircase and putting out your foot for the bottom step, but the bottom step isn't there...

Zandonella's eyes closed and her head lolled forward towards the table, falling asleep in slow motion. O'Mannion moved forward quickly, dodging around Dredd as she moved to Zandonella's side. She caught Zandonella's head and cradled it so it settled gently onto the table.

Carver and Darrid jumped to their feet in surprise. Dredd remained seated, calm and implacable.

"What the hell did she do?" said Darrid.

"She's some kind of necro-something," said Carver.

"A possessive necro-empath," said O'Mannion, brushing Zandonella's long black hair back so it revealed her oddly peaceful sleeping face. "Like Zandonella said, she has the power to hop into the body of the person who was closest to the deceased at the time of death."

"That's one spooky, sick trick," said Darrid. O'Mannion stared at him with level contempt then looked away, shaking her head.

"Our aim," said Dredd, "is for her to land in the body of the slaughterhouse foreman or someone else in a senior position at the factory farm."

"I see," said Darrid. "Then she just calls us with her location and we go and get her, and shut down the factory farm and arrest all the perps."

"Something like that," said Dredd.

Darrid chuckled and whistled. "Neat." He began stroking his long grey moustache with excitement.

"Will she be all right?" asked Carver.

O'Mannion shrugged. "We have no idea." She looked at the bucket of ribs on the table. "All the victims we've tried it on previously have been human." She shot a bitter glance at Dredd. "We've never tried this trick across the species barrier before."

• • •

The lights were red – a sweltering, uniform, ruby glare. That was the first thing Zandonella noticed. Then the red light hurt her eyes, so she closed them. And that was when she sensed the heat. Heat and steam and the smell of swill. Swill? How did she even know what the stuff was? It was an unfamiliar, disgusting odour. Zandonella had never smelled it before. Or had she? There was something terribly, eerily familiar about it, like an impression experienced as déjà vu.

Of course. She had never smelled swill before in her own body. But she wasn't in her own body. She was now in one of the personnel at the factory farm. Whatever human being had been nearest to the victim at the time of death. The victim being the poor pig who had ended up in that bucket of barbecued ribs.

Her mind was beginning to catch up with her new situation, finding itself in a new body like a bird that had knocked another bird off its perch. Her awareness gradually settled into its new surroundings. She was beginning to make sense of the situation. It was always like this after a jump. As the disorientation faded, Zandonella finally noticed another odour, stronger and more pervasive than the swill. It was also a more familiar odour, so familiar that she had ceased to register it a lifetime ago.

Pig stomm. Everywhere, all around her, filling her nostrils, the all-pervading stink of pig excrement. Now that she concentrated on it, it filled her sensitive nose, causing it to twitch with disgust as she detected every nuance of the bacteria-laden filth, the tang of residual stomach acid, the smell of cells sloughed off the gut lining of the pigs who had left the droppings. The stink of the swine excrement was the stink of information. An over-ripe, rotting stench of overwhelming detail which she sifted and analysed with her immensely sensitive nose.

There was a renewed waft of stench as a fresh pile of excrement spattered to the floor. Zandonella could distinctly hear it land, soft and moist on the unyielding metal bars. Her sensitive ears detected and analysed the sound. And her stomach rumbled with satisfaction as the flow of waste spilled out of her, dropping from her hindquarters, just beneath her curly tail, to land with a final splash on the metal bars of the floor beneath her trotters.

Her trotters...

Trotters. Curly tail. Large, pointed, hypersensitive ears. Refusing to believe what her mind was telling her, Zandonella stepped daintily away from the pile of excrement, giving it a final sniff with her long, sensitive, flexible snout.

Zandonella opened her eyes again and looked around at the big room full of red light. She was seeing the room from about a metre above floor level. That was the height of her head, as she stood here on her four trotters, her little tail testing the air behind her.

Gradually, like sipping a viciously bitter medicine, Zandonella let the truth trickle into her mind: the appalling, unavoidable, awful truth.

She had jumped into a new body all right. A body that should by now have been covered in the oily sweat of fear.

But pigs don't sweat.

Five hours had elapsed since Zandonella had gone into her PNE trance. After the first hour, O'Mannion had arranged for her sleeping body to be transferred to the med-unit in Justice Central.

The med-unit was a large white room with a domed ceiling illuminated by floating mobile spheres of brilliant white or intense glowing purple that hung in the air or moved freely around to those areas that were in need of increased light. The purple spheres were designed to kill insects and bacteria with their intense ultraviolet glow. The white ones were for providing illumination. They would swarm in close whenever a medical procedure required it, crowding together like a school of airborne jellyfish, hanging over the doctors and their patients, providing a steady, pure white light. The spheres were dimmed at night so the patients could sleep undisturbed, but only on the Judges' level.

This circular gallery where the Judges were treated over-looked another level below – a secondary hospital facility complete with a large number of holding posts – where violent criminals, who had been injured or wounded during arrest and were awaiting recovery, could undergo the full rigours of their sentences. From the circular balcony above, these miserable, condemned malefactors strapped to their holding posts could be looked down upon with satisfaction by convalescing Judges in the perpetual twenty-four hour light of the spheres.

But Zandonella wasn't convalescing. She wasn't even conscious. O'Mannion turned away from the balcony railing to look at Belinda Zandonella lying motionless in her spotless, white med-bed. She moved forward to check the computer readout on Zandonella's vital signs. Nothing had changed, of course.

"She's been out for five hours."

O'Mannion turned to see Judge Dredd standing there. "I know," she said.

"Zandonella's a resourceful officer. She should have found a way of communicating with us by now."

O'Mannion nodded. It was a bitter conclusion, but it was the truth. "Unless..."

"Unless she's in some kind of trouble."

"I agree." O'Mannion nodded. She turned to look at Zandonella lying in the med-bed. "Her trance is unnaturally deep and prolonged." O'Mannion looked at Dredd. His face betrayed no emotion. "There's no telling what happened to her."

Dredd watched her steadily with his cold gaze. "No telling what happened? I disagree. It's obvious what happened."

"Really? Enlighten me."

"Zandonella is trapped in the body of a pig. One of the pigs in the factory farm."

"Oh come on, Dredd. A PNE is presented with a corpse and jumps into the body of the person nearest at the time of death. The *person*. No one has ever jumped into the body of an animal."

"But no one has ever used the corpse of an animal as a subject before, have they?"

O'Mannion thought about the brightly coloured bucket of barbecue ribs and repressed a shudder. "No," she said. "And whose fault is that?"

Dredd stared at her. "We're going to find Zandonella. Whatever trouble she may be in, we're going to find her."

"I hope so," said O'Mannion. "Because if she is in the body of a pig, then that pig is in a factory farm waiting to be slaughtered."

Dredd looked away from her and said nothing. He moved away from Zandonella's bed, crossing to the rail of the circular balcony. O'Mannion moved to join him. He said nothing, staring down at the perps tied to the holding posts. She searched his face in vain for some telltale trace of emotion.

Far from looking upset, he was as cold and unmoved as ever. But there was something else. He was staring down at the perpsi with great concentration, as if he was looking for something in particular.

Something, or someone.

Dredd turned and looked at her. His face showed a brief ghost of a twitch that might have hinted at a smile of satisfaction had it been on the face of another man. "That was a Wiggly Little Piggly bucket of bootleg ribs, correct?"

"Correct," said O'Mannion, trying to work out where this might be going.

"And the main black market supplier for Wiggly Little Piggly is...?"

"Mac the Meat Man and the Barkin brothers," O'Mannion said automatically. "What's that got to do with...?" She fell silent, following Dredd's gaze down to the holding posts below. Dredd was looking with particular interest to the unmoving body of Theo Barkin.

O'Mannion turned to Dredd and smiled.

"Now, that *is* a good idea," she said.

Dredd nodded, his face expressionless. "I'll give orders for the news to be passed to our criminal informants," he said. "We'll get them spreading the word on the street right away."

· · ·

Mac the Meat Man shot a nervous glance at Blue Belle. "But our friend here can't just drop everything, can he?"

Blue Belle shrugged. "A man's got to do what a man's got to do," Belle said in what she intended to be a sardonic drawl.

Mac turned to Blue Streak. "But he has responsibilities to us. To his business partners."

Blue Streak shrugged. "I don't care what he does."

Mac turned away from the couple to look at Leo Barkin. The four of them were standing in the control room, with Leo's spindly robot standing by the door, like a parked appliance. Leo himself was busy in the weapons locker.

Rifling through the weapons locker, thought Streak, pleased with the pun. "But you have duties here at the farm," Mac was saying to Leo's back as he pulled guns and ammunition out of the locker and piled them on the floor.

"I'm not going to be gone long," Leo declared portentously, strapping a cartridge belt around his waist. "I'll look after my duties when I get back."

"Not gone long?" said Streak. "You're going to bust into Justice Central and try to kidnap your brain-dead brother while taking on every Judge in the Mega-City. You might find that will take a little while."

"I agree," said Mac urgently. "Think about this before you do anything rash, son."

"I have thought about it." Leo began to attach hand grenades on his ammo belt, arranging them carefully, as though he was adorning a Christmas tree with decorations. When he was finished, he looked at Streak, his eyes hot and moist and angry. He held up a finger. "Number one," he said, "I am not going to bust into Justice Central and take on every Judge. If you'd been listening you would have heard me say that Theo..." His voice trembled at the mere mention of his brother's name. "Theo is being transferred to a new secure facility by hover bus. I won't even have to set foot in Justice Central. We'll hijack the bus as it leaves the building." He glanced over at Boyard-27 standing by the door and then looked at Streak again. He held up two fingers. "Number two.

I am not kidnapping my brother. Kidnapping is what those bastard Judges did to him. I'll be setting him free. I'll be springing him. I'll be *liberating* him."

Saliva sprayed copiously from Leo's mouth. His voice was shaking with emotion. Streak wiped the moisture from his face as Leo held up three fingers. "And, finally, number three. My brother is not brain-dead!" His voice rose to a raw scream that silenced everyone in the room for a long moment.

When eventually someone dared speak again, it was Blue Belle, in a mild voice. "All we're saying is that you ought to be careful. I mean, you only just got this information about your brother being transferred."

"That's another thing," quavered Mac. "How do you know this information is accurate?"

"I just know it," said Leo. He struck himself on the chest, where there were now a number of ammo pouches bulging with refill magazines for his Rasterblaster RB-32. The mags clanged musically in their pouches. "I feel it in my heart," said Leo with a note of finality. The discussion was obviously over. He turned and marched to the door of the control room, heading for the launch chamber and the shuttlecraft. "Take those," he said, nodding towards the pile of weapons he'd left on the floor.

The robot obediently scooped up the guns and, clutching them to his metal breast, clanked out after Leo, the door automatically whispering shut behind them.

"Oh great," said Belle as soon as they were gone. "Now we have to look after the farm without him."

"Don't worry," said Mac. "He'll be back soon."

"Will he?" said Streak bleakly.

Mac cleared his throat, obviously uncomfortable with the subject of mortality. "I suggest we all get back to work," he said in a brisk business-like voice. "We have a farm to run."

"Without the Barkin brothers, it looks like," said Streak.

Mac either didn't hear him, or pretended not to. He slapped his hands together in a down-to-business gesture and said brightly, "Well, we'd better get cracking. Or should

I say, get crackling?" He chuckled for a moment or two into the uncomprehending gazes of Blue Belle and Blue Streak before falling silent and saying apologetically, "Just a little bit of pork dealer humour."

"Someone is going to have to take the latest shipment of tins of Sputam to Aquatomic for irradiation," said Streak. "I guess that will have to be me."

"Would you, son?" said Mac with fulsome gratitude. "That would be really fine. One other thing, could you take a couple of cases of gin along with you? For the boys at the irradiation plant?"

"I guess so."

"That would be just great. Those boys sure do enjoy a tipple. And it's a lot cheaper than paying them a bonus." He slapped Streak on the back as he walked towards the exit. When he was gone, Mac looked shyly at Belle. "Oh, and there's also something wrong with the Judas pig in chute S."

"The one I vaccinated?"

"That's right, Satan's Sow."

"What do you mean, something wrong?"

"She just isn't luring the livestock to slaughter like she should. Instead they have to be flushed out of the holding sheds with electric shocks run along the floors. And do you know how expensive that is? Not to mention putting voltage spikes on the grid which the Judges might be able to detect and identify as illegal pork production. No, no, much better to have another animal lead them unsuspecting into the killing chutes. Which is exactly what Satan's Sow used to do. In fact, she used to be our number one Judas pig. Something must have happened to her."

"All right. I'll check it out," said Belle wearily. She headed for the door.

"If she's sick or injured or anything," said Mac, "just replace her with another one from the population." He gave Belle a breezy smile. "And process Satan's Sow for table meat."

· · ·

Zandonella stared at her reflection in the metal wall in front of her. The red light distorted things, but not to any significant degree. She could see well enough to grasp the essentials. She was a pig all right – a big, bristling pink sow. Her mind had refused to accept the concept at first. But gradually acceptance had begun to seep in. It probably helped that she was thinking with a pig's brain.

There was something tattooed on her side. Alphabetic letters that formed words. Zandonella could see that they were letters. She knew that they formed words. But it took her pig brain a long time to connect up the letters and make meaningful phrases out of the words. This sort of abstract thought was alien to the pig's natural mental processes, but in the end Zandonella's persistent human mind forced the new patterns into action and the thoughts began to flow. She looked at the reflection and worked it out. The words read "Satan's Sow".

That wasn't very nice. Zandonella would have laughed if her new body had allowed her to laugh. Perhaps it was just as well that it didn't. If she had started to laugh, she would probably never stop.

She was trapped in the body of a pig. It was as simple as that. There was no denying it. And with the acceptance, shock set in. Her heart thudded and surged in her thick, solid chest. A low, bellowing squeal of terror rose from deep within her throat. Her guts gurgled and writhed with fear and her curly tail twitched as her bowels became fluid with panic.

Zandonella commanded herself to be calm. She was trapped in the body of a pig. So be it. She was a Judge. There would be a way out of this dilemma. And she would find it. She must find it. Judge Dredd and the others would be looking for her. She had to survive until they could find her and rescue her.

Zandonella forced herself to think rationally, to take stock of her surroundings. The room she was in was eerily familiar. She was standing in front of a raised metal platform fronted with a curving wall. She had been studying her

reflection in the polished surface of that wall. Above her, at
what seemed like a vast height but was actually less than
three metres, there was a railing and beyond that, out of
sight, the airlock that would allow her to escape this room –
if only she could get to it.

There were no steps leading up to the platform. It sat atop
the smooth, curved featureless wall. A wall she could not
possibly climb. When she had been a Judge, in a human
body, she could simply have jumped up to reach the railing
from the floor below. Now, as a pig, there was no way she
could make the corresponding jump. The smooth wall of
metal would have barely been chin-high to her human form.
But now it represented an insurmountable barrier.

Zandonella turned away from the platform. The room
stretched out behind her under the bloody red glare of the
lights. It was a vast shed with a floor of closely spaced metal
bars. Above her was the curved ceiling adorned with a giant
pink plastic pig with lettering on its side. She was able to
read the words more quickly this time, the patterns falling
into place in her mind. They said "Shop at Mac the Meat
Man's!" She remembered Dredd climbing up to this ludicrous thing to defuse the bomb that had been left there.

There was a sound behind her, the metallic clunk of a lock
releasing and the moist sucking of a rubber seal letting go of
metal, followed by a swift whisper of escaping air. Zandonella whirled around and stared up at the platform. She
couldn't see it, but she knew the airlock door was opening.
Zandonella scuttled forward and pressed herself against the
curved metal of the wall. With luck she would be out of sight
of whoever stepped through that door onto the platform
above. Zandonella had no wish to meet any of the humans
who ran this state-of-the-art slaughterhouse.

The sound of someone moving up above her on the platform could be heard. Zandonella held her breath. There was
silence for a moment and then came a deeply familiar noise,
a soft interrogative squeal that caused her heart to melt.
Porkditz! There was no mistaking it. Her roommate. Her kidnapped companion. Zandonella began breathing again and

instantly her keenly attuned snout identified the welcome odour of her little friend drifting to her from above.

Not so little now. In relative terms, he was almost the same size as her. Porkditz peered down over the rim of the platform, looking at her with his bright eyes and cheerful, almost-smiling face. "Out of the way. I'm going to jump and I don't want to land on you."

Zandonella moved obediently back from the platform as Porkditz grunted, then leapt down, landing heavily on the floor, his breath bursting from him in an explosive grunt.

"Are you all right?" said Zandonella, rushing to his side. Then she stopped dead. She had said something to Porkditz. And he had said something to her. They were talking.

Or, rather, they weren't talking. They were communicating by a strange blend of behavioural cues – body language, odour, the squeals they made – and something else. A strange extra element of intuitive communion, a bond between them that made them understand each other in a profound fashion that went beyond language. The whole blend of sensations added up to a kind of telepathy and, as a Psi-Judge, Zandonella didn't have any problem accepting telepathy, even in pigs.

Porkditz looked at her with amusement. "Don't worry about me. I'm swell, you beautiful fat sow," he said. "You seem surprised that I'm talking to you."

"Aren't you surprised, you handsome rutting little swine?" Zandonella found the string of affectionate endearments pouring out of her as naturally as breath. This form of communication gave rise to such terms as a matter of course. It seemed that undisguised emotional display was built into the very language of the pigs.

"Of course, I'm not surprised. I've always been able to understand you." Porkditz snorted with amusement. "It was only you who couldn't comprehend what I was saying. It wasn't your fault. You were handicapped by your stunted human nose and hopelessly vestigial ears. You were more than half-blind, oh swell sow-sister, but now you can see. You were deaf but now you hear! Now you have a fine long snout and huge flapping ears. And what a beautiful creature you are." Then suddenly the amusement vanished from Porkditz's manner. "But there is no time now to revel in each other, my plump beloved, to rub bristles or exult in the scent of one another's droppings. Instead we must move quickly, with purpose and a mission. Follow me."

Porkditz turned away from her and set off across the big room, his trotters ringing against the metal bars of the floor. Zandonella ran after him, panting with the effort to keep up. "What is it? Why must we hurry?"

"Because the next intake is about to arrive." Porkditz skidded to a halt. They had reached the far wall of the shed-like room, a featureless corrugated span of metal.

"The next intake?"

Porkditz spun around and started running again, in a new direction, moving parallel to the corrugated wall. "Follow me. They are coming." Zandonella fell in behind Porkditz, running as fast as she could, following his bobbing little tail. The wall blurred beside her as she ran. There was a deep grumbling noise and a tremor ran through the floor.

"They are here," said Porkditz. Zandonella glanced at the corrugated wall which was gradually rising up, lifting off the floor like a giant shutter.

"Hurry!" implored Porkditz. They were racing towards a dead end, the corner where the long wall of the shed joined the corrugated back wall that was now grinding upwards, opening all along its length. As the wall rose, Zandonella could glimpse the trotters of thousands of pigs standing there and she began to hear their terrified squealing and smell their overpowering collective fear. Porkditz had gone as far as he could now. He hit the side wall and bounced off, landing in the corner, his snout stuck under the corrugated back wall as it rose. "Swiftly! Join me, sow-sister." Zandonella slid to a halt beside him and stuck her own head under the rising door. She realised now what Porkditz was doing.

They were at the extreme edge of the mass of incoming pigs. Pressed against the wall as thousands of newcomers poured in...

"Now!" shrilled Porkditz. He wormed his way under the rising wall. As the mass of pigs began to pour into the room, Porkditz was slipping out. Zandonella followed him. Together they found a tiny pocket of space by the wall in the next room and waited there as the army of squealing, squirming pigs pressed past them, into the red glow.

"To their doom," she muttered.

"Doom indeed, sweet sow-sister." Porkditz beamed at her. The mass of pigs was thinning now. "Our fellow porkers know that the red lights of the holding shed spells their imminent demise. But what can they do about it? What is life but the short span between the breeding pits and the killing chutes? A short and cheerless span filled with suffering as we live out our ordained fate, to be tortured and slaughtered and then eaten by the *longghouls*."

"The *longghouls*?"

Porkditz shook himself with amusement. The wall had reached its full aperture and was now beginning to descend again with a renewed ugly grinding. The last few stragglers were trotting past, rushing by Porkditz and Zandonella, hurrying to enter the red gloom of the holding shed before the wall closed.

"The *longghouls*?" she repeated.

"You call them humans."

Zandonella tried to remember what human beings were, what it had been like to be one. But that all seemed a very long time ago. The corrugated wall was now locking back into place and the last of the red glow from the shed was abruptly cut off. Suddenly she was alone with Porkditz in a large, shadowy tunnel that led away into the curving darkness of the factory farm.

"What do we do now?"

"Something that I should have done a long time ago, you sultry, salty temptress," announced Porkditz in a debonair voice, promptly mounting her from behind. Before Zandonella had time to question what was happening, Porkditz

was ploughing into her in a copulatory frenzy. Her pig body
and pig nervous system immediately responded in a roller
coaster of sensation unlike anything she had ever experienced before. Explosion after explosion of raw ecstasy
detonated in her swinish brain.

"You're porking me!" she squealed. "Don't stop! Don't
stop!"

"Quiet, my beautiful, bloated beloved," murmured
Porkditz in her ear, gently nibbling at it. "We mustn't be
heard by the *longghouls*. Or much worse, the cabal."

Zandonella could barely heed his warning, or wonder
who the cabal were. Her rational mind was temporarily
melted by the hot pleasure of their united flesh. Only
gradually did full awareness return, after the act was over
and Porkditz had slipped back off her hindquarters and
they were lying together there in the slaughterhouse corridor, their individual aromas uniting in a magnificent
combined stink. Zandonella rolled over and looked at
Porkditz.

"I'm so glad you're safe. When I heard that you'd been
kidnapped I almost couldn't bear it. Those fools were
supposed to look after you." Zandonella's brain struggled
to remember Judge Darrid and Judge Carver. The walrus-
moustached old hack and the ill-smelling, gauche young
recruit. But their human characters were hard to fit into
her pig brain, and since there was no way she could
name them in the language of pigs, she let all memory of
them slip away and simply said, "Those treacherous
fools."

"I was fortunate," said Porkditz. "After all, I was kidnapped instead of killed outright. But I suppose I'm a useful
piece of merchandise to them."

Zandonella shuddered. "You mean they wanted to turn
you into meat."

"If necessary. But the *longghouls* also recognised my huge
intelligence."

"Surely not," murmured Zandonella. "Otherwise they
would never have allowed such an intelligent, dangerous,

subversive pig to exist. They would have slaughtered my plump, beloved, curly tailed one."

"True, they only sensed a small portion of my vast intellect. But that was enough for them to try and put me to use."

"What do you mean, my fine swine love?"

"They thought that they could use me to control the population of our brethren as they are being flowed to the slaughter, just as you are used. Or the body you now inhabited was once used, to lead your fellows to their death in the machines below."

"But how did you know it was me in this body? How did you know I was your human friend?"

"I sensed your power when I first came upon you, my bristly love. And when you arrived here I simply smelled your presence. Thank the Great Fates that it was so."

"Yes, thank the Great Fates," echoed Zandonella, letting the pigs' unique primitive concept of deity slot into her brain.

"And thanks to my knowledge of the farm and all of its secret passages, I was able to come to you and rescue you."

"Ah, yes," sighed Zandonella contentedly. "My brave rescuer."

"Excuse me for interrupting," came a gravelly utterance, "but I thought I'd better break in on you love-pigs before I spill my swill."

Zandonella and Porkditz leapt to their trotters and spun around to face the newcomer. He had emerged from the shadows of the tunnel and stood watching them, calm and amused. He was a scarred old boar with a large brass ring encrusted with mucus hanging from his nose. He shook his head as he spoke, and the ring wiggled and dangled, occasionally shedding a viscous drop of slime.

"Who are you?" quavered Zandonella. She looked at Porkditz. "Who is he?" But Porkditz didn't answer immediately. He just stared at the boar, his snout and ears vibrating with hostility.

"The little one wants to attack me," said the boar. "But he knows better."

Porkditz stared at Zandonella. "He is from the cabal." His voice held a note of doom. "They have found us."

TWELVE

"This sleeping beauty is Theo Barkin," said Judge Dredd, indicating the med-bed that was strapped down, filling the wide, bright orange seat that occupied the entire rear of the patrol wagon. The whole wagon was painted a ferocious fluorescent orange that was almost painful to the eye, the same orange as the jumpsuits that the prisoners wore. There were no prisoners on the wagon today, though. A normal load would have been twenty or more, all fully conscious and in relatively good health.

Tonight it was accommodating the sole, comatose form of Theo Barkin, and the vehicle had required some adapting for the purpose. O'Mannion had supervised the work of a team of droid fitters, installing straps to the seat that would secure the med-bed. She looked at the unconscious perp – the "Sleeping Beauty" as Dredd had so cruelly put it. Theo's face was as white as the polished surfaces of the med-bed that kept him alive. It looked like he was in an open coffin: a white coffin with a smooth curved surface dotted here and there with computer readout screens and control panels. Above his pale sleeping face were fitted two cylinders of pure oxygen which were mixed with a feed of anaesthetic and fed into Theo's nostrils through a thin transparent tube.

Looking down on him, like mourners at some bizarre funeral, were Judge Dredd, Judge Darrid and Carver. O'Mannion stood beside them. They were alone in the bus, which could accommodate up to three dozen prisoners. She checked Theo's life signs while Dredd explained the situation to the others.

"You'll remember that Theo Barkin was apprehended during the rescue of the Cetacean Ambassador."

"Of course we remember," said Darrid. "Don't we boy?" He nudged Carver, who flushed red with embarrassment and nodded wordlessly. "That was a hell of a good bust, wasn't it?" Darrid crowed. "We sure taught them a lesson."

"If we'd taught them an adequate lesson, we wouldn't need to be here now," snarled Dredd.

"Excuse me, sir," ventured Carver, "but what are we doing? I thought our assignment was to escort a prisoner."

"Here's your prisoner." Dredd rapped on the smooth surface of Theo's med-bed. "He received a massive head wound resisting arrest and is now on medical life-support. He's officially brain-dead."

"Brain-dead?"

O'Mannion nodded. "Yes. Ironically, the meat kingpin has turned into a vegetable."

"So why are we taking this vegetable anywhere?" said Darrid. "Surely the proper thing for him is to stay right here at Justice Central, in the medical unit. In the perp pit."

"We aren't taking him anywhere," said O'Mannion.

"But we've got him here on the bus," said Carver.

"He's a decoy," snarled Dredd. "It's a trap."

"Hoo boy, that's more like it," said Darrid. "A trap. A trap for who?"

"For Barkin's brother. He is our only link to Psi-Judge Zandonella who is being held against her will in the factory farm that Barkin runs."

"Against her will?" said Carver. He had turned pale.

"Yes. And we have reason to believe her life is in danger," said O'Mannion.

"So we need Barkin to lead us to her," said Dredd. He glanced impatiently at the open door of the cockpit at the front of the wagon. O'Mannion could see that he was itching to get started.

Dredd abruptly stopped talking and simply started towards the cockpit. Just before he ducked inside the amber-lit compartment, he called back over his shoulder to

O'Mannion. "You tell him the rest." He disappeared into the cockpit, slamming the security hatch behind him.

O'Mannion looked at Darrid and Carver. They were like a couple of baby birds waiting to be fed scraps of information. "We've spread a story through our network of criminal informants," explained O'Mannion. "A story to the effect that we're moving Theo into long-term custody. We expect his brother to emerge from the woodwork and try and ambush us on this wagon at some point on our journey tonight."

"Ambush. Oh boy," said Darrid happily. "That's the stuff." O'Mannion wished the old fart would shut up. There was a shivering jolt through the frame of the wagon as Dredd turned the engines on and brought the vehicle to life.

"Just take up positions and be ready for anything." She moved to sit beside Theo, pressing herself snugly in the corner of the back seat with her right thigh pressed against the cool surfaces of the oxygen cylinders. The other two Judges, after much fussing, chose seats on either side of the wagon just in front of her.

O'Mannion sighed. Through the bulletproof window next to her, she could see the pitted, oil-spattered concrete walls of the vehicle pool begin to drop away. The patrol wagon was lifting off the ground. It rose and then stopped a metre or so above the floor. There was a gentle rumble of acceleration and the concrete walls began to shift, floating past them as the bus surged forward.

"I guess even a vegetable has some uses," cackled Darrid. He glanced back at the comatose prisoner in his white, high-tech coffin. O'Mannion gestured for Darrid to keep his eyes ahead. She surmised that any attack would be coming from that direction.

Their bright orange patrol wagon floated under the harsh glare of the lights in the big concrete room, drifting above the oil-stained floor of the vehicle pool. Its shadow crawled forward, picking up speed and moving towards the three cruciform exit gates in the far wall. They were leaving the steel and glass sanctuary of Justice Central to fly out over the streets of the city. The four sliding sections of one of the gates began to groan open, revealing a mauve night sky and the white sizzle of neon beyond. A warm gritty wind blew in, spattering the windows of the wagon with particle pollutants. The vehicle rose gently up on the swell of the buffeting dirty air, then moved forward again.

"Where are the Karst sisters?" said Carver. "Shouldn't they be here with us?"

"They're on compassionate leave," said O'Mannion. "They've gone to the swimming pool."

"The swimming pool?" asked Darrid.

"It's therapy for her hand."

"Therapy? Won't her hand rust?" said Carver.

"No, she's got a special glove." To O'Mannion they sounded like two old women gossips.

Darrid was saying, "Did you say her sister went too? To the swimming pool?"

"Compassionate leave," explained Carver.

"Both of them?" Darrid's moustache twitched with indignation. "I can understand sending the short, fat one. You know, the one with the metal hand."

"Esma," said Carver in a tremulous voice.

"Yeah, that's her. Never can shut up for a second," babbled Darrid. "Just can't stop talking. Loves the sound of her own voice. But anyway, I suppose *she* deserves some time off. She can go to the swimming pool and splash around and take it easy. I mean she lost the gruddamned thing twice. Had her hand ripped out of its socket with blood spurting everywhere. And it happened *twice.*"

O'Mannion wondered if Darrid would ever stop talking. The bus eased forward, leaving the safety of Justice Central to ride the dirty air over the dangerous streets.

"But anyway, that other one," continued Darrid, "the tall skinny one who never says anything. Called Tit-Wrists or something."

"Tykrist," said Carver in an offended tone. He seemed sensitive on the subject of the sisters. O'Mannion wondered idly if he had a crush on one of them. Or, she repressed a shudder at the thought, both of them. The wagon rose gently on an updraft and the glass canyon of the Mega-City dipped majestically on either side. The great cruciform gate was biting inexorably shut behind them like a slow, terrible mouth. The bus started forward at a smooth speed under Dredd's expert control.

"Yes, Tykrist, that's the one," droned Darrid. "Why the hell are they sending her to the swimming pool? She didn't lose her hand."

"She's providing emotional support for her sister," said Carver, offended again.

"Emotional support?" shrilled Darrid. "What a load of hooey! If you ask me, deep down, all siblings actually hate one another. All this pretence of affection is just a cover for unholy blood-curdling rivalry."

O'Mannion leaned forward. "Do you have any brothers or sisters, Darrid?"

"No. I'm an only child, so believe me I know what I'm talking about."

"Heads up," said Dredd suddenly on the intercom. "We have company."

A lean shadow swung alongside the wagon, flashing past the window beside O'Mannion. It was a robot.

In one of its attenuated hands, the robot was clutching a long, steel cable attached to a vehicle that was flying above them, shadowing the patrol wagon. The robot swung gracefully along the side of the bus, flicking past O'Mannion's window, then the next, and then the following window, which was beside Darrid's seat.

"It's that robot again," said Darrid in a startled falsetto. For a man who had so recently been savouring the words "ambush" and "trap", he seemed disturbingly unprepared.

In the hand that wasn't holding the steel cable, the robot was clutching a chunky black device or weapon of some kind. O'Mannion leaned forward to try to get a better look at it as the robot passed the window beyond Darrid's. It reached out and aimed the device. The window exploded inwards in a fine spray of glass particles.

"Sonic shocker," said O'Mannion, but her voice was lost in the shattering of glass. The supposedly bulletproof pane had decomposed into fragments which were chunky and blunt and unlikely to injure. The robot swung through the hole where the window had been.

"Oh my grud!" screamed Darrid, still trying to catch up with the situation. "The robot's coming in."

O'Mannion was already rising from her seat, Lawgiver in her hand. The weapon was set for incendiary ammunition and would blow the robot into a neat heap of molten slag. O'Mannion took aim. At that very instant Darrid rose from his seat and wobbled jerkily around in her line of fire. He was wrestling with his own sidearm, trying to get it out of its holster. O'Mannion moved her gun to the left, tracking the robot, who was retreating back up the aisle towards the front of the vehicle.

As O'Mannion's gun moved, so did Darrid, jerking right into her line of sight, again and again ruining any chance of a shot. She moved and Darrid moved once more, in diabolical synchronisation, yet again blocking her shot.

And he was still struggling to get his own weapon out.

On the other side of the wagon, Carver wasn't doing much better, having just risen from his seat and only just beginning to reach for his gun. The rookie and the old fool seemed to share equally sluggish reflexes.

The robot was on the move, scuttling nimbly like a cockroach, heading towards the far end of the patrol wagon. There it would find the security hatch of the cockpit sealed and would be able to go no further. In fact, reflected O'Mannion, the robot would be trapped. Or at least it would be if she could get a clean shot at it. Darrid and Carver were still fumbling for their weapons as they moved away from their seats and crowded into the aisle, getting in each other's way. O'Mannion shouldered past them, pursuing the robot to the front of the wagon.

The robot reached the sealed hatch of the cockpit and whirled with a ratcheting sound to face her. O'Mannion finally had a clean shot at the thing, but unfortunately it also had a clean shot at her with the sonic shocker. The gleaming device was absolutely steady in the robot's mechanical grasp. The robot looked at her with the precision optics of its eyes and began to talk in a pleasant, informative voice.

"This instrument shattered the supposedly shatter-proof glass of your vehicle. That was when it was set on a diffuse beam. It is now set on a tightly focused beam which in turn is tightly focused on you."

O'Mannion was embarrassed to realise that this was true, and the point was illustrated further by a hot purple dot on her chest. "At this range, a tightly focused sonic wave will have a devastating effect on the organs in a human body. In fact, in *your* body." The robot emphasised the word suavely, as though selling her a patent medicine.

"So I would advise you to lower your weapon and simply allow us to go about our business."

"Us?" said Carver sharply. He was standing just behind O'Mannion. "You mean there's more than one of you?" Close behind Carver, Darrid was still fuming and blustering.

"Business? What business?" said Darrid. "What the hell is it talking about?" The old fool had evidently already completely forgotten his briefing. "Why don't you just let me shoot the damned thing?"

"Don't make a move," snapped O'Mannion. "I am your superior officer and I am telling you not to do a snecking thing unless I specifically advise you. Clear?" The purple dot was dancing in agitation on her chest. Didn't the damned old fool realise that a blast from the robot's device would cause all her organs to liquefy?

"All right, all right. Clear," Darrid subsided querulously. "But what's this business the stinking thing's yapping about?"

"I am here with my master to rescue my master's brother," announced the robot in its bright salesman's voice.

"Master?" said Darrid. "What the hell?" The old idiot fell silent as a loud clanking from above announced that someone had landed on the roof.

"That will be my master now," said the robot.

Sparks began to fly from the ceiling at the rear of the patrol wagon. First sparks, then a steady circle of flame that lapped around in a swift dance. "He is cutting through the ceiling with his thermic lance," explained the robot, as if it was narrating an infomercial. The hot white circle of flame turned to magma and began to melt in molten blobs that fell in spatters to hiss on the scarred black floor. The bright light of the burning metal shone in fierce reflections from the smooth white surface of Theo Barkin's med-bed.

A section of the ceiling about the size of a manhole cover came loose with a rush and fell clattering to the floor. Through the hole came a surge of night air followed by a blond young man with a black moustache whom O'Mannion recognised as Leo Barkin. He was wearing black combat trousers, a black T-shirt and numerous belts of ammunition. He was clutching a machine rifle in one hand and the glowing cherry-tipped rod of a thermic lance in the other. Waves of superheated air rippled and danced over the tip of the lance. O'Mannion wondered just how hot it was. Hot enough to cut through the armour of the wagon like a knife slicing cake.

"That is my master," said the robot helpfully. Just then the hatch of the cockpit hissed open behind it and Dredd stepped through holding what looked like one of the chainsaws they'd used on the raid on Featherman's forest. Dredd promptly sliced the robot in half across the ribcage with a violent screaming of torn metal and a sudden black gush of machine oil. The robot flapped to the floor in two separate pieces. Dredd brought one boot down on a hideously flapping arm, then reached down and took hold of the sonic shocker.

"It doesn't matter," said the robot confidently. "My master has full charge of the situation."

"That's right," said Leo Barkin. "I am here to liberate my brother from the iron clutches of you fascist drokkers." He was starting on an obviously rehearsed speech. With one hand he was pointing his machine rifle at them while still holding the thermic lance in the other. The lance was clearly heavy because Leo moved to set it down on his brother's med-bed.

"No, not there," said O'Mannion sharply. "Those are oxygen tanks."

"What?" said Leo. But the enormously hot lance had already eaten into the nearest tank.

"Get down!" yelled Dredd. He shoved Carver to the floor of the patrol wagon while immediately behind him, O'Mannion pulled down the struggling bulk of Darrid. They sheltered behind their seats as the oxygen tank blossomed into a bright bubble of superheated gas, then expanded in an explosive shockwave.

The entire rear section of the wagon blew out into the night sky.

The Barkin brothers went with it, tumbling from sight to disappear into the shadowed canyons of the Mega-City, bodies accelerating in free fall: Theo in his explosion-scarred med-bed, its severed tubes spilling fluid, and Leo still clutching his thermic lance whose glow lit their passage like a candle burning in the dark, until it finally vanished into the distance.

The Judges rose from the floor and stared out at the windy ruin that had been the rear of the wagon.

"Well, that went well," said O'Mannion.

"My master has escaped," announced the robot, lying dismembered on the floor.

"Your master is strawberry jam," said Dredd.

"My name is Rootmaster," announced the scarred old boar proudly. "Since our little friend shows no inclination to introduce us." He looked at Porkditz and shook his head with ponderous sadness, a pendulous gobbet of mucus swaying precariously on the brass ring that pierced his snout. "But this little one has never shown proper responsibility, nor respect for his elders. He is nothing more than a dreamer, a waster, a foolish little shoat." Zandonella understood the term and the insult implied. A shoat was a young male, not yet fit for breeding.

"On the contrary," Zandonella replied. "Porkditz is not a shoat but a proper boar. He proved that not more than a few squeals ago."

The boar called Rootmaster waggled his head in disgust. His ears flapped audibly and the precarious gobbet of snot went flying off his nose-ring and splashed onto the floor. "Yes, he's been rooting at your hindquarters in his inadequate, juvenile way. I can smell the stink of his futile little pizzle on you. Just as I can smell that you are not a proper pure sow of the true flesh. You have the stink of the *longghoul* on you." He moved suddenly close to Zandonella. She flinched as the scarred old beast drove her up against the wall. Porkditz moved to attack him, then checked himself. He remained standing where he was, his head hanging down with shame. She could tell he was terrified of the older pig.

Rootmaster sniffed at her, drinking in her scent with long, luxurious snorts from his scarred old snout. "Yes," he said. "You are possessed. A *longghoul* witch has possessed one of our beautiful sows. The true flesh is sullied by your presence."

"Leave her alone," murmured Porkditz. The old boar wheeled on him, smiling a vicious smile.

"At last he speaks," said Rootmaster. "Well, little shoat. What do you have to say for yourself?"

"Nothing," muttered Porkditz. He kept his head hung low, eyes on the floor, refusing to meet the gaze of the old pig.

"Nothing? Surely you have stories to tell, of your adventures among the *longghouls*?" He twitched his head around and looked at Zandonella. "What did he learn among you? Did he study your weaknesses? Did he find the vulnerable point for our attack? Was he plotting the strategy of a holy war?"

Attack? Holy war? Zandonella felt her human personality surface again as her mind responded to these terms with alarm. There was something going on here that a Judge needed to know about.

Porkditz lifted his head reluctantly and looked at the grizzled old boar. "No, I did nothing like that. I want no part of the cabal or their bloodthirsty plans."

"Bloodthirsty! At last the shoat speaks worthy words." Rootmaster glanced at Zandonella and his eyes gleamed with the disturbing light of the true fanatic. "The cabal shall indeed drink blood. We shall launch our campaign of right-eous war and holy slaughter and we shall do it with or without your help."

"Without," said Porkditz. "I will not help you. I am not flesh of your flesh."

"Clearly not." Rootmaster smiled at Zandonella. "Can you believe this little shoat is one of the greatest escape artists ever to grace our race? He avoided the slaughter tun-nels and blood hooks and sped out of this nightmare place, out of this world of pain, to a better life beyond. His fleet trotters carried him into the outside world; the world of sunshine, the fabled place where pigs can live without being butchered and turned into meat." His eyes clouded with hatred. "Meat for the *longghouls*. The vicious slaugh-tering cannibals who take their brothers who run low to the ground and make captives of them, pen them and breed them, and then kill them and chop them and turn them into meat for their greedy mouths." Viscous ropes of saliva flowed from the boar's mouth. He shook his head as though waking from a bad dream and looked at Porkditz. "The Great Fates allowed you to escape into the outside world, and yet you did nothing to help your brothers in the cabal."

"You are not my brothers. I want nothing to do with the cabal or your plans for vengeance."

"Vengeance? Do you mean justice?" Saliva flowed from Rootmaster's mouth in a steady stream. "Justice and fit ret-ribution for the millions of intelligent swine who lived a short, hellish existence in the death farms before being bru-tally torn apart by the blades of the *longghouls* and being turned into what they call bacon, what they call sausages, what they call chops and ribs and hams and loins, but what I call my people. My poor, suffering brothers."

"Your brothers, yes," said Porkditz. "But what of your sisters?"

Rootmaster glanced at Zandonella. "Sisters?" he murmured. "What do you mean?"

"The cabal is a brotherhood," said Porkditz.

"The one true brotherhood. The only hope for swinedom. We shall lead pork-kind out of the years of suffering, and into the light of freedom." The old boar's rhetoric had the intoxicating passion of a true zealot. Zandonella herself was almost swayed by it.

But then he said, "Females, of course, can never be part of it."

"What?" snorted Zandonella.

"See how she is infected by the diseased thoughts of the *longghoul* witch?" Rootmaster wiggled his head with satisfaction, his ears flapping. "A female of our species understands that she is the inferior. No sow could ever be part of the cabal and they know that. Their only duty is providing pleasure for the males and rearing young."

"So when you say you're leading pigs to freedom," said Zandonella, "you only mean male pigs."

"We shall take our women folk with us. They can continue to serve our needs."

"That's very generous of you," said Zandonella.

"Don't make him angry," begged Porkditz in a whisper.

"You mustn't worry about me," said the old boar placidly. "I won't fly into a rage. There is no need. This is the happiest day of my fine, fat swinish life."

"What do you mean?" said Porkditz. Zandonella could see that Rootmaster's peaceful demeanour worried him more than any amount of hostility.

"You see, today is the day," crooned Rootmaster. "After long years of suffering, our revenge against the *longghoul*s is finally at hand. Now it is their turn to die by the millions."

"By the millions?" said Zandonella. Perhaps the old animal was insane. He certainly seemed to be talking nonsense. How could domestic animals, trapped in a slaughterhouse, threaten the mass murder of human beings?

"Perhaps tens of millions," cried Rootmaster, saliva gushing from his mouth. His little piggy eyes glowed brightly.

"The furnace that burns atoms," breathed Porkditz.

"Yes, the furnace that burns atoms," exulted Rootmaster. "We shall cause it to explode, like the hottest and most violent flatus that ever rippled from the bowels of a pig. It will explode and spread its poison everywhere, among the *longghoul*s, killing them in their multitudes."

"A furnace that burns atoms?" Zandonella looked from Porkditz to the old boar. "Do you mean a nuclear reactor?"

"They take the bodies of our murdered brethren to the furnace," murmured Rootmaster, as though intoning a prayer. "They kill them and slice them and grind their bodies to a pink paste and squirt it into tiny metal turds. Pointy turds."

Metal turds? He must mean tins. Pointy tins. Zandonella remembered the pyramid-shaped tins they had seized in the shoplex. The tins were full of processed pork. "Sputam!" she said.

"That is what the *longghoul*s call it. Our fine, brave brethren ground to paste. They take it to the atom furnace and let the deadly glow of the furnace play over the metal turds."

"Radiation. You mean they irradiate the tins," said Zandonella.

"Yes. Even in death our fallen comrades might find a way of striking back and harming or slaying those who try to eat them. But the glow of the atom furnace finally defeats the brave spirit of our brothers, subduing them utterly, turning them to food."

"They irradiate the tins of Sputam to prevent food poisoning," said Zandonella.

"Spoken like a true *longghoul*."

"And you think that somehow you'll be able to blow up the nuclear reactor – the atom furnace, as you call it?"

"It will explode with a hideous blast like the richest, foulest fart ever farted by pig," declared Rootmaster with satisfaction.

Zandonella decided the old boar was definitely out of his mind. It was time to call his bluff. "But how can you possibly achieve that, trapped in here?"

"We shall not be trapped in here. We shall leave this place on a glorious mission and lay down our lives. We shall blow up the atom furnace."

"A suicide attack?" said Zandonella. She still couldn't see how it was feasible.

Rootmaster licked his face with satisfaction. "We shall slay the *longghoul*s in the millions, in return for the millions of swine who have died to satisfy their greed."

Zandonella looked at Porkditz. "He can't do it," she said. Porkditz said nothing. He just stared at her with infinite, inexpressible longing in his warm, liquid eyes.

"I can do it; with the help of my brothers in the cabal. And you two are coming with us."

"Coming with you?" squeaked Porkditz.

Rootmaster chortled. "If you could not serve the cabal in life, little brother, you shall at least serve it in death." He shifted his gaze to Zandonella. "And this poor sow possessed by the *longghoul* witch shall also join us. She is contaminated and she must die. We shall all do it for the greater glory of pigdom. We shall all die together. Rejoice, brothers."

"Rejoice," echoed two pigs in a powerful guttural snarl. The two pigs stepped out of the shadows. They were both boars, both larger than Rootmaster and far younger and stronger. One of the young boars had white and brown colouring and large spots that covered his powerful body. His companion was pink in colour, covered with fine, blond bristles, with one ear irregularly notched at the edge where it had been viciously bitten and torn in a fight.

"Take them with us," said Rootmaster. "They shall die for the cause."

"Are you off to Aquatomics?" said Blue Belle. Her face was smiling out from the screen on the wall of the launch chamber. Blue Streak stood sweating in front of it. He had manhandled most of the latest shipment of Sputam into the detachable cargo hold of the shuttlecraft that was standing nearby, filling the launch chamber. Streak had been working steadily for half an hour and he had just added the two large cardboard boxes containing a dozen litre-sized plastic bottles of gin each. With these, the operators at the irradiation plant would be able to drink themselves silly. Streak decided that he would head back for the farm as soon as he'd made his delivery, before they could start drinking seriously. He would be glad not to be anywhere near those drunken fools in charge of a chunky and powerful nuclear reactor.

He was almost finished loading up the last of the Sputam. Now all he had to do was load one last palette of tins and make sure that the cargo was snugly stored. He would have been finished already if Belle hadn't appeared on the communications screen to wish him goodbye.

"I'm just about ready," said Streak.

"Please darling, be careful," said Belle. She was sitting in the control room. He could just make out Mac the Meat Man moving around in the background.

"I will," said Streak gruffly. His voice had suddenly betrayed him. He was deeply moved by Belle's sudden concern for his well-being. She'd never wished him goodbye like this before.

"Be careful and hurry back." Belle blew a kiss from the screen. She was being very affectionate. She was never normally this nice to him. Streak mentally shrugged and told himself not to question a good thing. Enjoy it while you can.

He blew a kiss back at Belle. On the screen she reached for the control panel, getting ready to break contact. "Wait a minute," said Streak. Belle stopped and looked up at him, a flash of impatience in her eyes.

"Yes?" she said. "What is it?" There was a note of hostility creeping into her voice and Streak felt a familiar sinking feeling. He'd done something wrong but he had no idea what it was.

"I was just going to say, I thought you'd gone to find that pig. The one that disappeared, the Judas pig. Satan's Sow."

"Oh, her." Belle shrugged. "I've been on every camera in the farm using recognition software and there's just no sign of her."

"That's odd," said Streak, scratching his head.

"Never mind," said Belle gaily. "I'm sure she'll turn up." She reached for the control panel again and this time the screen went black. But just before it did so, Streak saw Mac step into shot, moving towards Belle. He stared at the dead screen for a moment before returning to his task, feeling a strange unease that he couldn't identify.

Streak went back to the open cargo hold at the rear of the shuttlecraft. In front of the hold, the last loading palette floated just above the ground, laden with glistening pyramid-shaped tins, packed upside down and right side up in alternating layers so as to form one large cube. He shoved the palette and sent it floating towards the open rear of the craft. According to his calculations, he should be able to fit one more in. The palette connected with the guide track; a metal flange on its underside engaging with a metal groove on the floor of the cargo hold. It locked into place with a satisfying clunk and began to slide forward. But after a moment it came to a sudden halt.

Blue Streak cursed and leaned against the pile of tins, trying to force the palette into the cargo hold. He grunted with effort but it was no good. The palette slid forward a fraction then stopped with a sudden squeal. Streak backed away in alarm. Had he managed to jam the palette onto the guide track? That squeal had sounded like metal binding onto metal in a disastrous lockdown. If so, he would be spending the rest of the day trying to get the damned thing unstuck.

Sweating, he grabbed hold of either side of the palette and tried to waggle it gently free. To his surprise and immense relief, the palette came loose immediately. He pulled it back out of the cargo hold, its hover-unit cutting back in with a hum as it slid free of the craft and back over the floor of the launch chamber, bobbing over its shadow. Streak guided it carefully back to the rear of the chamber and left it parked there for the next trip.

He'd obviously miscalculated; there was no room for it this time. He took one last look at the neat loads of Sputam and then he turned and pushed a button on the hull outside.

As he walked away, the hatch of the cargo hold began to slide shut.

As it snapped into place, the hold was plunged into darkness. Shapes moved in the darkness, stirring in the narrow spaces between the pallets stacked with tins.

"Which of you idiots made that squeal?" demanded Rootmaster. "You almost betrayed our presence to the *longghoul.*"

THIRTEEN

Two minutes after the lurch and roar that indicated take-off, Rootmaster led them forward in the darkness of the cargo hold. The two young boars kept close to Zandonella and Porkditz, forcing them to move and preventing any chance of escape. They were hemmed in between pallets stacked with tins of Sputam and some boxes full of plastic bottles labelled "Jumpin' Juniper – Finest Mega-City Gin". At the far end of the hold there was a glowing amber hexagon on the wall with some lettering on it. The lettering was in Russian, which Zandonella couldn't read even when she was in her own body. To her pig eyes the symbols were utterly meaningless. Rootmaster seemed to have an understanding of what they said, though.

The old boar reared up on his hind legs and hit the glowing panel with his snout. A hexagonal door in the wall slid open, allowing light to pour into the cargo hold. Zandonella could see the cockpit of the shuttlecraft. There were two acceleration couches jammed at the rear of the small chamber and, beyond them, two chairs for the pilot and navigator. Only the pilot's chair was occupied by the young man with the tattoos. Zandonella struggled to remember the man's name, or at least his street name. She had heard it at a briefing only a few days earlier. She wrestled with her swine brain, trying to force it into human patterns of thought. Then the name popped into her head. Streak. That was it. Blue Streak.

Streak didn't notice the door of the cargo hold opening behind him or the five pigs slipping in and concealing themselves behind the acceleration couches. The octagonal door whispered shut, but the sound of it was drowned out by the rumble of the engines and Streak's eyes remained fixed on the screens above the control panel.

One of the screens showed the view from the rear of the shuttlecraft, looking back at the spot from which they had just launched. It showed a glittering spread of greenish water, waves stirring across its surface in the wind, lights glinting in flickering reflections. As they rose higher, the body of water was revealed to be in the shape of a large, ragged star. It was surrounded on all sides by towering factory complexes. Zandonella immediately recognised the distinctive body of water: Condoleezza Rice Municipal Swamp, a drainage basin for the multitudinous toxic effluent from this industrial district. There was a milky spot of turbulence in the centre of the swamp, shrinking now until it was just barely visible, and then disappearing altogether. Zandonella realised that this must be the disturbance on the water left by their shuttlecraft when it had broken the surface, rising from below.

The factory farm was under water. No wonder they'd been unable to find it. It was an ideal hiding place and the space station, designed for use in a vacuum, would have required only minimal modification to make it water tight.

Streak wasn't paying any attention to the screen showing the swamp dwindling and sinking below. Instead he was staring at the centre screen, busy on the communications band. So far the link was audio only. The screen in front of him was a bluish blur with the words "Waiting for Visual Feed" flashing on and off in blinding white. Zandonella was able to read the words with ease. Fear and stress were sharpening the human components of her hybrid mind.

"Come in factory farm. Come in. Mac? Belle?" The tattooed man made some adjustments on the control panel. "Are you receiving me? Urgent. I repeat, urgent."

"Ah, hello, yes," a man's voice, full of forced joviality, came out of the speakers. "We, I mean I, I mean we, we are indeed here, son. We indeed hear you loud and clear. Ah, this is Mac the Meat Man. Over."

"Mac, I saw something..."

The flashing white words on the screen changed to "Visual Feed Established" and they disappeared, to be replaced by the image of an old man with an extremely red, sweating face and large white eyebrows. He said, "Son, shouldn't you be concentrating on flying that old jalopy?"

"I've put it on autopilot. It's on course for the Aquatomic."

The Aquatomic. Zandonella remembered the combined leisure pool and nuclear reactor facility. Its gala opening had been in the news recently and the response of the Mega-City's fickle populace had been sufficiently enthusiastic for the operation to become an overnight success. Zandonella shuddered inwardly. The place would be packed with citizens happily splashing in the reactor-warmed water. Families. Children. They would be the first to die if Rootmaster had his way. She glanced at the old boar crouching beside her. His plan was obvious. He was going to seize control of the shuttlecraft and crash it into the nuclear facility.

The families and children would be the first to die, but only the first. If the Aquatomic reactor exploded, the detonation and ensuing fallout would seal the fate of a vast swathe of people. What had Rootmaster said, tens of millions?

"Well, that's just grand, son," said Mac the Meat Man on the screen. "So why don't I just leave you to it?" The red-faced old man started to reach for the controls that would cut the communications link.

"Mac," said Streak urgently. "Listen to me. I saw something as I was taking off."

"Saw something? What?" There was a sudden note of alarm in the voice from the speakers. "You mean in here in the control room? You saw something in here? With us? I mean, me? I mean us."

"No. Not you in the control room," said the young man impatiently. "I saw something in the sky. During take-off."

"In the sky? During take-off?

"When I launched the shuttlecraft, yes. As I was leaving the vicinity I noticed an incoming vehicle."

"Incoming?"

"Yes." The young man leaned over the control panel and checked some data. "I calculated its trajectory and destination and it seems to be headed straight for the swamp."

"For the swamp?" The red-faced man kept repeating Streak's words like a parrot.

"Affirmative. It looks set to break surface and dive straight down to you."

"Well, then son," said the voice over the speaker, becoming more firmly jovial, "that's good news."

"How do you figure that?"

"It's probably just Leo's shuttlecraft returning from his mission."

"I ran a check on the vehicle silhouette. And yes, it does look like one of our shuttles."

"Well, there you are then, son. It's Leo coming back. In fact we felt a little shudder a moment or two ago and that must have been him docking. The boy is back, the prodigal returns. We shall make him welcome."

"Only do that if you're sure it's him."

"What do you mean?"

"If it's Leo he would have contacted us to say he was coming in."

"Son, you are such a pessimist. If it isn't Leo then who else can it be?"

"Judges."

"Judges? Why, how on earth...?"

"They might have captured Leo's shuttlecraft. And it had a homing device that allowed it to return to the mother ship. Which means the space station. Which means the farm. Which means you."

"Now son, you're just being paranoid. He's just worrying without reason. Isn't he, my dear?"

"That's right. Stop worrying Streak darling," said a young woman in a solicitous voice. The camera automatically panned to take in the new speaker and revealed a half-naked young woman with tattoos all over her torso and breasts.

"Belle," said the young man. "You're undressed."

"Stomm," said the girl, realising she was on camera. She hastily covered her breasts.

"What's going on?" said Streak, his voice shrill with outrage. "Has he taken your bra off? You old bastard."

"He's the least of your worries, creep." Judge Dredd's face suddenly filled the screen. "You're under arrest, and so are your friends we caught here with their pants down."

"I didn't have my pants down," shrilled Belle. She appeared on the screen, still without shirt and bra, but now wearing handcuffs. "Just my shirt off."

"You bitch," said Streak. "You were my girlfriend."

"We never said anything about exclusivity," said Belle.

"Two-timing me with that old sack of lard. How could you?"

Mac the Meat Man stepped back into shot. He too, was wearing handcuffs. "As it happens, Belle here has something of a hankering for the more mature gentleman. You can hardly blame her."

"Blame her?" A fine spray of spittle burst from Streak's mouth as he addressed the screen. Zandonella could see blue veins standing out on his forehead in rage, like a new set of tattoos. "She's just doing this to get back at me because of that moustache on the tattoo. But she knows it was just an accident. She knows it's not my fault. But she's vindictive. She holds a grudge."

"Look, just shut up, all of you," said Judge Dredd, appearing on the screen again. He stared directly down at Streak from the screen. "As for you, punk, if you're so upset about your girlfriend's amorous adventures, why don't you come back here to discuss it with her."

"I think I will," said Streak.

"Streak, don't do it," shouted Belle. "They'll arrest you."

"That's right, boy," said Mac. "Think of the consequences. The Judges have no idea where you're heading. They didn't bust into the control room until we'd finished discussing your destination. You're free as a bird. Don't throw it all away by coming back here."

"I'm through listening to either of you," said Streak venomously. "I'm coming back there and I'm coming back with a gun. I don't care how many Judges they've got protecting you."

"That's right, punk," said Dredd. "You come back. We'll be waiting for you."

"All right," snarled Streak. "I will. I'm switching off the autopilot and coming right back."

But as he reached for the controls, Rootmaster gave a signal to the boar with the torn ear and the animal launched itself forward, leaping over the acceleration couch and landing on top of Streak. Before the man could react, the pig had sunk its teeth into his arm. Zandonella's keen ears could hear the clipping of teeth on his bones. Streak began to scream as Rootmaster scrambled over the acceleration couch and thrust his bulk up against the control panel, striking at the communications panel with his snout.

"Pig, put that man down," said Judge Dredd, in the instant before the screen went dead. Blue Streak continued screaming.

"You can release the *longghoul* now," said Rootmaster, and the pig let go of Streak who sank to the floor clutching his damaged arm. "If he tries to reach for the controls again, bite his fingers off." Streak stared at the pigs, frightened and uncomprehending. He had no idea what was being said, but he showed no signs of resistance.

Rootmaster turned triumphantly to face Zandonella and Porkditz, who were still skulking behind the acceleration couches with the brown and white boar guarding them. "Well, little shoat?" demanded Rootmaster. "Well, *longghoul* witch?"

"What do you want us to say?" said Porkditz.

"I want you to congratulate me and my fine brave brethren. The cabal is now in command of this flying turd and we are going to send it crashing into the atom furnace. Our mission will soon be completed. No one can prevent us now."

"What makes you think you can control this craft?" said Zandonella. "What makes you think you can find this so-called atom furnace?"

"We don't have to," snorted Rootmaster. "The *longghoul* has done all the work for us. He has told the mechanical brain of this flying turd where he wants it to go, and unless anyone interferes with it, it shall soar straight to its destination. The *longghoul* was about to change the orders to the mechanical brain when I sent Ripped-Ear to attack him. Fortunately, Ripped-Ear got to him in time, otherwise the *longghoul* might have spoiled everything."

Zandonella cursed inwardly. Despite his rather quaint phraseology, Rootmaster seemed to have a good rudimentary grasp of the control systems on the ship and how they operated. He might have an incomplete understanding of computers and autopilots, but that hadn't stopped him successfully hijacking the craft.

However, the old boar's understanding was indeed incomplete, thought Zandonella, and that was precisely what could stop him completing his attack on the nuclear facility. This was because the autopilot, left to its own devices, would not only fly them to their programmed destination, but it would also implement a soft landing, bringing the shuttlecraft down gently and safely on a suitable surface. Rootmaster's dreams of destruction were nothing more than a wild fantasy after all. For the first time in hours Zandonella felt fear ebbing away and she began to relax. All she and Porkditz needed to do was sit tight and soon the shuttlecraft would be safely parked at the Aquatomic Fun Pool and Fission Reactor Complex, waiting for the Judges to discover it.

Rootmaster smirked. "Look at the *longghoul* witch. Pig excrement wouldn't melt in her mouth. She thinks she knows something I don't."

"What do you mean?" said Zandonella. The fear was coming back now, in waves.

"You think I don't have enough knowledge to make this flying turd crash and burn. I could see the relief and happiness in your face, smell it on you. You haven't been a pig long enough to hide your emotions. Your assumptions are wrong. I know that when we are approaching the atom furnace, flying at top speed, I must wait for the last possible moment and then do exactly what the *longghoul* tried to do." He nodded at Streak who was still lying on the floor, murmuring weakly and clutching his bloody arm.

Zandonella felt a deep, profound chill. Rootmaster was going to turn off the autopilot just as they came in for landing. That would do the trick all right. The shuttle would crash, and if it crashed anywhere near the reactor, they would blow it to Kingdom Come.

It had taken a few minutes for the Judges to work out the controls at the factory farm. Most of the equipment still bore Cyrillic labels from its tour of duty as a Russian space station. But eventually they'd got the hang of things. It was Judge Dredd who had worked out how to switch off the red illumination in the holding shed and replace it with white light in the daylight wavelength. It enabled the Judges to see properly but it wasn't doing O'Mannion any good.

She was standing at one end of the shed. Beside her, on the floor, was the eerie form of the comatose Zandonella. Her sleeping body lay enclosed in the white shape of a portable med-bed. As she lay there under the gaze of O'Mannion, thousands of pigs filed past her, being driven by groups of Judges equipped with riot clubs that they used occasionally to nudge along any reluctant animals. The pigs passed by Zandonella's med-bed, moving in a continual stream, entering at the far end and leaving through the open section of wall which had previously led down to the slaughter chutes. The pigs were understandably reluctant to pass into the abattoir darkness, reeking of the death of their kind. But they had nothing to fear. Dredd had switched off the killing mechanisms and the animals passed through unharmed to end up in one of the loading bays where a further detachment of Judges were loading them onto transport vehicles to be carried to safety.

Judge Dredd came into the shed, climbed down from the platform that led to the airlock and joined O'Mannion. He didn't waste time with greetings. "This isn't working," he snarled as he watched the endless line of pigs shuffling past Zandonella's med-bed. "What do you expect to achieve?"

O'Mannion glanced at Dredd in irritation. "I expect that the pig that is hosting Zandonella will step out of the line and come over to the bed here. Then we'll simply have to bring it into contact with her sleeping body and the consciousness exchange will take place. We'll have her back safe and sound."

"There's just one problem with your plan."

"Oh really? And what's that?"

Dredd looked away impatiently. "What if the pig containing Zandonella isn't here?"

"Isn't here? Where else could she be?"

Dredd frowned. "When I was talking to Blue Streak on the communications link I saw that there were some pigs in the shuttle with him. And one of them bit him just before they broke contact."

"Bit him? But if he was attacked by a pig..."

"That pig might have been the host for Zandonella, trying to break free of her human captors."

"Well, can't you trace the communications signal and go after the shuttle?"

"Negative. They were using a signal-bounce algorithm. We can break it using the computers at Justice Central but that won't do any good. It will take an hour or two and then all it will tell us is their flight position an hour or two ago."

"Isn't there any other way to track the shuttle?"

"Not unless they broadcast an unguarded signal. Otherwise they're just lost in the traffic pattern."

O'Mannion stared at the unending line of pigs waddling past. "Maybe you're wrong," she said. "Maybe Zandonella's pig isn't on the shuttle. Maybe she'll turn up here."

"Maybe," said Dredd grimly. "But if she doesn't, I've got a hunch time is running out for her."

．　．　．

Blue Streak had crawled onto one of the acceleration couches and was lying there nursing his maimed arm, moaning occasionally, under the alert, baleful gaze of the boar called Ripped-Ear. Having bitten the man, the pig seemed to be taking a proprietary interest in his fate. The other young boar, the brown and white specimen called Splatter-Pattern, was keeping a close watch on Porkditz and Zandonella.

The Judge was waiting for an opportunity to try to do something – anything that might improve their situation – but no such opportunity had presented itself and she was beginning to wonder if it ever would. Rootmaster was lolling comfortably on the other acceleration couch and seemed entirely in control of the situation. The shuttlecraft was roaring along on autopilot, and if nothing happened to disrupt its flight, they would all too soon be arriving at their extremely final destination.

It was Porkditz who broke the silence. "So we are to die with you, Rootmaster."

The old boar stirred on his couch and gazed down at Porkditz. "Has that knowledge only now penetrated your thick skull, little shoat?"

"It is only now that I am beginning to accept it, old warrior," said Porkditz humbly. Zandonella wondered what he was up to. This sort of humility was quite uncharacteristic of the cocky little pig.

"Ha," snorted Rootmaster. "It is never too late to kneel before your betters and pledge allegiance to the cabal. Is that what you have finally decided you want to do, little shoat?"

"What I want, old master, is to spend my last moments in this life expiring in pleasure and happiness."

Rootmaster squinted at Porkditz suspiciously. "What do I care about your pleasure or your happiness, runt?"

"Nothing at all, wise master. But equally, why should you want to prevent it? Since it is nothing to you, I might as well end this life as joyfully as I can."

"Joyfully? Your joy means nothing, runt. It means nothing to the cabal or myself or the vast uncaring world."

"If the world is uncaring, then it makes no difference if I am happy or sad. So, I repeat, why shouldn't I be happy?"

Rootmaster squirmed to the edge of the couch and peered down at Porkditz. Zandonella could see that the old boar was becoming dangerously angry. What was Porkditz up to? She prayed that he knew what he was doing.

"Your happiness is less than nothing," sputtered Rootmaster. "It is the droppings from the anus of a diseased old sow, shortly to die. It stinks, it spatters, it revolts me. Better you should suffer than be happy. Suffer for the cause of the cabal. Exult in our glorious deaths, in our victory which will strike a blow like a killing hammer against the vile *longghouls*."

"True, my happiness is nothing, mighty master, but what of your own and that of my brave brothers?" Porkditz nodded at Ripped-Ear and Splatter-Pattern. "Sure such courageous members of the cabal deserve blessed rapture in their final moments in this life?"

"Pleasures of the flesh mean nothing to the brothers of the cabal," snorted Rootmaster. "We are above such primitive gratifications as rutting with this sow." He stared at Zandonella with his mad fanatic's eyes. "I assume that is what you are suggesting. A last orgy with this pitiful, inferior creature."

"On the contrary, master," said Porkditz quickly. "That was not what I had in mind at all."

"What then? A last meal? Are you suggesting that we rip out the intestines of that *longghoul* and feast on them?" He glanced over at Blue Streak, who was lying motionless on the other acceleration couch. He looked at him thoughtfully. "The brothers and I had a huge feast before we set off on this mission. But still..." Rootmaster licked his chops.

"No, master," said Porkditz hastily. "As tempting as that is, I had something far better in mind."

"Far better? What, then? Speak, little shoat."

"Mighty warrior, I was speaking of the delicious drink that is being carried on this vehicle."

"Delicious drink? What nonsense is this?" For the first time Rootmaster sounded intrigued and Zandonella felt the first faint stirrings of comprehension and hope.

"I saw it in the rear of the craft, and smelled it, when we were hiding there in the darkness."

"Nonsense," said Rootmaster. "There is nothing back there but the bodies of our brave brethren, churned into meat and packed into metal turds for the *longghouls* to devour."

"I beg to correct you, oh mighty boar. There are indeed many metal turds containing that disgusting and obscene confection. But there are also a few boxes of the delicious drink I mentioned. It is the finest and most cherished drink that the *longghouls* have created for themselves. I learned of it in my time among them." He looked across at Zandonella, a quick surreptitious glance. She remembered sharing her gin martinis with Porkditz back at her con-apt. It seemed a long time ago now, in another life. But all that mattered was that Porkditz had a plan and she was beginning to guess what it was.

Rootmaster glanced over at the brown and white pig who came towards Porkditz. "You lie," said Splatter-Pattern. "There is nothing back there but the metal turds full of meat."

"I beg to correct you, brother," said Porkditz evenly. "There are many bottles of this fine concoction."

"He lies," snarled Splatter-Pattern.

"Go back and check," Rootmaster said, licking his lips. The young boar headed for the rear of the cockpit, shooting a poisonous look back at Porkditz. He disappeared through the open door into the shadows of the cargo hold.

"If you are lying, if you are trying some kind of mischief..." Rootmaster left the rest of the statement to their imaginations. A moment later there was a dry scraping noise as Splatter-Pattern came nosing back, pushing one of the cardboard crates in front of him.

"This is the drink," he said. "I can smell it."

"Then root some out," ordered Rootmaster. Splatter-Pattern looked at the crate for a moment and then lunged forward and began to chew savagely at it, sending scraps of cardboard flying. A row of litre-sized bottles were revealed through the cardboard, each adorned with an image of a drunken London Palace Guard that owed more to enthusiasm and imagination than painstaking historical research. The logo on each bottle read "Jumpin' Juniper Gin". Zandonella's heart pounded in her wide, low-slung chest. She had pieced together Porkditz's plan. Would it work?

Splatter-Pattern stuck his snout in the box and rooted out two bottles and sent them spinning across the floor of the cockpit. The plastic bottles bounced with the loud *thump* of sealed liquid.

"Thank you oh mighty brethren," squeaked Porkditz. "Now if you will just allow myself and the lowly sow to drink our fill..."

Rootmaster ignored him. "It is I who shall drink." He hopped down from the acceleration couch and waddled over to the nearest bottle.

"You won't like it," said Porkditz quickly.

"I shall be the judge of that." Rootmaster bit into the plastic bottle and it burst open, the clear fluid gushing out, splashing into his mouth. The old boar swallowed a mouthful, licked his chops and then bent his head to lap out the remaining contents of the ravaged bottle. "It's good," he murmured, looking at the other bottle that had spilled from the crate, his eyes full of piggy calculation. After the briefest of pauses he trotted over to it, bit into it and drained it with a few, swift greedy swallows. He knocked the torn bottle aside with his trotter and sent it spinning across the cockpit.

"More," he said, looking at the young boars who were watching his drinking with avid interest. Rootmaster's gaze seemed slightly askew, but his voice was powerful and clear and commanding. "Get me more of that drink. And help yourselves."

Porkditz spoke quickly and nervously. "But surely you three brave brothers don't need to drink any more. Leave it for myself and the sow."

"Greedy little shoat. You want it all for yourself. Just for that you shall have none."

"None," quavered Porkditz. "But it was my idea."

"At least you have contributed to the cabal and our fight against the *longghoul*s. That is more important than satisfying your own selfish thirst. You have helped in our cause, offering refreshment to brave soldiers. For that you should be grateful, and gratitude should be enough."

Porkditz turned his long, handsome face towards Zandonella. One of his eyes flashed shut then opened again. She could have sworn he had winked at her.

"Given up your identity parade?" snarled Judge Dredd.

O'Mannion shook her head. "I've left Judges Norbert and Westhope in charge. Their orders are to station themselves beside Zandonella's med-bed and let me know if any of the pigs walking past show any kind of response to her sleeping body."

"Sounds like a plan," said Dredd. "Why didn't you stay yourself and supervise?"

"Because I think you're right. I think Zandonella is out there on that rogue shuttle." She walked across the control room and joined Dredd. The pale green readout flashing across the computer screen was reflected on Dredd's stony countenance. O'Mannion glimpsed a stream of Russian text, broken into blocks, followed by entries in English that looked like addresses.

"What are you doing?"

"We can't trace the shuttle, but we can hack into the farm's business files, and we've got a list of addresses for deliveries."

"Of course. They're in the black market meat business. That's probably where the shuttle is going. It's a brilliant idea. Who thought of it?"

"It's not so brilliant," said Dredd sourly. "There are hundreds of addresses here."

"So what are you going to do?"

Dredd's face was grim. "Cover all of them."

The entire cockpit stank of gin. Blue Streak lay on the acceleration couch, going in and out of consciousness. He was vaguely aware that he was in the shuttle and that it was on autopilot, hurtling through the air with a bunch of escaped pigs on the loose.

Somehow the animals had found their way in, escaping from the mainstream farm tunnels and getting into the launch chamber. They'd got on board the craft and got loose during the flight. And one of the bastards had bitten his arm, clear through to the bone. The pain danced up his arm in bright red flashes that filled Streak's brain and caused him to black out briefly before waking again to wait for the next fat red throb.

Blue Streak was vaguely aware that he was in shock as a result of the bite. And those stinking pigs were milling about freely in the cockpit as he lay there, injured and helpless.

As he drifted in and out of consciousness, Streak saw the pigs basically having a party. They had somehow managed to push one of the crates of gin out of the cargo hold, tear it open and chomp into the bottles. The flimsy plastic bottles gushed gin and the greedy mindless pigs lunged forward and lapped it up. Soon they were as drunk as lords.

At least, three of them were. The little one and the sow didn't join in the drinking. The other pigs got more and more drunk, finishing all twelve bottles and then dragging out the second case of gin, tearing into that, chomping into the bottles, lapping it up and finally rolling around the floor in a total drunken stupor.

As they did so, the little pig and the sow edged towards the controls of the shuttle. They peered at the flight panel curiously, their fat heads and long snouts bowed over it. He prayed that they wouldn't accidentally hit any of the buttons.

But then the sow jerked her head abruptly forward and triggered something on the control panel. From the flashing lights and the audio alert, Streak could tell that she had triggered their distress beacon. Oh well, it could be a lot worse. It wouldn't affect their flight or the autopilot, it would just send out a mayday signal.

This was not a totally inappropriate result for a craft whose pilot was drifting into unconsciousness while pigs ran wild in the cockpit.

The flashing lights woke up the three drunken pigs and they attacked the sow, jumping on her and dragging her away from the control panel. That was the last thing Streak saw before a big red pulse filled his head and he was gone.

The sound of the mayday signal continued to reverberate throughout the cockpit, as it pulsed out to receivers in all directions.

"I'm going to take this glove off."

"You can't do that."

"The damned thing is hurting my wrist."

"Do I need to remind you that you need the glove? The glove is waterproof."

"The glove is uncomfortable. The glove is killing me."

"Your hand is made out of metal and is it a good idea to expose a metal hand full of expensive micro-electronics to the water of a swimming pool? No, it is not."

Esma did not reply. She sighed with disgust and then let herself float away from her sister. The swimming pool was a large, irregularly shaped "lagoon" with plastic boulders and real palm trees fringing the water. The floor of the lagoon was blue neon under glass, which caused the water to glow eerily. Beyond the palm trees Tykrist could see the rooftop of the building, and beyond that, the purple sky of the Mega-City night.

At the centre of the lagoon was a plastic island with a large house of glass set on it. Inside the glass house, activity was revealed on three floors where shrouded figures in lime green radiation suits and yellow goggles hurried around, attending to the everyday business of running a large nuclear reactor. Every corner of the glass house was full of flourishing green plants that seemed to be thriving in the warm humid atmosphere and possibly also the stray radiation. Dotted around the glass house's island and on the outer perimeter of the pool were diving boards and towers containing lifeguards wearing full-body radiation suits and goggles.

Esma and Tykrist were situated between a diving board and a lifeguard tower, lolling in balmy shallows beside a

plastic pirate's chest that gaped half open to reveal plastic
gold coins and jewels. "Look at that," said Esma suddenly.
"It's Carver."

Tykrist looked across the pool to see Judge Carver wading
shyly towards them, wearing lividly gaudy swimming
shorts.

"What's he doing here? He must be off duty."

"He doesn't have a bad six pack," said Esma.

"Just so long as he doesn't start farting," said Tykrist.

"Oh ugh, yes, can you imagine it, bubbling up in the
water?"

"It's the synthetic crap he eats. I'm beginning to wish
they'd make pork legal again."

"What kind of talk is that?" cried a jovial voice. Tykrist and
her sister turned in surprise to see Judge Darrid in the water
a couple of metres away, wading inexorably towards them,
his pale pot belly, sparsely matted with wiry grey hairs, jutting in the water like the prow of a ship in front of him. He
was wearing a pair of swim shorts even more garish and
hideous than Carver's. Above and below the painfully brilliant colours of the shorts, his bulging belly and spindly legs
were slug white. "Legalise pork? That's no way for a couple
of Judges to be talking. Especially two such beautiful ones."

"What are you doing here, Darrid?" demanded Esma.

"They gave us the rest of the night off. We were supposed
to be assisting Dredd on one of his crackpot, hare-brained
schemes. It went wrong, of course. Turned into a fiasco.
Poor planning, as usual. And after, they gave us the rest of
the night off. Me and young Carver." He nodded to the distant edge of the pool where Carver had stopped in his tracks.
He had spotted Darrid and looked as mortified as the sisters.

Darrid moved closer to the women, his bulging paunch
threatening to touch them. Both sisters bobbed back in
alarm. "This Aquatomic pool is quite something, isn't it?"
And he proceeded to give an utterly unnecessary explanation of how the pool worked.

"You see, the water flows in there under the reactor complex, and some of it is turned into steam, and some of it

flows through the cooling bays where it cools the reactor and circulates back out, making the water nice and warm for us, and keeping the reactor at a safe temperature." He went on and on, endlessly explicating the obvious. "And they take the power they produce with the steam and sell it to the grid," he concluded. He tapped his nose. "Shrewd business sense, that."

Then, suddenly and awfully, Darrid ran out of small talk, like a machine grinding to a halt. There was a terrible, awkward silence while Darrid stared at the sisters, panic growing in his eyes. He had no idea what to say to them and the sisters felt the embarrassment as acutely as he did. Finally Darrid clapped his shaking hands together and said, with mortifying forced cheeriness, "Now why the hell doesn't Carver get his smelly butt over here and join us?"

Carter was still standing on the other side of the pool. But he wasn't looking at them. He was staring up into the sky. Tykrist followed his gaze. Then Esma and Darrid looked up. Soon they were all staring at the same thing, a long grey craft with Russian symbols painted in white on the side. It was some kind of shuttle and it was hurtling through the sky, towards the Aquatomic rooftop.

"Why, that damned fool has dropped out of the traffic pattern," said Darrid, squinting upwards. "It's a disgrace, driving like that. Somebody should arrest him. I'd do it myself if I wasn't off duty."

The shuttlecraft grew larger, dropping like a stone. "Doesn't the damn fool know this is a no-fly zone?" said Darrid indignantly. "After all, it's a nuclear power plant." He edged closer to Tykrist, making a transparent attempt to stare down the top of her swimsuit. She automatically edged away as she continued to stare up into the night sky.

As the shuttle fell towards the rooftop, a second shape appeared in the night above it. It was a small, glowing shape trailing a tremulous lavender flame. "Why, it's a jet pack," announced Carver. "Some other damned fool is getting in the way with a jet pack. It's not bad enough we have this clown who can't park his shuttle but now there's this joker. We're getting them all tonight."

"It's a Judge," said Esma, staring up at the figure in the jet pack as it swooped towards the dropping shuttlecraft.

"It's Dredd," said Tykrist. The figure with the jet pack had matched velocities with the shuttlecraft. The lavender flame cut out as Dredd dropped towards the shuttle and seized hold of hand grips on its hull. He was now clinging to the vessel as it fell, like an ant on a watermelon.

"What the hell does he think he's doing?" demanded Darrid, answering himself an instant later. "He's using the emergency access shuttle. He's going on board. What the drokk?"

Dredd disappeared inside the shuttle which continued to plummet towards the rooftop. Tykrist looked down from the falling craft to the point where it was going to hit: right on top of the glass house containing the nuclear reactor. Her mouth went dry and hollow, and a cold feeling began to spread across her stomach. She started to silently formulate a prayer. Then the shuttle twitched in the air, altered the course of its fall, and began to move under its own power again.

It pulled out of the dive, clearing the roof of the glass house by two or three metres, rising back into the night sky to circle cautiously, then rejoin the traffic pattern.

Darrid watched these events with a sour, discontented expression. Finally, he shook his head. "Imagine Dredd getting involved in a trivial traffic violation like that. You'd think he'd have better things to do, what with Psi-Judge Zandonella missing and in danger and all. And using the jet pack like that. Flagrant misuse of departmental resources. The egotistical show-off. Someone should report him..."

FOURTEEN

Zandonella only spent one night in the med-bay, back in her own body and recovering from her recent ordeal. She was discharged the following morning and arrived back at her con-apt to find Porkditz waiting for her. The pig followed her happily into the kitchen where she opened the refrigerator and took out a bottle of gin.

"We never did get a drink on the shuttlecraft," she said. The pig grunted happily, as if he understood her, and he watched avidly as she dug out the ice and vermouth and a lemon. She mixed and poured two generous dry martinis, setting one on the floor for Porkditz. "You saved my life, you know," she said.

He looked up at her brightly, snorted once, and began to lap up the drink. The doorbell rang and Zandonella sighed and set her own glass down beside the sink. She wasn't surprised to see O'Mannion there, but Judge Dredd was with her and so were Carver and Darrid, both looking sheepish. They must have learned how close they'd been to a radioactive death at the swimming pool last night.

"Come in," said Zandonella. "We were just having a little victory celebration." She looked for Porkditz but he remained in the kitchen, shyly hiding.

"You deserve it," said O'Mannion, stepping into the living room. "With your help we've crushed the biggest black market pork ring in the Mega-City. Tell her the good news, Dredd."

Judge Dredd shrugged. "The Council of Five has decided that you will receive a decoration for uncommon valour."

"A decoration? You mean a medal?"

"Correct."

Zandonella discovered that, despite herself, she was glowing with pride. "When is the ceremony?"

"Tomorrow afternoon. It will be held in the rooftop forest we seized from Featherman," said O'Mannion. "In fact, it's going to be the site of the departmental picnic. All the Judges involved in the recent crackdown on pork will be invited to attend." She scrutinised Zandonella. "You'll be expected to attend and to receive your medal."

"Of course," said Zandonella happily. "Will I have to make a speech?"

"No," said Dredd.

"Perfect." Zandonella smiled at them. Why did they all look so glum?

"That's the end of the good news," said O'Mannion. "Now for the bad news."

"What do you mean?"

Dredd looked at her. His face was expressionless. "The Council of Five has studied your report very closely."

"I imagine so," said Zandonella. There was something in his voice that chilled her, and she responded with an edge of sarcasm as she spoke. "I imagine that's why they're giving me a medal."

"And you deserve it, Judge. But what concerns us here is the Council's conclusions concerning the mutant pigs."

The chill that Zandonella felt suddenly deepened. "What conclusions?"

"It's clear from their attempt to blow up the Aquatomics nuclear reactor that the pigs are even more intelligent than we suspected."

"Than *you* suspected," said Zandonella acidly.

"More intelligent," continued Dredd, "and much more dangerous."

There was silence in the small room. Zandonella thought she could hear Porkditz moving around quietly in the kitchen. Her mouth was so dry she found it hard to speak. "So what?" she managed to say.

O'Mannion shrugged. She looked tired. "The combination of high intelligence with the desire for revenge against human beings..."

"Well of course they want revenge," snapped Zandonella. "We've been torturing them and slaughtering them and eating them for generations."

O'Mannion sighed. "I'll get to the point. The Council has decided that the mutant pigs are too dangerous to be allowed to roam free in the Mega-City."

"So what are you saying?" said Zandonella. "That they'll be exiled to the Cursed Earth?"

Once again there was silence in the living room. "No," said Dredd finally. "That's not what we're saying." He looked her in the eye. "The Council of Five is still mindful of the nutritional value of the mutant pork."

"Nutritional value?" said Zandonella. But her voice was only a whisper.

"That, combined with the intelligence and the obvious hostility of the pigs towards humans, a hostility which your report describes in detail, Judge Zandonella, has led the Council of Five to a decision."

"Oh no," said Zandonella.

"Is that pig you call Porkditz here, Judge?" Dredd's cold gaze bored into her. Zandonella nodded in the direction of the kitchen. Dredd signalled to Carver and Darrid. They moved towards the kitchen.

"No." said Zandonella. Carver and Darrid wouldn't meet her gaze. They disappeared into the kitchen and a moment later they reappeared, dragging Porkditz by his hind legs. The little pig was agitated and squealing so loudly it hurt her ears. Zandonella tried to go to him, but Judge Dredd restrained her. Carver and Darrid dragged the squealing Porkditz out the front door. Just before the door slid shut Porkditz's gaze met Zandonella's, his eyes intelligent and imploring and hopeless.

Zandonella began to cry. Judge O'Mannion touched her on the shoulder briefly and headed for the door. She was gone in an instant, eager to be on her way. Only Dredd was left in the con-apt. He looked down at Zandonella.

"You'll be there for the ceremony tomorrow, Judge," he said. "No excuses."

It was a beautiful warm day with just enough breeze to blow the pollution away and leave a clear blue sky above Feather-man's forest where there had once been a plastic dome. The only fumes were those rising in hot smoky waves from the barbecue pit. They rose to combine with the clean green astringency of pine scent from the surrounding trees.

In a patch of sunlight in a clearing in the forest stood the tank of the Cetacean Ambassador. The dolphin was in the middle of a speech that was being broadcast from speakers rigged in trees all over the rooftop. Among the hundred or so Judges present was Psi-Judge Zandonella, standing erect and tall in her dress uniform, the bright yellow and blue ribbon of her new medal fluttering on her chest.

The dolphin's voice came from the speakers, sonorous and mellow in its human translation. "I am here to congrat-ulate all of Mega-City's Judges on their successful battle against the vendors of black market pork. You are here to enjoy a well-earned reward in the form of symbolic hon-ours," the dolphin glanced at Zandonella, "and ritual feasting. But you may be asking yourself why I am here, with my tank and translator, when my people so recently insisted on citizens' rights for that same mutant pork." The dolphin spun in his tank, looking at the Judges ranked in front of him. Near Zandonella stood the Karst sisters, Carver and Darrid, and Judge Dredd, tall and implacable.

"My advocacy on behalf of the pigs was based on their unquestionable intelligence," said the dolphin. "What I and my people didn't know at the time was that this intelligence was bent purely on destruction and bloodshed: blind, vicious vengeance against all human beings, as senseless as a shark among the infants of the pod. Just as the pod must protect itself against the shark, you must protect yourself against the threat constituted by these intelligent swine."

The Cetacean Ambassador paused for a moment. The breeze carried the cooking smells from the barbecue pit to the waiting line of Judges. O'Mannion glanced at Zandonella and then looked away again. "The wise and pragmatic decision of your Council," said the dolphin, "is to legalise once and for all the consumption of pork in the environs of the Mega-City. This is a most shrewd judgement, since it allows exploitation of a rich source of food while also ridding you of a threat. You are going to eat your enemies."

The dolphin paused, bubbles rising in his tank. "I and my people are also pragmatists and applaud the elegant economy of that solution. What's more, your Council of Five has decided that as the factory pigs are reared for slaughter and prepared for your tables, they will also be dumbed-down by genetic manipulation so that future generations won't prove so troublesome. The gene sequence for their reduced IQ is to be taken from a human source: the Mega-City's least bright – but most tractable – citizens."

There was laughter and sporadic applause from the Judges. The merry smile on the Cetacean Ambassador's face seemed to grow wider. "Let the festivities begin! While I feast on snow crab generously provided by your city, you shall celebrate with a special barbecue."

There was loud and sustained applause from the Judges for a minute or two, then people began to make their way to the barbecue pit and return with full plates. The sizzle and smell of pork floated lavishly on the air. Zandonella turned and walked away from the pit and the cooking smells, passing among the pine trees. In a moment she came to another clearing full of sunlight. In the golden light a team of caterers were busy laying out glinting cutlery and white linen napkins on a wide table with a red and white checked cloth spread across it. Food was heaped in the centre of the table. Zandonella realised she had stumbled onto the VIP's table. But before she could turn to go, one of the caterers set a wide silver platter down on the table. On the platter was a pig's head, roasted, with a cooked apple in its mouth. Even with the apple, the gaping mouth and the closed eyes, the pig's face was unmistakable. Zandonella could still hear the screams he had made as he was dragged from her con-apt.

She turned and blundered blindly out of the clearing, back through the trees, fleeing what she had seen. She emerged from the forest and almost collided with Carver, who was carrying a plate stacked high with roast pork. He stared at Zandonella who stood trembling in front of him. "Would you like something to eat?" he said.

"Eat?" said Zandonella.

"Sure. Why don't you try some?" He dug a fork into a thick slice of pork and offered it to her. Judge Zandonella said nothing. She just turned and walked away from him, away from the other Judges, and away from the greasy smell of the barbecue.

"What's the matter with her?" said Carver.

The rich aromatic smoke rose up from the pit and disappeared into the clear blue sky.

ABOUT THE AUTHOR

Andrew Cartmel was the script editor of the legendary science fiction epic *Doctor Who* before moving on to become senior script editor on another BBC hit, *Casualty*, which he helped to launch on its record breaking run. His television career also encompasses a stint as lead writer on the cult sword and sorcery classic *Dark Knight* for Five. Outside the realm of television, he has also scripted comics for *2000 AD* and for *Marvel UK*, written a successful stage thriller, *End of the Night*, and has published several novels, including *The Wise*.

THE BIG MEG GLOSSARY

Black Atlantic Tunnel: A tunnel located below the Black Atlantic that connects Mega-City One to Brit-Cit.

Citi-Def: The City Defence Force (a civilian militia): a voluntary civilian army organised on a block basis that saw action against the Sov-Bloc invaders of the Apocalypse War in 2104.

City Bottom: The pre-Atomic rockrete foundations of Mega-City One, littered with the architectural, human and sub-hume refuse of the city. Also known as The Pits, this area is not recognised as one of the three city levels, and is often the last stop for Slummies who do not wish to live within society.

Council of Five (The): The central ruling council of Judges, consisting of the heads of the main divisions of the Justice Department, that acts as the Chief Judge's advisory body.

Cuidad Barranquilla: Located in the former Buenos Aires, 'Banana City' is considered to be one of the poorest and most corrupt cities in the World.

Dave the OrangUtan: Widely regarded as Mega-City One's finest mayor, Dave won a landslide mayoral race after gaining fame by appearing on the Tri-D show Tipsters Tonite. Sadly, Dave's term of office only lasted a couple of years as he and his owner, Billy Smairt, were murdered by Billy's best mate, barman Mo Molinsky.

Heatseeker Round: Also known as a Hotshot, this specialised ammo is made by capping a guided warhead onto a standard execution round, and rarely misses its target.

Hondo City: Also known as Hondo-Cit; the Japanese counterpart of Mega-City One.

Iso-Cube: The standard imprisonment for criminals; a huge block full of very small, plasteen, isolation cubes.

Long Walk (The): A tough journey a retired Judge decides to make to bring Law into the Cursed Earth or the Undercity. Once gone, few Judges are ever heard from again.

Luna-City: Also known as Luna-1, Luna-City is a colony on the moon established and maintained by the American Mega-Cities.

MAC (Macro-Analysis Computer): Referred to as the 'brain' of Mega-City One, MAC can even predict crimes before they happen, as well as being the information centre for all citizens and Judge activity.

Otto Sump: This extremely unattractive citizen won sixty million credits on the Tri-D show *Sob Story*, and started a chain of beauty parlours with his winnings. When the beauty treatments started turning people ugly, the look caught on and created a subculture of 'Uglies'. As Sump's new products were deemed unhealthy, a hefty 'Ugly Tax' was established. Despite this, demand for Sump's anti-beauty products have still persisted.

Pedway: A pedestrian-only pathway found all across Mega-City One at all levels. Motorised pedways are known as slidewalks and eeziglides.

Power Tower: A controlled volcano, the Power Tower obtains red hot lava from beneath the Earth's crust to provide most of Mega-City One's energy supply.

Robot Wars (The): In 2099, a renegade construction droid called Call-Me-Kenneth waged war against the Judges, killing thousands of cits and Judges. Dredd was able to bring the rebel droid down with the help of other loyal robots and Weather Control.

Sector House: A miniature version of the Grand Hall of Justice, of which there are hundreds located around the city. Sector Houses carry out all routine judging activities for their area.

Statue of Judgement: A massive rockcrete statue of a Judge erected for the second time in 2117, found in Sector 44. Unbeknownst to the public, the Public Surveillance Unit is housed within the statue's head.

Tri-D: The shortened term for three-dimensional holovision; thousands of both legal and pirate channels are available in Mega-City One.

Troggies: The blind descendants of a group of people who remained underground, the troggies have adapted to their dark environment, and have also in the past made violent and dangerous forays into the city above them.

Umpty Candy: Formerly the most popular confectionary in the city, it was eventually banned due to its extremely addictive nature. Later, the Mega-City Jong family procured the recipe from its creator, Uncle Ump, before killing him, then proceeded to establish the Umpty black market, selling the substance as a fine powder.

Undercity: Formerly New York City and Washington DC, this area was covered with a huge slab of concrete upon which Mega-City One was built. The Undercity is populated by a small number of mutants called 'troggies', who have adapted to live in the cold and dark.

Wally Squad: A group of undercover Judges who infiltrate criminal organisations. Wally Squad Judges are not well thought of by other Judges, as they are prone to become perps themselves.

Wreckers: Also known as street pirates, these armed gangs raid moving vehicles and rob them.

TOUGH FICTION FOR A TOUGH PLANET

JUDGE DREDD

Dredd vs Death
1-84416-061-0
£5.99 • $6.99

Bad Moon Rising
1-84416-107-2
£5.99 • $6.99

Black Atlantic
1-84416-108-0
£5.99 • $6.99

Eclipse
1-84416-122-6
£5.99 • $6.99

Kingdom of the Blind
1-84416-133-1
£5.99 • $6.99

The Final Cut
1-84416-135-6
£5.99 • $6.99

STRONTIUM DOG

Bad Timing
1-84416-110-2
£5.99 • $6.99

Prophet Margin
1-84416-134-X
£5.99 • $6.99

Ruthless
1-84416-136-6
£5.99 • $6.99

ABC WARRIORS

The Medusa War
1-84416-109-9
£5.99 • $6.99

ROGUE TROOPER

Crucible
1-84416-111-0
£5.99 • $6.99

Blood Relative
1-84416-167-6
£5.99 • $6.99

NIKOLAI DANTE

The Strangelove Gambit
1-84416-139-0
£5.99 • $6.99

DURHAM RED

The Unquiet Grave
1-84416-159-5
£5.99 • $6.99

The Omega Solution
1-84416-175-7
£5.99 • $6.99

NEW LINE CINEMA

Blade: Trinity
1-84416-106-4
£6.99 • $7.99

The Butterfly Effect
1-84416-081-5
£6.99 • $7.99

Cellular
1-84416-104-8
£6.99 • $7.99

Freddy vs Jason
1-84416-059-9
£5.99 • $6.99

The Texas Chainsaw Massacre
1-84416-060-2
£6.99 • $7.99

FINAL DESTINATION

Dead Reckoning
1-84416-170-6
£6.99 • $7.99

Destination Zero
1-84416-171-4
£6.99 • $7.99

End of the Line
1-84416-176-5
£6.99 • $7.99

JASON X

Jason X
1-84416-168-4
£6.99 • $7.99

The Experiment
1-84416-169-2
£6.99 • $7.99

Planet of the Beast
1-84416-183-8
£6.99 • $7.99

THE TWILIGHT ZONE

**The Twilight Zone #1:
Memphis/The Pool Guy**
1-84416-130-7
£6.99 • $7.99

**The Twilight Zone #2:
Upgrade/Sensuous Cindy**
1-84416-131-5
£6.99 • $7.99

**The Twilight Zone #3:
Sunrise/Into the Light**
1-84416-151-X
£6.99 • $7.99

**The Twilight Zone #4:
Chosen/The Placebo Effect**
1-84416-150-1
£6.99 • $7.99

THE UNQUIET GRAVE

Durham Red

Mutant, vampire, total babe – careful boys, she bites!

PETER J EVANS

DURHAM RED
THE UNQUIET GRAVE

1-84416-159-5

£5.99/$6.99

THE OMEGA SOLUTION

PETER J EVANS

DURHAM RED
THE OMEGA SOLUTION

1-84416-175-7

£5.99/$6.99

2000 AD

NIKOLAI DANTE
THE STRANGELOVE GAMBIT

Swashbuckling, drinking, womanising...
it's a tough life being an outlaw!

DAVID BISHOP

1-84416-139-0
£5.99/$6.99

ABC WARRIORS
THE MEDUSA WAR

1-84416-109-9

£5.99/$6.99

WWW.BLACKFLAME.COM
TOUGH FICTION FOR A TOUGH PLANET